The Trouble with Love and Ink

HARRIET ASHFORD

Published by Phillips House

Book Cover by My Lan Khuc

Editing by Sherri Shackelford

Proofread by Ramona Mihai

For my favorite business analyst—who also happens to be my favorite
human.
Thanks for believing in me.

Author's Note

This book was written by an adult for adults, and as such, contains explicit language and open-door intimacy scenes. If you are one of my former students who has found me, I love you but put the darn book down.

You can find trigger warnings on my website by clicking on the tab labeled "The Trouble with Ink" and scrolling toward the bottom.

Chapter 1

The day my promotion was stolen, I was supposed to be on vacation. I spent the morning decorating my cubicle as if sprucing up my workspace would compensate for losing the trip.

I replaced my mousepad, which looked to have survived Y2K, with a fresh find patterned in vibrant green banana leaves and dropped a collection of pens into a new holder—this one a golden pineapple.

I'd just finished hanging a group of hexagon tiles decorated with water-colored hibiscus when Anna waddled by my cubicle. She stopped to sniff audibly.

"What's that smell?" she asked. "It's so tropical."

I inhaled deeply but couldn't pick up the scent yet. "You and your superhuman pregnancy nose." I gestured toward the parrot-shaped wallflower. "It's coconut."

"Wow. And I thought I was nesting." She reached to examine my new dollar store pineapple pen holder, and her round-tight stomach brushed past me. "This wouldn't have anything to do with the vacation you should be taking right now, would it?"

My eyes flicked to my desk calendar. Though crossed out, the words Key West might as well have been a neon sign. I didn't need to look at the itinerary to know that my sister and I had planned to go on a dolphin watch and snorkel cruise today. In an alternate universe, I was two pina coladas deep with Nemo and friends.

In this twisted timeline, a new company within our business went live five days ago, the swing of which hacked my trip like a guillotine. So, instead, I'd spend the day trudging through support tickets, and my sister Hailey was enjoying Florida with my replacement—a DJ she'd met at a wedding two months ago.

The timing had been romcom-level perfect for them. After I bailed on Hailey, she had the choice to cancel the trip altogether or go to Florida alone. Then she met Braxton, who was headed to Florida for a DJ gig. It was as if the universe had tilted the frame, knocking me from the picture to make room for Braxton, the DJ.

I stood so suddenly that I almost collided with Anna's baby bump. "We'd better get going. Meeting is about to start."

"That's right," Anna said as I folded my laptop. "Big announcement today. You ready to get that promotion?"

The promotion was only a slight step up. It's not like I was going to be a supervisor or in any kind of management position. Still, I would have superiority when making decisions on projects, and, more importantly, I'd be making more money. I tamped the rising excitement.

"We don't know if I'm getting it," I said. "There are lots of deserving people on our team."

Anna looked at me and snorted. "Who else on our team is senior-level material?"

"If you weren't leaving, we wouldn't have to worry about who will fill your position," I deflected with a pouty lip.

I was mainly just teasing, but the pain rang true. I knew she'd make priceless memories—staying home when little Grace arrived, but a bitter taste always hit the back of my mouth when I pictured coming to the office and not having Anna to get me through the day.

"Exactly. You should be thanking me. My leaving is forcing management's hand. Because God knows you would never risk rocking the boat by asking for something you deserve." Anna lowered her voice as we neared the conference room, where most of our team already waited. She grabbed the box of donuts off the conference table and extended her arm. "Here, have one of these. It will make you feel better."

I plucked a pink frosted sugar bomb from the offering and took a less-than-lady-like chunk out of it before greeting the rest of the team.

"Oh! I almost forgot." Anna reached into her cardigan and pulled out a lavender sticky note. "Can you add Georgia to the mailing list for the baby shower? She's my cousin. And I haven't seen her in forever, but I know there will be drama if I don't invite her."

I laughed, mouth still full, and took the note from her. "Can't have that."

"Are you sure addressing the invites isn't too much right now? Work is crazy."

Understatement of the century. I kept promising myself I'd start on the envelopes, but the earliest I'd left last week was seven-thirty. And I'd been so exhausted that I'd flopped down on my couch, still fully clothed, and had fallen into a light coma. I'd woken in a cotton-mouthed panic to my alarm the next day—my phone barely hanging on at seven percent battery life.

If I waited until work slowed to get started on addressing the invitations, then I might as well forget the baby shower. Instead, I'd be addressing invitations for Grace's first birthday party.

I could admit to Anna that work had me pulled tightly in too many directions. After all, I wasn't letting her pay me for the service. She could find someone in time to get them done if she started looking now. But I didn't want her to.

"I'll find time," I said as much to myself as to her.

Calligraphy was one of the few things I looked forward to. I needed to make time for the things I enjoyed.

Not long after we joined the team at the conference table, Wesley—our supervisor—strode in. Behind him was someone I didn't know.

He looked about my age, so he was probably in his late twenties. Everyone in the conference room dressed professionally, but this guy looked sharp. His dress shirt had to be upwards of a thousand or so thread count. However, his wind-blown curls offset the crisp look.

"Thank you for waiting," Wesley said, taking his place at the head of the table like the good papa he was. Good at delegating. Good at leaving before four-thirty every day. Good at taking credit for things he had little to do with. Good at making more than twice what I made, all for pointing his finger and continuing the patriarchy. "Everyone say hello to Beckett At—"

"Please," the new guy said with a wince. "It's just Beck."

"Beck," Wesley corrected, "our new senior analyst."

The room stilled. My ears felt like they'd been stuffed with cotton. I couldn't hear anything beyond my hammering pulse.

They'd hired out.

I wasn't getting the promotion.

Anna's eyes cut to mine. I felt the gaze of everyone else in the room, too. I flushed, sure my pale complexion had turned the shade of a cardinal. Chin lifting, I forced myself to look at Wesley, try to smile, or at least act like I was listening instead of swirling the drain of a doom spiral.

He introduced us to Beck, giving a little backstory on each team member. "This is Emily Lane," he stated, nodding toward me, the human turned cadaver.

I'd given up on a social life for this job.

I'd foregone dating for this job.

I canceled my vacation for this job.

"And this is Anna Nguyen," Wesley said, having made it around the table with the introductions. "You'll be shadowing her in the next two months to provide a seamless transition when she leaves."

Anna gave the new guy a chilly once over, and when Wesley moved on to his next agenda item, timesheets, she met my gaze with a *What the hell? You were supposed to get my job!* look. I attempted a shrug, but the moment felt too heavy to lift a shoulder at, resulting in a clumsy elbow winging out. I couldn't feign nonchalance any more than AI art could get the eyes on a portrait right.

But the more I looked at Beckett—Beck, the more my poor-pitiful-me mood melted with a fit of smoldering anger in my chest. And I realized I should take the hit with grace, but I was too pissed. I'd worked at The Arlow Group for five years and had nothing but positive feedback from my supervisors. In our one-on-ones, I frequently received an earful of "leadership material" and "really took the initiative with this project."

Yet, nothing ever came of it. And damn it, with this last go-live, I'd brought my A-game. Staying until seven-thirty or eight on most nights. Making myself available on the weekends. And don't even get me started on the ass kissing, which had involved lending a shoulder to cry on as Wesley navigated through his fresh divorce.

I should have been in Florida, getting tipsy before noon and arguing with my sister about whether we should try a haunted tour or go barhopping on Duval. Instead, I stared at the man who stole my promotion, with his nice hair and even nicer shirt.

Seriously, this guy shows up with his Egyptian fucking cotton button-down and grabs the position I'd been slotted for for years? And why?

I knew the situation had to be more complicated than how it seemed. Still, it was all too easy to imagine some, *he's a golf buddy, or I went to college with his old man* bullshit.

I didn't know the meeting had concluded until my teammates gathered their things and headed for the door. Usually, during meetings, I took meticulous notes. Today, my note page sat blank.

Anna leaned forward. "You deserve an explanation. He practically promised you this position," she whispered fiercely.

I shook my head. "It's fine," I whispered back. "This doesn't need to be a big deal."

"It's already a big deal," she hissed. "Either you say something, or I will."

My eyes widened. Anna was only going to make things worse for everyone. "Fine!" I shooed her away. "I'll talk to him."

Wesley shuffled toward the exit like everyone else, but before he could make a full retreat, Anna called out, "Wesley, Emily needs to speak with you."

He sighed. He knew where this was going. "Of course."

Anna gave me one last commiserating look before closing the door with a soft clink. Now that I had Wesley's attention, I hesitated, unsure where to begin. My mind swarmed with angry thoughts buzzing in and out of my train of thought.

I landed on, "I think I may have misunderstood. Didn't you say the promotion was all but mine?"

"Emily," he said carefully. "No one in this office works harder than you. Sometimes, I wonder if the team could even function without you." I crossed my arms, not in the mood to be buttered up, but then, fearing I resembled a sulking child, uncrossed them. "You've always made sure all the little details line up. And we need that."

"But?" I prompted, sensing the lingering word.

"But Beckett had stellar recommendations from some big names." Finally, the real truth. Beckett knew people. That's what it always came down to, didn't it? "Besides, he'll bring a fresh perspective to the team. We could use that." Wesley's hand rested on the door handle. He was done with this conversation. "I know this is a lot to process, but try to see this as an opportunity for growth."

I attempted to smile, but my facial muscles seemed to think that would be an act of mutiny. "Sure," I managed.

Because, really, what else was there to say? They'd already hired Shirt Guy. It's not like the powers that be were going to say: Oops! We forgot we had a totally competent employee for the position until she whined about it.

It was a done deal.

Wesley looked at his phone, claiming to have a Zoom meeting with corporate. So, I returned to my cubicle, immediately pulling up an email I'd gotten from a headhunter a month ago. I wondered if she was still looking for a business analyst fluent in AX.

I'd start by updating my resume. I'd worked at The Arlow Group for five years. I had experience now. Certainly, I could find a pay range to match that. Maybe I could even find a job with a healthy work-life balance. If those even existed.

I pulled my resume from Google Docs but stopped, mouse hovering by the reply button. I let out a long breath. I wasn't in any position to make life-altering decisions, not when this angry, anyway.

I worked in a big, clean office in a beautiful location with mostly good people. My job was secure, and I made enough money to afford rent.

The grass wasn't always greener on the other side. I clicked out of my resume and dropped the idea of quitting.

I didn't have time for fantasies. There was a reason I'd had to cancel my trip with Hailey. I opened my inbox to find eighty-three unanswered support tickets. My stomach dropped at the daunting day ahead. Not even my new mouse pad or coconut plug-in could save me now.

At six o'clock, Anna shuffled past my desk, tote on her shoulder. "Don't let them keep you late," she said with a yawn. "At least you won't be alone. The new guy is burning the midnight oil too, wants to get through as many orientation videos as possible."

My eyes flicked in the direction of his cube, but I had no intention of discussing Beckett. He may not have intentionally stolen my job, but I was still sore about it. "I'm not staying much later," I said to her original comment. "One more ticket, and I'm out of here. Ten minutes tops."

Except the last ticket I opened proved to be quite the challenge, and before I knew it, I found myself lost in the puzzle. By the time I realized the complexity of the problem, I'd already dove too deep.

I emerged from the office two hours later than Anna, eyes burning from staring at my computer screen too long, shoulders aching from my rigid posture. The only perk of leaving the office late was the view of the Woodlands waterway. Our building was nestled among boutique shops, several restaurants, and my gym. All of which sat right on the bank. At night, they illuminated the stringed lights on the trees, which reflected romantically on the water. There was no arguing; it was a great location.

Or so I thought.

As I pulled my keys from my bag, a piece of paper knocked loose. The wind picked it up, and the note tumbled to the waterway, where it snagged on a low-hanging branch reaching toward the water like a witch's gnarled hand.

I squinted at the paper, only inches above the water, hating littering but sure I wasn't missing anything important. Then I made out the lavender square. It had seemed like seventy years ago Anna had given me her cousin's address on that sticky note.

Damn it! Can't forget Georgia.

I dropped my bag near the tree and tested a perpendicular branch—a skinny thing—but it seemed sturdy enough. Gripping tightly, I leaned out and over the water, my free hand stretching toward the note.

My fingertips grazed the paper when I heard the crack.

I barely had time to register the branch had snapped when water enveloped me—cold and unwelcoming. I doggy-paddled upward, forgetting all other strokes until I surfaced, gasping and sputtering. My hand slapped against the concreted edge, and I pushed myself up—something I do every morning after swimming laps at the gym—but my arms buckled, and I slipped right back in.

"Here, I've got you," a deep voice called. "Grab my hand."

With hair and water in my eyes, I could only make out a squatting figure on the bank in front of me. I reached out. My hand met a muscular forearm, and I held tight as he easily pulled me up.

"Th-thank you," I said, pushing soaked hair away from my face.

As soon as I did, I locked eyes with my rescuer, Beckett—Beck, The Arlow Group's newest senior associate. It took half a second for my gratitude to dissolve into embarrassment. Had he stayed this late trying to get ahead of those orientation videos? No one worked this late on our team . . . except me.

"Are you okay?" he asked, helping me to my feet.

Can you die from embarrassment? "Yes. I'm okay. I just dropped something, and I—"

Beck's eyes trailed down to his arm, where I'd soaked his nice dress shirt from wrist to elbow. And as quickly as my gratitude had flipped to embarrassment, his concern turned to disgust.

"I'm sorry," I said, cheeks and ear tips flaming.

Beck looked back at me. "What could you have possibly dropped to warrant diving for it?"

"I didn't dive for it!" My voice rose with the need to defend myself. "I fell in."

Beck ignored that. "Because even if it had been a hundred-dollar bill—"

I sure as hell wasn't going to tell him I'd gone for Cousin Georgia's address. I'd already kicked myself over it. I didn't need any help. Anna could have written the address out for me again. No water involved. But still, Beckett here didn't have to be an ass when I was clearly freezing and already embarrassed beyond repair.

I couldn't imagine treating a practical stranger like this, let alone someone I had to work with for the foreseeable future. Maybe he didn't recognize me from the conference room. Maybe the wet hair skewed the picture he'd stored away as my mental profile picture. Or, more likely, he'd met dozens of people today at his new job and couldn't possibly remember all those faces. Good. Then, I could treat him like a stranger instead of a slightly superior coworker.

"It wouldn't have covered half the bill for that shirt, I know," I said sharply. Beck opened his mouth, but I didn't want to hear it. He'd stolen my promotion. I wouldn't let him steal the last crumbs of my dignity. My bag still waited by the tree. I shouldered it. "Well, this has been fun."

"Wait. I'm sorry. I—" His gaze dipped, and I followed it to my floral, now translucent blouse. I slapped an arm over my breasts and glared back at Beck, but he'd at least had the decency to avert his eyes. "I have a jacket in my car," he said to the sky. "I can go get it for you."

"No need. I'm headed straight home if that wasn't obvious." The strap of my bag dug into my shoulder, but I managed to shift it while keeping the other arm safely pressed against my boobs. "But thanks. You're my hero in damp Egyptian cotton." I had to work against the violent chattering of my teeth.

I didn't so much as spare him another glance, but I could feel the weight of his gaze as I forced my legs toward the parking garage, leaving watery footprints in my wake.

Chapter 2

When I got to my Prius, I blasted the heater and unfolded the sticky note, careful not to tear the wet paper. The letters dripped down it, an inky mess, but I could still make out the address.

Georgia, you'd better come to this baby shower. Better not just bring diapers either, I thought, pulling out of my parking spot. *Better be a car seat or, at the very least, a fancy sound machine. One that can belt out Ava Maria or have such a high resolution of sound that you can feel salt spray when you pick the ocean setting.*

I squirmed in my seat. Nothing like the feeling of your wet ass on pleather. I fantasized about getting to my apartment: *I'll start with a steaming hot shower and end bundled in a fleece blanket.* The thought could have made me purr. But home sat just outside Houston, a thirty-minute commute, which equated to an eternity when converted into dripping-in-wet-clothes time.

Hailey's apartment, on the other hand, was a ten-minute drive—if the red lights were favorable. Besides, I was supposed to be watering the plants for my sister while she sipped mai-tais with her new boyfriend. And *shit.* Hailey had been gone for five days, and I hadn't stopped by once. Most house plants would be fine, but, of course, Hailey had to have a high-maintenance Boston Fern and a depressed orchid among a plethora of other leafy problem children.

I should have let Hailey's neighbor take care of them like she'd suggested. But I'd felt so guilty for abandoning her and the trip, I thought watering her plants could soften the blow. If only by a little bit. Now I imagined Hailey coming home to a living room of crumpled brown.

Not if I could help it.

I took the exit for Hailey's apartment. I could shower at her place, borrow some of her clothes, and hopefully drown the plants in enough water and love that they'd forget all Auntie Emily's neglect. *Heck*, I thought sourly, *I could conserve water by ringing out my clothes over them.*

Hailey's apartment never failed to smell like some sort of fruit arrangement. Today's choice was peach. I loved her place. Deep corduroy couches adorned with an eclectic collection of throw pillows made a nest in her living room. Stringed bulbs allowed for softer lighting and a basket of blankets all but said, *Cuddle up on the couch. Make yourself at home.*

Every time envy crept up on me while at Hailey's, I tried to remember that her savings account could probably cover a week's worth of groceries. Meanwhile, mine looked pretty good. Mainly because I was obsessed with saving up for a mortgage.

That's why planning the vacation to Florida had been such a big deal. It had taken Hailey months to convince me to go with her. Finally, after collecting Groupons, agreeing to drive instead of fly, and finding a dirt-cheap Airbnb, she'd convinced me . . . only for work to veto the trip by needing me.

Still shivering on the way to Hailey's bedroom, a quick look at the plants lining the sliding glass window told me they were sad but that they would probably, possibly, hopefully, make a full recovery. Preferably before Hailey's plane touched down on a Texas tarmac in a few days. Hailey had always been my person. And while I practically buzzed with excitement to have her back, I didn't need the lecture about letting one of the plants shrivel up.

I could hear it now, *You're supposed to be the responsible one!* I always had been, even though she was the older of us. On the other hand, Hailey had the most fun and lived life to the fullest.

After a shower so warm and long, I was sure I'd stolen the chance for any of Hailey's neighbors to use hot water for the next forty-eight hours, I helped myself to a T-shirt and shorts from Hailey's dresser.

I then grabbed a blanket off Hailey's floor, wrapped it around my body like a cocoon, and sank into her mattress. After a shitty day, I missed Hailey, but I couldn't call her and vent. I'd messed up her vacation enough already.

Instead, I called my mom. She answered on the second ring.

"Hey, sweetie." Her voice was like grabbing a mug of coffee and letting the warmth seep into your palm.

"Hey, Mom."

"What's wrong?"

The corner of my lip pulled up. That's all it took. Two words, and she knew something was off.

"You know that promotion I was talking to you about?"

"Yeah?"

I swallowed around the lump in my throat, feeling emotional. "I didn't get it. They hired out."

"Oh, honey. I'm so sorry."

"It's okay." A tear fell free, and I hastily wiped my cheek.

"I just can't believe it. Your supervisor said you were in line to get it. Didn't he?"

I sniffed. "Yeah." I shrugged, even though she couldn't see me. "They just found someone better." I tried hard to keep my voice even, but it wavered at the end of the sentence.

She paused, and I could sense she was contemplating how to broach a subject. "I know you don't want to hear this. But I think it's time you find a different job, Emily."

"It's a good job, though," I argued.

"No. It's a secure job. I know that's what you crave, but you have a master's degree and five years of experience. I'm sure there are plenty of opportunities out there."

Probably. But The Arlow Group was safe, established. I knew what I was doing there. Sure, it came with a crazy workload, but I was good at it.

"Hold on a minute, hun." Something crinkled on the line, then, "That looks great. What color are you going to use to highlight here?" My mom's voice sounded muffled, then a clear, "Sorry about that."

"Mom, are you in the middle of class?" She taught art lessons at a small studio downtown, sometimes late into the evening, to fit around school and work schedules.

"Oh, no!" she denied like it was a ridiculous conclusion. "Not a whole class, just a private lesson tonight."

"You should have said something," I said, smacking my forehead. "Go back to teaching. We can talk later."

"Okay, but please think about what I said."

"I will," I lied. "Bye, Mom."

As I hung up, my gaze drifted to the floor. Where the blanket had been, there, in the middle of a pile of laundry, laid a deep green envelope with delicate gold lettering.

I slipped off the bed, curiosity thoroughly piqued by the envelope. I picked it up, appreciating the lettering—how each swoop was perfectly even. Each descension held the same boldness. Each ascension flicked with the lightest feathery strokes.

The envelope was addressed to Reagan Dawson. California sat on the bottom line of the address. Did Hailey know a Reagan from California? That, in itself, wouldn't have been too strange, but Hailey's name wasn't on the return address.

Why does Hailey have this? I wondered, setting the envelope on her desk.

That's when I noticed the Dalmatian-like ink blots on the cedar desk. It reminded me of my workspace at home. I removed a hoodie from the desk, revealing a set of pointed pens that would put my collection to shame. Then there was the Rhodia paper. I flipped through it and found rows and rows of drills. Loops and curves, names all in delicate calligraphy. I looked up, flabbergasted, and saw the bookshelf full of stationery. I ran my fingertips over the different color and weight options.

"What the hell?"

Calligraphy was *my* thing. Always had been. I'd started in eighth grade, and while Hailey had always seemed impressed with the skill, she'd never seemed interested.

I returned to the desk, desperate to know more—either to justify or quell the growing sense that I didn't really know my sister after simply finding some pens and fancy paper. I opened Hailey's planner, completely disregarding any right to her privacy.

But it didn't take long to find names and even some detailed notes: *addressing for Victoria's wedding, bridal party glasses for Jones's wedding, and live lettering at Henson Winery.*

I backed away from the desk, feeling both impressed and hurt. Hailey had done what I'd been too afraid to even consider. She'd started her own calligraphy business.

And she hadn't told me.

Me? The one who'd taught her how to do a fishtail braid, who settled on being Flounder for Halloween so she could be Ariel, who wrote her finance paper in college because the thought of completing it made her cry. I baked pistachio macarons for her birthday every year; they were an absolute pain, but I did it because Hailey loved them.

Yet she couldn't mention buying a jar of ink, let alone that she'd decided to make a side hustle off my favorite pastime.

Dazed and a bit shell-shocked, I picked up my phone. Hailey didn't answer my call, so I settled for a message instead, but as I typed, my hands shook. The betrayal ran hot, and it ran deep.

I found the pointed pens. You have a lot of explaining to do.

Chapter 3

"Please, don't let him recognize me from yesterday." My voice was low enough so that only Anna and, hopefully, a higher power could hear. "I pray to the old gods and the new," I said as we walked from my coconut-scented cubicle to the conference room.

"Is that from . . . Game of Thrones?" Anna asked, scratching the tight bump under her blouse.

"It covers all the deities, doesn't it?" I clutched my notebook and laptop to my chest, shielding myself from the coming embarrassment.

"It doesn't matter if he recognizes you. *He* was the ass. You have no reason to be embarrassed."

She'd obviously taken my side when I told her what happened. I appreciated her fierce loyalty, but I gave her a look, because, really? Can you fall in a waterway outside your place of work—reaching for a sticky note—without feeling embarrassed?

"Okay," she conceded. "You don't have as much to be embarrassed about. I'd rather slip into Lake Woodlands than be a jerk to a new coworker."

"Keep your voice down," I said out of the corner of my mouth as we approached the nearly full conference room.

The team gushed over a Shipley's box in the middle of the table. I hated that I zeroed in on Beck. Also annoying, he wore an equally nice shirt as the one from yesterday, this one a forest green—it paired well with the browns of his hair and eyes. His stern brows furrowed at our entrance.

Damn it. He definitely recognizes me.

Susan turned the box of kolaches our way. "Beckett brought these." I noticed Beck wince at the full use of his name. Like garlic to a freaking vampire. Noted. "Here, Anna, there's a jalapeno one."

Anna craved all things spicy. Any time we ate out for lunch, she ordered the item on the menu with the most little red peppers next to its name. She'd recently told me if a meal didn't make her sweat, it wasn't worth her time.

But instead of grabbing for the kolache, she searched my face as if to ask, *Are we accepting gifts from the enemy?* A true testament to her loyalty.

I responded by picking up a sausage and cheese pastry. I was petty but not on a level where I'd turn down food to make a point. I sank my teeth into doughy heaven.

Beck approached, and I froze mid-bite. "Hey," he said, hushed. "Can I talk to you for a sec—"

Thankfully, Wesley interrupted with an overly enthusiastic entrance. "I would say I hope you all had your Wheaties this morning, but it looks like someone took it a step further," he said, plucking a kolache from the rapidly emptying box.

"Maybe later," Beck offered as we all took our seats. I nodded politely but hoped not. I could do without circling back to one of the most embarrassing moments of my life. I'd already done plenty of ruminating the night before.

"Today," Wesley continued. "We start the convergence of family office with corporate, which will be a doozie."

I used to love new beginnings, but now I felt slightly sick at the prospect of starting over. While Wesley prattled about efficiency, deadlines, and workflows, I pulled out my phone, checking for approximately the seven hundred thousandth time to see if Hailey had responded to the message I'd left last night.

I furiously typed out another one.

I swear to God, if you don't call me back by the end of the day, I'm assuming you are dead, and I'm launching a full-blown investigation. We're talking the FBI. Liam Neeson's character from the Taken movies. The whole nine yards.

"Who can I count on to compile meeting minutes?" Wesley asked, pulling my attention back to the conference room.

I averted my eyes. It was gorilla rules in the conference room—no eye contact. He would sense my weakness, and I'd get suckered in. Just like I always did.

I looked up just enough to see him use a kolache as a pointer, swiveling to each of the faces at the table. No one offered because, to my knowledge, none of us are masochists who would like to add an extra hour to the workday by sifting through everyone else's meeting notes and then typing them up in a clear and consistent order, especially with this new project on the rise.

"No takers?" Wesley asked. Then, "Sorry Beck. The new recruit is honored with meeting-minute duty."

My eyebrows shot up in surprise. I pictured Beck and the disgusted look he wore yesterday after pulling me out of the water, all too easily imagining him with that look as he painstakingly compiled notes from today's meeting. I pretended to be very interested in one of the daisy-shaped buttons on my cardigan until I could get a grip on my smile and force it back to a neutral position. *I guess all that glitters is not gold.*

"That is, if no one else volunteers as tribute." Wesley waited for someone to chime in and then chuckled at his joke.

No one else joined. I might have participated a couple of days ago, but my ass-kissing days were done now that he'd given my position to Beck.

"No problem," Beck answered.

I thought about how late he'd stayed the night before and wondered if he'd had a chance to finish the videos for orientation training. If not, he'd have quite the workload.

Not my problem, I thought, capping my pen as if to snap that empathy closed.

"Great," Wesley said, thumbing through his notebook. "Next order of business—Ow!" He yanked his hand back and shook it, but then looked at me, amusement sparkling as he held the paper cut close to his body. "Can't let Emily see. Wouldn't want her passing out again."

Wesley looked at Ted, and the two started snickering.

I passed out once at the office two years ago, and they still wouldn't let me live it down. It had happened when Ted showed an X-ray of his jammed thumb and explained how the doctor had to yank it back into place. Feeling nauseous, I'd stood—planning an escape for the hallway—but immediately blacked out. They'd called an ambulance. It was a whole thing.

I'd tried to get them to stop fussing over me, telling them I was fine. Because it had happened before. I was a fainter.

It usually only occurred after I gave blood. In fact, it had happened so many times at blood drives that they told me to stop coming back. Like, my fainting spells were such an issue they'd rather pass on healthy blood than deal with the literal fallout.

Telling my officemates that bit of information had saved me an ambulance ride, but it was ultimately a mistake. The next day, Wesley sent an email to the team with the words Employee of the Month and, under it, a fainting goat gif. It had been a running joke since.

"Har, har," I said, wishing I could keep my cheeks from reddening.

I risked a glance at Beck, who seemed to be making a mental note of the exchange. *Redhead that likes to dive into questionable bodies of water also blacks out at the slightest mention of blood. Got it.*

Kill me now, I prayed to those gods of old and new. But a lightning bolt never obliged.

My phone vibrated just as Wesley wrapped up the meeting. Hailey's picture popped up on the illuminated screen. I packed up quickly and rushed to a stairwell a few doors from the conference room.

Before I could even utter a greeting, Hailey started rambling, "Okay. So I know I should have told you about starting a calligraphy business, and I was going to, but I wanted it to be more established when I asked you."

"Asked me what?" I demanded.

"To join me," she said like *duh, keep up.*

My mind reeled, picturing the calligraphy in Hailey's room, her business, and trying to see where I landed in all this.

"Like . . . as your business partner?"

"I know you hate your job, and you've always been so in love with calligraphy. It just makes sense."

None of it made sense. No part of this week made sense. At that point, I felt like I'd stumbled into The Upside Down in *Stranger Things*.

I pinched the bridge of my nose. "What I don't understand is how it makes sense for you?" My voice sounded angrier than I intended. "Since when has calligraphy been your thing?"

"Well." A pause. In the silence, I imagined her plotting the safest course for this conversation. "It started out as a relaxation thing. You always seem so Zen when doing calligraphy." Her voice rolled out softly as if we walked on eggshells here. And we did. "But then I got good at it and started to wonder if it could be more for me. I started up my business, and things were going well." The soft edges crested to something more robust, her voice swelling with pride.

"How well?"

"Well enough that I quit bookkeeping a few months ago."

I gaped. Calligraphy was an art. And just like any other art, it was subjective, a luxury, which made the industry incredibly flaky. And yet Hailey had decided to lean wholeheartedly on it. Let it feed her. Shelter her. The whole idea made me sweat.

"Are you sure that's a good idea?" I asked, not able to help myself.

"I made more from calligraphy last year than I did bookkeeping. Not by much, but my business is just starting."

I wanted to protest further and mention that bookkeeping was the secure choice, but I realized I'd sound just as jealous as I felt. So instead, I ground out a "That's great, Hailey."

I couldn't make my tone match the words, though. Instead, it sounded hollow, like the feeling in the pit of my stomach. The one that came with figuring out my sibling had whimsically decided to try something I'd been perfecting for decades only to be some fucking prodigy at it.

The universe wasn't even trying to hide the Texas-sized middle finger it was shooting at me. I'd worked my ass off at my job. I practiced drills and perfected my lettering. But none of that mattered. People like Beckett and Hailey were just cosmically blessed.

"I never meant to hurt you, Emily. I swear. I was going to tell you when the business got bigger—gained more traction. I know you need stability—"

I exhaled through my nose. "You act like I'm paranoid for wanting solid ground to stand on. Everyone wants stability."

"I know, I know. And you should, especially after the summer we lived out of Mom's van."

Precisely. That summer had jaded me, shattered my sense of security—like someone had turned my life upside down and rattled all its contents loose.

"But all of this is coming to light at a good time," she continued. I didn't like the overly cheery tone her voice had taken. "Because." She took a deep breath. "I'm moving to Florida with Braxton."

I gripped the railing, dizzied by Hailey's words. "What?"

"I'm staying in Florida. Braxton has been speaking with the owner of the venue he DJ'd at. This wedding was a test of sorts, and he passed with flying colors. They want to hire him full-time. He'll be working exclusively for the venue instead of having to find individual clients. It's a huge step for his career. And he wants me to move in with him. I really like it here."

"Everyone likes Florida, Hailey. That's why you visit. You don't live there permanently. Have you ever watched the news? It almost always starts with 'Florida man . . .'"

"Emily—" I could hear the eye-roll in her tone.

"You were supposed to be just visiting."

Something like panic gripped my chest. I was already losing Anna. I couldn't lose Hailey, too. Her boyfriend of two whole months couldn't just steal her away from me. I wanted to reach through the phone and yank her back home. And the worst part about it—I'd been the reason Hailey had gone to Florida with Braxton, the reason they'd started dating. If work hadn't stopped me from going on my trip, we would have had a great time *visiting* Florida, not setting down roots.

"I know, Emily, but I like it here. I love it," she amended. "The water here is blue—you can see all the way to the bottom like a swimming pool." My mind immediately drew up the brown waters of the gulf we grew up swimming in, muddied by river sediment. "And it's more than that. I can picture my life with Braxton here."

I was losing my footing in this argument. She'd already made up her mind, but I decided to throw one more punch. "You don't even know him! You just met. He could sell whale organs or make wigs out of pubes for a living—"

She laughed. "He's a DJ!"

"But that could just be a front. You wouldn't know because you just met him. Seriously, Hailey. I don't like this. Going on a fling vacation is one thing. Moving to a different state with someone—who probably doesn't even know your middle name—is crazy. I'm just going to say it. This is crazy, even for you."

An icy silence fell on the other end. I swallowed. But her retaliation came out quiet, calm. "Well, I would rather take risks than live like you. Hating life because you are too scared of change."

That comment stung even more than her secret calligraphy career. "That's not true."

"Emily, please. You won't even look for a different job, and you hate it there."

"So what? Everyone hates their job."

"No, they don't. But even if they did, you are like that even with your relationships."

I scoffed.

"Just look at your last boyfriend, Chad?" I rolled my eyes. Of course, she just had to bring up Chad. "He'd been hanging out with his *best friend*—" I didn't have to see her to know she used air quotes. "—*Mia*, the whole time. You tried so hard to make it seem fine until you found them fucking on his couch."

"Yeah. I was cheated on. Way to victim blame."

"I'm not! I'm just saying that you tend to try and force things to work when there is obviously a problem. So, excuse me for passing on your relationship advice. I have to go. Braxton is taking me to his favorite bakery."

"Hailey, wait."

"I just wish you could be happy for me," she said before hanging up.

I looked at the disconnected phone, resisting the urge to lob it down the stairwell. Judging by the jumble of thoughts in my head and the tight feeling in my chest, a breakdown was impending. But I took some steadying breaths, gripping the rails until my palms ached. I didn't want to cry at work, and more importantly, I didn't have the time. The tears would have to wait. I allowed myself one long shuddering exhale before heading back into the building. But before I could, the door to the stairwell swung open, and I had to back up to keep from being hit.

"Oh, sorry," Beck said, realizing he'd nearly smacked me with the door. "Anna said she saw you go this w—" He stopped. His brows furrowed into what looked like concern. "Are you okay?" His voice rumbled so deep, so quiet, I could have imagined it.

I might not have allowed myself to shed a tear, but he was probably asking because my traitorous eyes were red-rimmed. And knowing my pale complexion, the argument had more than likely left red blotches on my chest. Why was it that I couldn't act normal around him?

"I'm fine," I said way too quickly to be believable.

He looked at me, obviously skeptical. For someone with sharp brows, he had soft—almost sleepy—eyes, and they searched mine. It was like he expected to read what had happened in my irises.

"You were looking for me?" I asked.

My tone came out harsher than I'd intended. Yeah, he'd been a jerk yesterday, but I'd planned to be civil with him. At this point, though, he was at the wrong place at the wrong time—just a casualty in the falling out with my sister.

"Uh—yes. I need your notes to compile them for the meeting minutes."

I ripped the pages out of my notebook with all the grace of a second grader tearing pages from a workbook. The edges were as jagged as I felt. "Anything else?" It took great effort to keep the trembling out of my voice.

"No," he said quietly, but the look on his face contradicted him.

Before he could ask me again if I was okay or, worse, bring up what happened yesterday, I made for my exit.

"Then I'd better get back to work," I said, brushing past him.

Back in my cubicle, I inhaled the coconut aroma from the new wallflower, trying—and failing—to get my mind off Hailey so I could work. If I didn't get busy soon, I'd be working late enough for the custodial staff to kick me out. Finally, I decided to pull up another IT ticket. Distracted working would be more efficient than not working at all.

I didn't surface until hours later. I'd declined to get lunch with Anna. Declined to refill my water when my throat got parched. Just forced myself to keep plowing ahead. It wasn't until my bladder threatened to unleash on my swivel chair that I relented. For the journey there and back, I kept my head down. I couldn't afford to have someone stop me for casual conversation. I needed to trudge through these tickets as quickly as possible before we started tackling the first phases of the convergence project.

"Hey, Emily. Real quick." Beck waved me over. Apparently, I hadn't mastered the unapproachable look I'd been aiming for. "Jordan from family office emailed me about this budgeting error." He pointed to the screen. "Have you seen it before? I'd ask Anna, but she left early for a doctor's appointment."

I leaned in, noticing that he had a fresh scent, an *I just stepped out of the shower* smell. If I could bottle it up, I'd plug it into my wallflower. Trying to keep my breathing even, instead of taking the deep inhales I wanted, I checked the error. I didn't recognize it. Could I figure out a solution? Sure. A quick Google search would do the trick. But it was his time versus mine; I wasn't going to take on his workload along with my own, especially knowing my paycheck probably dwarfed compared to his. Part of me knew my resentment was childish. He probably didn't know he ran me over to get the promotion. He was new and asking for my help. I should have obliged. Made him feel welcome.

But after all that happened yesterday and today with Hailey saying she wasn't coming back home, I felt like the strings of a violin pulled too tight during tuning. You can only endure so much pressure before you snap.

"No. I don't recognize the error. But then again, *I'm* not the senior analyst."

Beck turned to face me, looking to see if I was teasing. When I held a level gaze, he gave a short laugh. "I was just seeing if you'd encountered it before. Sorry for asking," he said, swiveling back to face the screen.

I retreated to my cubicle and tried to work until the guilt simmered in my chest, causing me to relent. I looked up the error. It was a simple fix. I decided to email Beck, afraid if I faced him again, I'd bite his head off for something else. I copied his email from a group message Wesley sent.

Most people would have opted for first initial then last name at The Arlow Group dot net. Not Beck. He was just Beck A. How professional. I couldn't remember what Wesley said his last name was. I checked the signature of his previous email. But it was just Beck A. there, too.

I thought it must be a bad one, and I found myself curious, running through the last names that started with A. But I shut it down quickly, frustrated at the time I'd already wasted stopping at Beck's cube. It didn't matter what his last name was. I closed out the email I'd been about to compose. He was a big boy. He'd figure out the error.

By the time four o'clock rolled around, I'd plowed through all my IT requests and made some impressive headway on our next project. I wasn't used to being done so early. It was liberating. I knew I had my acute anger and the laser focus that came with it to thank.

At four-fifteen, I watched Wesley make his exit. Same time he did every day. It must be nice to leave in your Bentley while the sun is still out because you are good at delegating to your lackeys.

I considered getting a head start on processing workflows, but my hand hovered over the mouse. I hadn't eaten anything besides that ko-lache. My stomach rumbled. My eyes burned from staring at my computer and trying to keep from crying over my sister. My brain felt like it had turned to oatmeal in my skull. I needed a break.

I thought of Anna and her baby shower invites. In a snap decision, I logged out of my computer. My bamboo pajamas, calligraphy pens, a bowl of instant ramen noodles, and spending the rest of the evening braless called my name. I gathered my things, high on the idea of taking a break to work on something I enjoyed.

Leaving the office before five felt like breaking the law. But somehow, that little act of rebellion filled me with new life. Until Beck joined me on the elevator. His shoulders drooped as he looked up and noticed his ride buddy was me: Emily, who liked to jump into waterways, fainted at the mention of papercuts, cried in the stairwell, and demeaned you when you asked for help. Not my best couple of days.

The ride down was quiet, rigid. Standing close to him, I felt small. He wasn't all-star tall, but he had my 5' 5" beat by a head. The elevator had a mirror panel in it. I glanced over. He stared at his shoes with tight eyes, looking as tired as I felt.

When the elevator stopped, he motioned for me to leave first.

"Did you figure out the error?" I asked, surprising myself.

"Do you care?"

My head whipped in his direction. One corner of his mouth seemed on the verge of twitching upward, drawing my attention to his full lips.

I snapped my eyes back to his. "If you don't figure it out, Jordan will email me next. So yes, I care."

"It's handled," he said, holding the doors to the waterway open for me. "Have a nice swim home."

I gaped. Well, I guess someone had to bring it up. I put my arms in akimbo. "I'm just impressed by your bravery," I said, indicating his shirt. "Continuing to put your Banana Republic collection at risk after what happened to the other one."

He sighed. "My reaction yesterday wasn't about you. And it certainly wasn't about a shirt." I expected him to explain further, but he just nodded and tossed, "Night, Lane," over his shoulder.

Not Emily. First names were for friends. If I had known his last name, I would have given him the same sendoff. Instead, I remembered how Beck had cringed in the morning meeting when Susan used his full first name. My goodbye would be even better.

"Night, Beckett," I said, enjoying the way he halted briefly, letting me know I'd hit my mark.

Chapter 4

With my jammed door, there was no graceful entry into the apartment. I had to channel my inner linebacker, shoving my shoulder into the dense wood to get it to budge. All the while, the neighbors squabbled on the floor below. Once I finally made my forced entry, I could hear every other word hurled at each other. Today, they appeared to be arguing about a comb, of all things.

Hailey detested my apartment. When she first helped me move in, she nearly packed the rental truck back up and made me come home with her. She'd taken one good look at the broken security gate left ajar and told me her older sister senses were tingling. On the outskirts of Houston, my apartment had been on the cheaper side, which, Hailey had informed me, also equated to the more dangerous side. I'd rolled my eyes at her concern. So, the apartment wasn't perfect. It had character. And though the people in my building could be eccentric, they all had good hearts.

Besides, the price was right. I had student loans to pay off, and I ultimately wanted to save up enough to afford a down payment on a house. I considered living in a less-than-ideal apartment a tradeoff for owning a nice home one day.

I'd finally convinced Hailey to let me stay by saying we just needed to make the place more welcoming, and after a few trips to my favorite consignment shops and dollar spots, we'd made a valiant effort. A vase sat on the coffee table, fake lavender proudly stretching out of it. A print of an adorable café adorned with a wall of pink flowers hung in the living room. And the couch had throw pillows with the same palette as conversation hearts.

I'd been going for a Frenchy pastel vibe, but in the apartment with its bent blinds and the water-stained ceiling, we'd only marginally increased the value of my new living space. Still, Hailey had relented with a playful eye-roll. "You and your glass-half-full vision," she'd said. At the time, I'd considered it a compliment. But now, thinking about what she'd said about my past romantic relationships, I suddenly didn't think she intended it that way.

Great. Now, I'd be analyzing every conversation between us to see if she'd been dropping clues on how she really felt about me all along.

I didn't come home to sulk, I thought, trying to pep talk myself into being productive. *I have invitations to address.*

First order of business, I reached under the back of my shirt, un-hooked my bra, pulled it through my sleeve, then sling-shotted it across the room. It almost made the edge of the hamper.

Bit by bit, I traded my work clothes for pajama bottoms with a garden party—flowers and teacups—and a U of H shirt I'd washed so many times you could barely make out the lettering. Finally, I pulled my cop-pery, right-at-the-ribs-length hair into a messy bun at the nape of my neck.

Seated at a desk that took up a disproportional amount of space in my living room, I picked up a workbook with pages and pages of drills: upstrokes, downstrokes, turns, loops, curves, letters, and words, words, words. Though I'd never consider myself an artist, I even had pages of embellishments: floral arrangements, leaves, berries, and frames to put words or phrases in.

I fell in love with calligraphy in eighth grade. It had helped me cope—to find some control in my life—after the summer Mom had quit her stable career to pursue her love of painting. I'd learned firsthand that the grass isn't always greener on the other side. Her paintings didn't sell as she'd hoped, and we'd been evicted from our apartment just to move in with her emotionally abusive art buddy. I didn't think things could possibly get worse and then he kicked us out, and only one door slid open—the one to Mom's minivan.

I'd never felt fear quite as potent: not knowing when I'd eat next or where the meal would come from. Never slept as restlessly as when only a sheet of metal stood between us and the rest of the world.

So, when Mom got a job teaching at an art studio, effectively placing all our feet back on solid ground, I sought out control in any form. Another teacher at her studio taught calligraphy, and I clung to her lessons like they were the last life preserver on the boat. I dedicated myself to the craft, becoming almost religious about practicing my drills.

Only recently, with my job, had I been unfaithful. The entries for my drills had grown farther and farther apart. And though I didn't think my skills had suffered, I knew they would eventually if I kept abandoning them.

I'd once upon a time dreamed of letting my calligraphy be something more than the occasional addressing of envelopes for friends or quotes daintily scribed and framed as Christmas presents. I really thought one day I could make it into a side hustle. I still had the books about opening a small business, highlighted and tagged with sticky notes, on my bookshelf, but starting my own business belonged among all the other fantasies on the shelf. Because that's all it was.

Even if I had the time, I doubt I could have done what Hailey was doing. I was too afraid that something I loved deeply might end up being another disappointment, another heartbreak.

Honoring my old ritualistic routine, I lit a nearby three-wick candle—pineapple-scented—before starting an acoustic playlist. Going through these motions put my mind in the right place—like a baseball player tapping his bat in a certain pattern before taking a pitch.

The stack of blush envelopes and the list of addresses waited in my desk drawer. I pulled these out along with all the other tools of the trade: a pencil, a jar of ink, nibs, an envelope stencil, a ruler, and a laser level.

I lost myself in the magic of it all. Hailey had called calligraphy Zen, and she wasn't wrong. I mapped out each name and address, looking at the descenders of the name to tell me how to best center it, and chose the right nib to place into the holder to make my weapon of choice—the pointed pen.

Then, I took it to the envelopes.

If you watch calligraphy on TikTok, chances are you think it's quick work—each address looped and curved in a minute or less. However, most of those videos are sped up. In real life, the process is methodical and deliberate. In other words, slow. Calligraphy is slow.

I used a pencil first. For the address, I etched block letters, and then, with careful, practiced strokes, I used calligraphy for the name. I erased imperfections and added embellishing swoops before my pen ever touched the paper.

But when the nib finally connected with the page, the magic happened: heavy strokes going down, followed by the lightest of upstrokes. It reminded me of following music in choir. Every downstroke belted a proud fortissimo, and every upstroke sang a delicate, hushed pianissimo. I loved using the pointed pen. I'd initially tried it because I wanted to feel more like a Hogwarts student, dipping my pen in ink. I'd kept using it over the years because its sharp tip allowed for the slightest wisps of lines—very useful for details—but it also forced me to slow down. To take my time, just live and breathe and enjoy. When else did I ever do that?

Each envelope took me about ten minutes, give or take. With a list of fifty addresses, I finally put the pen down at just ten, eyes bleary from focusing so intently, with still thirty to go. I wanted to do more, but I had work in the morning.

Ugh. Work.

The next day had all but laid itself out in front of me. Meetings that should be emails. A mountain of support tickets. And Beckett—Beck, shirt enthusiast, promotion thief, and a handsome face marred by a smug smile.

I thought of the comment he made earlier.

Well, have a nice swim home.

What an ass.

I hated that I'd let him get under my skin—that I'd been rude back. That wasn't me. But ever since yesterday, ever since he'd entered the picture, I hadn't felt like myself around him.

I needed space and time to clear my head. Tomorrow was Friday. Maybe I could call in and have a three-day weekend to gather myself.

Even as I daydreamed about a self-care day, the idea of coming in on Monday to a pile of work, stank up the fantasy. I imagined teachers must feel the same way when taking a sick day. *Sure, rest would be nice, but someone had to write the sub plans.*

So, begrudgingly, I climbed into bed and tried very hard to keep Beck out of my mind, which is precisely why he was all I could think about.

I yawned even as my flip-flops slapped across the indoor pool deck of my gym.

I'd debated skipping my morning swim. I could have capitalized on forty-five extra minutes of sleep if I had, but even as I shut off my alarm and turned over, I knew I'd get up, knew I'd find my ass in the pool that morning because as much as I loathed that first freezing plunge, it electrified me awake better than any espresso ever could. And today, I needed all the energy I could get.

Putting my swim cap on, my hand slipped, causing it to smack against my ear. I rubbed the side of my head, thinking sourly about what a *great* day it already was.

There were only two lanes at Power Gym. An elderly couple always took one, and I used the other. My freestyle swimming routine looked bland next to all the aqua jogging and frog kicks done on the other side of the lane rope.

The older gentleman waved. I waved back, but he was already off, a pool noodle under his arms as he kicked leisurely down the lane.

I smiled until I dipped my toes in the water. I'd chosen Power Gym because it was conveniently located a few buildings down from my office, but while the gym boasted an eighty-degree pool, my toes determined that was a lie.

Self-preservation told me to back away from the chilly water. I ignored the instinct and plunged in. I came up, gasping from water that felt mighty close to being the preferred bath temperature for the Narnia witch. Eighty degrees, my ass.

Still shivering, I slipped on my Aftershocks. The water-proof head-phones had been a game changer for swimming, and halfway down the lane, I found my muscles loosening and my mind giving way to the rhythm of my freestyle while I enjoyed some light-hearted acoustic music.

Two laps in, I wondered what Beck would think if he saw me now—if he knew swimming was my cardio of choice.

Have a nice swim home.

I gritted my teeth underwater.

I hated myself for allowing Beck to permeate this space. Swimming was something I'd picked up in the last couple of years, and while my strokes wouldn't be winning any gold medals, I looked forward to the time in the pool, where the water muffled out the rest of the world, and the dappled light hitting the depths was far more relaxing than the blaring light of my monitor.

Even with my calming music and calming atmosphere, my thoughts kept orbiting Beck, like I'd somehow drifted into his solar system and couldn't pull myself free.

Over and over, I kept thinking about how I'd brushed him off when he'd asked for help. How I should have just lent him a hand because, God, it was only his second day, and I'd been a bitch. Even if he'd started it first, I didn't have to match his energy.

At the end of my third lap, I discarded my headphones at the side of the pool. I needed to get my mind off everything, and the soft playlist didn't have the power to pull me away like I needed.

So, I pushed myself, working my arms and legs furiously until the burning in my lungs and muscles took the stage, leaving me with little room to fret or worry about anything else. I knew I'd be sorry tomorrow for hitting it so hard today, but I didn't care. I needed the relief, especially before the looming workday ahead.

Chapter 5

"**N**o." I rubbed my temples, trying to preemptively soothe an emerging headache. "That isn't going to work, not the way we set up the attributes in the system."

This was supposed to be a simple meeting—have the order management team give an output for all the fields available in the management system. They were not supposed to take a sledgehammer to said system entirely.

"Then it looks like you'll have to reset some of those parameters," Frank said, unyielding.

I didn't know him well, but his reputation preceded him. The man, twenty or so years my senior, worked for the family office and had a knack for bullying his way through meetings.

I'm not one for confrontation, but I hadn't spent the last week setting up the parameters just for Frank to come in like a wrecking ball, Miley Cyrus style. "We defined these attributes together."

"Maybe *your* team agreed on them. I surely didn't."

I looked at my team for backup, but Susan had checked out long ago, finding a chip in her magenta shellac nails far more pressing. Jefferey scrolled on his phone, and Ted's head drifted downward as he sank quickly into sleep. Anna and Wesley had attended a meeting with accounting. Which left . . . Beck.

It had been about two weeks since he started, and he still had the courtesy to pay attention during meetings, or at least act like it, but we hadn't spoken much since our tiff outside the office.

My throat felt cottony just thinking about asking him for help, but—a true sign of my desperation—I swallowed it back. "Beckett," I managed, the use of his full first name eliciting the slightest twitch in his jaw. "Can you please pull up the meeting notes from last Tuesday?"

"Sure."

He at least attempted a polite smile as he angled his laptop for me to see. Leaning close, I got a whiff of his fresh scent and had to hold back a little sigh of contentment. Then I mentally whacked myself with a ruler over the knuckles for momentarily forgetting the task at hand—standing up to Frank, the office place bully.

Focus.

Without asking, I commandeered his laptop, scrolling down the document to where the team had discussed—

Aha!

There it was: the notes on the defined attributes. I eagerly scrolled until I got to the end of that section. Something in my stomach dropped.

Wait. No.

My eyes went back up to the start of that section, scanning for anything about the parameters we had agreed upon, but— "It's not here," I voiced, unable to save face by keeping the disbelief at bay.

Beck leaned in. "Let me help. Which part are you looking for?"

"The notes I gave you after our meeting last week." I knew I'd written at least a page on all the details. My notes were missing entirely from the section, possibly the whole document. It had probably just been an oversight, but he hadn't liked me since I got his sleeve wet, and now my notes were conveniently missing. It left a bitter taste in the back of my throat.

He scrolled for a bit but had to start from the beginning when he didn't find what we searched for. "I don't know." He had the decency to sound remorseful. I'd give him that. "I thought I included them. I'm sorry."

"Well, I guess it's settled then," Frank said, stretching back in his chair.

And it was. Nothing I could do about it now except wallow in both work and self-pity.

Back at my cube, I couldn't concentrate, not with the meeting replaying in my mind. I rested my head on my desk, trying to climb out of my pity party, but I was wedged in. I took a few deep breaths but nearly gagged. The coconut scent had put my cubicle in a tropical fog, and while everyone else complimented the aroma, I found it less and less tolerable every day.

Coconut used to be one of my favorite scents, but the aroma therapy had backfired. Now, I'd never be able to smell coconut without thinking of work. I unplugged it, but the thought of sitting and waiting for the scent to dissipate made me nauseous.

I decided to take an early lunch instead, venturing to the steps on the walkway before finding a spot in the sunshine. March in Texas was a dream—that sweet in-between from a soppy winter to a hellishly hot and humid summer. *This is what I need,* I thought as I closed my eyes, chewing my chicken salad sandwich. *Some sunshine. A break.*

I pulled up Pinterest on my phone and started a new vacation board. I was going to do it: go on a vacation. Work wouldn't stop me this time. I spent about ten minutes poring over tropical locations with white-sanded beaches. But then I stopped. Who would I go with? Hailey wouldn't plan a vacation with me now. Not when I'd flaked on Florida and then lectured her over a life decision she'd been excited about.

It had been two weeks since our argument. We'd fought before, but this felt big. I could barely stand the thought of her living in a different state, let alone losing her to a stupid fight.

I pulled up our text message thread, suddenly frantic for contact.

Me: I miss you.

I sighed. She was probably snorkeling with Braxton or sailing, or maybe they took an overnight trip to Disney.

But then my phone pinged with a message from her.

Hailey: I miss you too, babe.

I racked my brain, trying to think of ways to get her to warm up to me.

Me: Send me a picture of you enjoying Florida. I need to live vicariously through you.

Hailey obliged, sending one of her in a wide-brimmed hat and a flowy coverup dress. Hot pink bikini straps peeked from her neckline. She was laughing as a turquoise wave crashed at the back of her knees.

Me: Looks like you are having the time of your life.

Me: I'm happy for you, Hailey.

I kept adding on, desperate to fill the space and silence between us.

Me: I'm really sorry about what I said before. I was having a bad day and your news just sent me over the edge.

I winced at my phone, afraid I'd severed the olive branch by bringing up our argument. Then, it vibrated with a video call.

"Hey," I said, answering.

"What happened?" Hailey asked, her nose and cheeks a tad pinker than normal and, overall, more freckly.

Though her complexion still couldn't compare to the collection on my face and shoulders.

"Just work stuff," I said before taking another bite of my sandwich.

"Tell me."

I swallowed down the bite, trying to decide how to calmly relay the events back to Hailey. "Well, you know the promotion Wesley has been waving in front of me like a carrot?"

"Yeah?"

"They hired out," I said, taking another chunk of sandwich to disguise the inevitable rising emotion.

"Are you fucking shitting me?"

I nearly choked on my sandwich. Hastily, I looked over my shoulder, double-checking that no one from the office had the same idea to eat lunch outside today. But it was just us.

Having another person on my side felt good, which led to me opening up and letting it all out. "The worst part? The guy they hired is an absolute waste of space. Today, I needed him to just pull up the notes that I *handed* to him, but did he have them ready? No!" My pulse quickened at the memory of facing Frank empty-handed because Beck had, what? Purposefully omitted my notes? "Forget senior-level associate. He's more of a senior-level asshole."

Hailey gave some sort of remark, but I didn't hear her over the rush of my pulse in my ears as the aforementioned senior-level ass rounded the stairwell near me.

I eyed the paper bag in his hands.

Oh God.

He must have gone out for lunch. He didn't slow as he passed me, but he did give a smug, almost imperceptible look as he headed toward the building.

He hadn't heard me, had he?

"Emily, hello!" Hailey said, pulling my attention back to her. "What are we going to do about this? Cover his office in sticky notes? . . . No," she said, answering herself. "That's too tame." She snapped her fingers. "We can hide a dead fish in his desk."

"Wait. What are we talking about, and why do you sound like a member of the mafia?"

"Hazing the new guy until he quits. Keep up."

I laughed. "We are not hazing anyone, Hailey."

"He stole your job and is making your life miserable. He's office enemy number one. He's got to go. It's called taking matters into your own hands."

I smirked. "You know, a *normal* sister would just say, 'I'm sorry about your job.'"

"No. I think any normal, *loving* sister would react this way. But I am sorry about your job. I really am. They don't deserve you, Emily."

I shrugged. "Them's the breaks."

"Have you given what I said any thought?"

"The fish thing?"

"No." She seemed suddenly very interested in something off-screen. She had a habit of tugging on the hem of whatever clothing covered her thighs when she felt nervous. "About taking over my business."

The last thing I wanted was to shut Hailey down after just smoothing things over, but her idea sounded like something a preteen dreamed up:

flowery and unrealistic. "I don't know, Hailey. Work is just psychotic right now."

Definitely not a lie, though not the only reason for my decline. Somehow, placing the blame on work seemed like cushioning the blow.

"It always is." Hailey stopped playing with her hem. She looked into my eyes with newfound righteous indignation. "Which is kind of my point. You have busted your balls for that company for years, and they still haven't promoted you. Even after you carried the team with the last go-live."

"You've only heard my side of the story. You're biased," I said, balling up the foil from my sandwich.

"No. I know you, Emily. You are a perfectionist. You don't half-ass anything. When you do something, you are committed. Maybe it's time you take your talent elsewhere." She looked at me pointedly. "I'd love to see what you can do with Lettering Lane," she added with a playful, lilting voice.

"Is that the name of your company?" I asked, delighted by the not-so-subtle placement of our last name.

Hailey blushed. "Yeah. I know. It's a little cheesy."

"I kind of love it."

She smiled brilliantly at the compliment.

"Hailey, I have to be honest. I'm jealous. I can't believe you did it—started a calligraphy business. You're so fearless." She tried to wave me off, but I kept going. "No. Seriously. I wish I could be more like you."

"Now's your chance." She looked at me through her long lashes, daring me.

"Hailey—"

"Run my business. Try on my life for a bit."

"It's just—" *Messy, risky.* "Complicated." The thought of losing my benefits alone turned a few of my hairs gray.

"Please, at least consider it. If not taking over Lettering Lane, at least apply for a different job. Surely The Arlow Group isn't the only company in need of a boss bitch business analyst."

"Sure, I'll think about it," I said because I'd already been on the steps for thirty minutes. There was work to be done. "I gotta go."

"Hey, real quick. I'm going to be in town this weekend."

"You will?" My voice took on a new octave.

"Yup! Mom's coming over Saturday if you want to swing by."

"Sure, yeah. That sounds like fun."

"Thanks! I need all the help I can get."

I narrowed my eyes. "Did I just unknowingly agree to help you move?"

"Yup! I've got to box up all my stuff, so come ready to work."

I groaned, but I'd be happy doing just about anything with Hailey. Even if that meant wrapping her mugs in newspaper and wiping down her silverware drawer.

When Beck visited my cube, I had thirteen tabs open and was ready to stick a pen in my eye if it meant I could take a break from the spreadsheet in front of me.

Out of my peripheral vision, I'd seen someone approaching. Then I got the whiff of his scent. I let out a long exhale.

"How can I help you?" I asked without taking my eyes off the screen.

"Can you clarify something in your notes," he said, sounding about as enthused to be there as I was to have him.

I spun away from the screen to face him, trying to rub the burning blue light from my eyes without messing up my eyeshadow. "Sure. What's your question?"

He showed me a bullet from the notes I'd given him over our most recent meeting with Frank. "Well, here you defined this attribute as header level information, but it's supposed to be line level, isn't it?"

"No, you are thinking of purchase orders, which, if you look on—" I reached over and flipped a couple of pages. "—This page, you will see that here." I worked to bite back the words that had been simmering all day. I reminded myself that I was a professional. There was a calm way to bring issues to the table. He probably had a good reason for not having my notes, but as I looked at him, these words came spewing out: "Not that it matters what I wrote since you are going to inevitably omit all my information in the meeting minutes."

Shit. So much for professionalism.

"I knew that would come back to haunt me," he said, leaning against the wall of my cubicle. God, I hated how long and lean the action made him look.

"Come back to haunt *you*? *I'll* be the one redefining attributes for a week. Minimum. On top of everything else I'm already doing."

"Look, I'm sorry. I promise I didn't intentionally leave out your portion of the notes for that part of the meeting. But can you blame me? Your notes aren't notes. They're dissertations," he said, thumbing through my pages from earlier as proof.

My jaw opened, then shut, then opened again. "I'm detail-oriented."

"Then maybe you should be the one compiling the meeting minutes."

"Because I'm detail-oriented, I *shouldn't* be doing the meeting minutes. When I used to do them, I had to have everything perfectly aligned.

It took me forever." I scrunched my nose in mock sympathy. "Guess that's the perks of being a senior-level associate."

I turned back to my computer, ready to face the spreadsheets over another minute with Beck, but he hovered near the opening of the cubicle.

"Look, I really am sorry about screwing up with Frank. I made sure to add his changes to the new meeting notes. The newly defined attributes he requested are highlighted and bolded in case we need them next time." I nodded but didn't look back at him. "And I'll help you with the reconfigurations, but it will have to wait until tomorrow. I have to go."

My eyes darted to the time at the bottom of the screen. "Do you leave at four-thirty every Thursday?" I asked, turning back to face him.

He quirked an eyebrow. "Are you keeping tabs on me?"

My cheeks warmed. "I told you. I'm detail-oriented."

Beck shrugged, stepping toward the exit. "I guess leaving early on Thursdays is just another perk of being a senior-level asshole."

My mouth dropped open in horror.

Senior-level asshole.

He *had* overheard my conversation with Hailey.

Before I could do more than gape like a fish, he turned to go. "Night, Lane."

I'd just flopped onto the couch to inhale a steaming bowl of beef instant ramen noodles, a great celebration dinner for finishing up the invitations for Anna's baby shower, when I realized I had an unread message from Hailey. She'd sent it several hours ago.

Hailey: I have a bride who wants to meet next month. Have you thought about what I said? About taking over my business for a while?

Try on my life.

Her words echoed in my head: a sweet succulent dare out on a limb like a peach for the taking. But I couldn't just try on her life. This wasn't akin to squeezing my ass into her skinny jeans.

The idea was ridiculous.

And yet.

The possibilities rolled out in front of me. Days with the blinds open, the sun spilling onto my latest project. Listening to my favorite acoustic playlist while working my magic. Invitations dipped in gold foil. Envelopes sealed with wax. Names written on flower-embellished place cards. Menu items on glass in a flirtatious font.

It surprised me—how badly I wanted it. Maybe because I hadn't given calligraphy as a side hustle any serious thought in years. Work was too busy to indulge in such fantasies. Besides, it was risky to start a business, let alone one considered a luxury service and, therefore, an unnecessary one.

Calligraphy added an elegant and personal touch, but when budgeting for an event gets tight, calligraphy is easily one of the first things to go. And, let's be honest, if it were my wedding and I had to choose between pretty place cards and a three-tiered buttercream cake, buttercream would win every time.

Somehow, Hailey had managed to do it, started this business and found success, enough to make a living off her earnings.

I sent her a message back before I could chicken out.

Me: What platform do you use to keep in contact with clients?

Hailey: I created a Gmail just for Lettering Lane.

Next, she sent over the address and the password.

The organization of the account pleasantly surprised me. Each client had her own folder. Notes filled the calendar with due dates. It jarred me, all this coming from the girl whose backpack in high school had contained an avalanche of loose papers and half-empty snack trash.

Me: Who is the client?

Hailey: Victoria. I already completed all the invitations and signage for the shower. So there's just some signage for the wedding and she wants live lettering at her shower.

I frowned. A lot of calligraphers did live lettering. I'd seen plenty of YouTube videos on it. They'd set up a table, and guests would come over to have a favor signed—or a product if done in a store. I typically practiced calligraphy alone in my apartment, braless. The idea of having an audience made me sweat, but I supposed I could do it.

Me: What does she want to be signed?

Hailey: Capiz shells

Me: When is the shower?

Hailey: Last Saturday in April

That would give me over a month to mentally prepare. I opened Victoria's folder and started clicking through the email threads. It looked as though Hailey must have been communicating with Victoria through a wedding planner, Amanda.

I studied the shower invite sample with its deep green envelope and gold lettering and immediately recognized it from the letter I'd found in Hailey's laundry pile. I made a mental note to mail the lost invite the next time I was at Hailey's.

Clicking through emails, I found Victoria's color scheme. It seemed like Hailey and Amanda must have done a lot of communicating over the phone because I didn't see much about the signage or live lettering Hailey had referred to.

I opened the most recent email, which had been sent to Hailey today. Amanda had requested a meeting. Victoria wanted to get with each vendor to ensure everyone was on the same page about deadlines and expectations.

As an almost P.S., Amanda asked if Hailey could do something for the wedding similar to the attached picture—a pane of glass brushed with bright colors, then in the middle of the splash of color, a Mr. and Mrs. Last Name in white calligraphy letters followed by a wedding date.

I considered it. I hadn't done a project exactly like that, but I felt certain I could pull something like that off. I'd do it in layers. My lettering on the glass would come first, possibly gold instead of the white in the example photo. Then I'd add her colors to the back: a swipe of sweet coral followed by a mellow magenta, all backdropped by a deep plum.

My heart rate picked up at the prospect of it. I set my phone down, trying to rein myself in. Because I shouldn't have even been entertaining the prospect. The idea of getting to use my calligraphy skills, to show off what years of practice and dedication could do . . . it was exhilarating. And that felt dangerous, like I was standing too close to the edge of the Grand Canyon. If I got distracted by the beauty of it, I'd fall into its depthless, gaping hole.

But then again, what was the risk? I wouldn't quit The Arlow Group. Hailey had already done the heavy lifting—getting the business up and running. I just had to keep it that way.

I'd wanted a vacation. Maybe, in a way, this could be it. A much-needed distraction from the brutally long workdays.

I replied to Victoria's message.

Me: I'd love to meet and about the glass pane, let me see what I can do.

Chapter 6

I'd been too excited to sleep last night. It reminded me of being in elementary school, that last night of summer when you lie awake in bed knowing only your new teacher's name. That fear and thrill of the unknown, being on the cusp of change, heart thrumming, and mind reeling with the possibilities. Taking on Hailey's client, accepting the job, had awoken that feeling in me.

But now, getting ready to dip my toes in the cold pool, all I felt was grumpy, possibly a little doubtful of the decision. I should have slept on it before being so quick to decide.

It's fine. It will be fine. I can still back out, I reminded myself, nearing the lanes. The first of which had my favorite elderly couple. The man backstroked down the lane while the woman pumped her arms, moving along in the aqua jogger.

What wasn't expected was the guy in the other lane, the *only* other lane. Barring the elderly couple, I hadn't ever seen anyone else in the pool at the time I swam. And this guy had the form of a pro. He gave off Michael Phelps vibes, the way he glided across the water, pulling himself forward with strong arms.

Peeling my eyes away from the Poseidon in the pool, I benched my duffle and mentally prepared myself for sharing a lane with someone who obviously had something serious to train for. Whether that be an Ironman or just to keep his back and shoulders chiseled, he was serious about it. I hated imposing, but I already had on my damn swimsuit, hair tucked into my cap, goggles suctioned around my eyes.

He stopped to get a gulp from his blender bottle, and I knew it was now or never to approach him. He might go for a marathon swim and not come to the surface for hours.

As I got closer, I couldn't help but admire the ink wrapped around his forearm: floral work with beautiful, intricate lines. The flowers popped in shades of red. I didn't know flowers, especially ones so delicate, could look masculine, but they did on this guy.

Poseidon of the gym pool noticed me and pinched a spot on his headphones, seeming to pause them. I crouched down to say, *Mind sharing a lane?* But as my goggled eyes fell on him, I realized, with horror, I recognized that confident jawline, the sharp eyebrows, those full lips.

My request died in my throat. Instead, I sputtered, "You're in my lane," to my office enemy.

Beck pulled off his goggles, laughing. "I'm sorry. This is my first day." He made a show of looking around. "Where can I find the reservation for this lane?"

"What are you doing here?" I asked because seeing him in my lane, in my pool, was like running into your gynecologist at the grocery store.

Worse. This was one of the few places I could unwind, and now I had to share with someone who flustered me to a point where I felt unrecognizable.

"Swimming," he answered with a flash of perfect teeth. "What are you doing here? I thought you only did open water."

"Har. Har." I looked around at the sad-looking, two-lane pool. This was like the Dollar General of gyms. "There have got to be natatoriums in the area that better suit your standards."

"What standards?"

I motioned vaguely toward his well-defined physique. He looked as if he'd been sculpted in pools with more lanes, pools more akin to an Olympic standard in every aspect.

He hiked an eyebrow, waiting for me to elaborate. But when I just shook my head, he said, "As I'm sure you are aware, this one is convenient, being so close to work."

"It used to be convenient," I muttered.

Beck smirked, and I suddenly became painfully aware of how un-dressed I was, crouched only a couple feet from him. While swimming might have tightened my arms and shoulders, I still had thighs that tattled on me for never turning down cake. And though I generally felt comfortable in my own skin, I found it difficult being half-naked in front of someone who probably ate kale for breakfast. Seriously, I could have guessed he had a nice body under those button-downs. But what I was seeing was . . . more than just nice. It was unholy.

A flicker of flight response kicked in. I could leave, kiss my swimming spot goodbye, and probably save myself the embarrassment of Beck scrutinizing my very liberal freestyle. But leaving wouldn't be saving face. Not really. It felt like losing to him, and I'd done enough of that lately.

Instead, I slipped into the biting water, clamping down on the urge to gasp at the polar plunge. I wouldn't give him the satisfaction of seeing a sign of weakness so early in the workout.

"Just stay on your side," I said.

Then I hit play on my headphones, pushing off from the wall before he could retort.

On a normal, pre-Beck day, I'd get lost in the serenity of my all-acoustic playlist and in the way the light dances across the bottom of the pool. Today, Beck's body took up all my headspace with his lean, muscular frame, which only made me angry with myself. I could not appreciate Beckett's—Beck, AKA Senior-level Asshole—body. Not allowed.

He kept darting past me, never seeming to tire. Annoying as hell with his graceful kick turns, while I had to stop and push off the side of the wall to go the other way. He had a desk job, for Pete's sake. Why did he need that much endurance?

I'd stopped every three hundred meters for a break, but toward the end of my workout, Beck finally stopped too, barely out of breath while I thought I'd pass out, trying to keep my huffing from him.

As he paused for another drink, my eyes were again drawn to his tattoo. I tried to guess what the flowers were—peonies, maybe—which stemmed from two bold, black bands. The space between the bands seemed empty. And I couldn't help but contemplate the meaning behind it. Was the negative space deliberate?

Beck caught me staring. He raised an eyebrow as he drank, his Adam's apple bobbing past a singular freckle on his throat.

"I wouldn't have pinned you as a tattoo guy," I said, taking my own sip of water.

"I don't know if I'd say I'm a 'tattoo guy.'" He held onto the wall, then pushed against it with his legs, stretching his arms and back. I definitely did not admire the chords of muscles beneath his skin. "It's just the one for now."

"You really into flowers or something?" I asked, trying to dig a little but also because I found myself genuinely curious.

He made a clicking noise of disapproval. "No. Not really into flowers."

"Then what's the story?"

He stopped stretching, a playful glint in his eyes. "I'll tell you when you beat me at one hundred."

Pssh. Two laps against Aquaman. I didn't have a prayer. "Fine. Keep your secrets."

"Come on. It will be good motivation."

"You've seen me swim. If you can even call it that. It's more like aggressive floating."

He laughed. Actually laughed at that. His eyes crinkled at the corners. The amusement was so authentic that I found myself smiling with him until I realized what I was doing.

"Well," I said, fixing my face back to a safer, neutral expression. "I'd better get back at it. The rest of us mortals have several more laps to catch up to you."

He'd started to reply, but I was off, not willing to spare another minute with him—the man who'd stolen my raise. Who'd embarrassed and insulted me out on the waterway.

Last night, I'd been right. Things were changing. I simply never would have guessed it would include sharing a smile with Beck.

Beck and I got to the office elevator at the same time and rode up in an awkward silence. Why was it that I constantly found myself in tight quarters with Mr. Beckett A? And now that I knew what he was hiding under that button down . . . The doors dinged, and I stalked out quickly, ready to put distance between me and those pectorals.

Then I realized we were headed to the same place—a huddle room with Anna to discuss the changes we needed to make based on Frank's request.

When I'd relayed the meeting to Anna, she'd been furious and cleared her schedule to make this task priority number one. She didn't want me to have to try and untangle this mess on my own, which was one of a million reasons why I dreaded her leaving. Who else would have my back like Anna? The rest of the team would watch me drown in work and throw another file folder at me instead of a life preserver.

Except for Beck. He had offered to help. Though, one could argue he'd been the one to get us into this mess by not having my portion of the meeting notes in the minutes. I'd tried to let him off the hook—told him Anna and I would knock it out, but he'd been insistent on helping. Besides, Anna thought it would be a good idea for him to attend since he'd been shadowing her anyway.

Anna looked up as we entered. Her eyes played ping-pong between us. "Is it raining outside?" I scrunched my brows, not sure why she was asking that. "You both have wet hair," she explained.

I scrunched the damp tips. Flustered after my swim, I barely had enough time to shower, let alone finish drying my hair. "Turns out Beckett here is a swimmer. I found him in my lane this morning."

Her lips pursed to an *oh* as Beck and I took seats on opposite sides of the table.

"Again, my apologies, Lane. I had no idea it was taken."

"Does that mean you won't be in my lane tomorrow?"

"No." He flashed a smile. "So, I extend my apologies in advance." So cheeky.

"Apology not accepted," I said, straightening some copy paper left on the table.

"Your last name suits you since you guard the lanes of Power Gym so well."

"Apparently not well enough," I muttered.

"Oh-kay," Anna loudly interjected. "Let's review the new parameters we are working with."

I happily obliged. I could be professional. Even with Beck, Senior-level Asshole.

After thirty minutes of working through the system, that theory was being tested by fire.

"What if we did this?" I said, sharing my screen with the others.

"But the system has what? Millions of orders? The customer will have to wait forever to search for an item. It's not user-friendly," Beck said.

And damn it. He was right. I'd been so focused on the in-house use that I hadn't even considered the customer's side, but it would be an issue. Beck might actually prove to be . . . competent. But I willed my expression to remain flat.

I tilted my head. "What if we schedule a job to store an index with header-level information in our own database? It will allow a quicker search of the orders themselves without going outside the ERP system."

"That—" I could see the spark in his eyes, an argument on his tongue. Then he stopped, really sampling my words. "Isn't a half-bad idea."

"Don't look so surprised, Beckett." He glared at how I weaponized his full first name, and I gave an overbearing smile, complete with a crinkled nose.

"Okay," Anna said tentatively, looking between us like she might have to jump up and play referee at any moment. "That will probably work. But we'll need to get some real-time data on this, make sure it is functional."

Beck and I nodded. We could at least agree with Anna.

"I'll get started on that," Beck offered, closing his laptop.

We watched him go. When the door closed, Anna looked at me pointedly. When I didn't offer anything, she said, "Are we going to talk about what just happened?"

"What do you want me to say, Anna? He's insufferable. He's been a thorn in my side ever since he pranced in here and took my promotion."

She gave me a long, assessing look. "You know I'm always on your side, and you should have gotten the promotion. Hands down," she began in a gentle voice, which immediately clued me in that I wasn't going to like what she had to say next. "But, and don't hate me, he's been really helpful to me."

I gasped. "Traitor."

"Hear me out," she said, palms up in a defensive pose. "He's a quick study. He's already taken the lead on many of my tasks, shouldering the burdens without me having to ask. And this last doctor's appointment, he offered to take over our scheduled Zoom meeting with the family office so I wouldn't have to be at the meeting during the visit. Do you know what it's like having to carry on a conversation with your colleagues while in stirrups? I mean, I turn the camera off. But still!"

I shuddered.

"Exactly."

"How are the doctor's visits going?" I craftily turned the conversation from my issues with Beck because Anna was talking about him as though he spent his free time rescuing kittens out of trees. "My Gracie Girl being good to her mommy?"

Anna rubbed her tight, round belly. "She's doing fine. We're doing fine." She read my expression. "Don't worry. I still have another two months before she arrives. From what I've read, the first one is usually stubborn about evicting. I'm sure I'll be here until forty weeks." Anna let out an exhausted sigh and shifted positions on her office chair.

I hated seeing Anna uncomfortable, and I knew she was so ready to meet her daughter and be a stay-at-home mom. But I was selfish and wanted Anna for as long as possible. Even still, I knew these two months would fly by.

Before I could get choked up at the idea of life in the office without my work wife, I pulled a Ziplock from my canvas bag and placed the neatly stacked pile of envelopes in front of Anna.

The recognition hit her face immediately. "You finished the invites?" Bright, contagious excitement replaced her exhaustion. She pulled them out, carefully inspecting the invitations: black strokes on the sweetest blush paper. "Oh, Emily."

"You like them?" I asked, that anxious feeling bubbling over my chest at someone examining something I took so much pride in.

"They are beautiful," she gushed. "Better than I imagined."

I was good at my job. Over the years, I'd evolved into quite the problem solver. But nothing ever matched up to this, someone appreciating my art—my calligraphy bringing someone joy. That never happened over spreadsheets.

I deflated for a moment until I remembered my secret life, taking over my sister's business, tucked safely away in my pocket.

Chapter 7

The weekend arrived, and I had to ignore the sick, swelling feeling in my chest that told me I didn't have time to help my sister pack when I had laundry, groceries, meal prep, checking emails, and support tickets. Saturdays and Sundays were slotted for catching up on work and tending to all the other tasks that ensured I could survive as a functioning adult.

But I didn't know when I'd have a chance to see my Floridian of a sister, and I looked forward to catching up with my mom, too. So consequences be damned.

Hailey barely got the door to her apartment open before nearly knocking me down with a hug. I squealed and put a foot down like a kickstand to keep us upright.

Then, Hailey pulled back to give me a hard pinch on the arm.

"Ow!" I said, rubbing the area.

"That's for letting my orchid die." She moved aside to let me see a shriveled papery flower hanging limply from a woody stem.

"I'm sorry! I lost my sister to Florida. I wasn't thinking about your houseplants. Look on the bright side. That thing is finally out of its misery."

Hailey went for another pinch, but I dodged. "I brought boxes," I offered, trying to extend an olive branch.

"Come on." She led me past a maze of cardboard and a half-packed living room. "You can get started on my calligraphy collection."

"You going to let the real expert pack up the supplies?" I asked with a smug smile.

"No. I just want to give you a task I think you can actually handle." The words were mean, but they held no bite.

"Ouch," I said, a hand dramatically flying to my chest.

Mom already sat cross-legged on the floor, pulling clothes out of Hailey's dresser.

"Hi, sweetie!"

I squatted to hug her and got a dose of serotonin that comes with catching the scent of home. "Hey, Mom! How's it going?"

"Same old, same old," she answered. I noted the blots of paint on her shirt. Same old, indeed. "What about you?"

"Just work, work, and more work," I said, eyeing Hailey's desk to map out the best plan for organizing the area.

"Hailey says you agreed to be her business partner," Mom said brightly.

"Did everyone know about your business *but* me?" I asked, not even trying to mask my hurt. I mean, geez, I was her sister. Her compadre. The one who brought her Mr. Goodbars when she was on her period. And watched horror movies every Halloween with her—even though I hated scary movies. In high school, we'd fawned over the same boys and avoided the same mean girls.

We'd made a preteen pact that we would be each other's maids of honor—drawn up a contract on notebook paper. We were close, to say the least. But not close enough for her to tell me she was making a business out of my passion, apparently.

My mom sighed and put down the shorts she'd just folded. "Sweetie, I think Hailey just wanted you to really consider joining."

"And I knew you wouldn't unless it was established," Hailey cut in, not nearly as gentle as Mom.

I made myself very busy then, lining the pens up and laying them in the zipper pouch. "You act like being careful is a deficit."

"It can be," Hailey muttered, snapping open a trash bag.

"It's not," Mom said. "Especially not after what happened to me—to us."

And that did it. Hailey and I shared a look. *Truce.* Because any time Mom brought up the summer that had uprooted our life, we did whatever we could to keep her from feeling guilty.

My eyes fell on the hunter-green envelope I'd found in Hailey's room weeks ago. The one that had been a window into Hailey's secret life. Before, the envelope had been a startling revelation. Now, it was an easy way to change the subject.

"Hey," I said, frisbeeing the invitation onto Hailey's bare mattress. "You might want to mail this off soon."

Hailey picked up the invitation, then her eyes widened as she realized what it was. "Oh shit! This is for Victoria's shower. I mailed the others weeks ago."

"Hopefully, Ms. Reagan Dawson can find a gift in time."

Hailey rolled her eyes. "The shower is still a month away, and we live in the era of Amazon Prime. I think she'll be fine." Hailey went back to boxing her bookshelf. "Besides, you can hardly blame me for missing one; with 145, it's bound to happen."

I nearly dropped the stack of paper I'd been straightening. "You mean 145 guests. Total," I supplied. But even that number seemed too high.

"No. Her guest list is 230 people."

I gaped.

"What?" Hailey asked, seemingly annoyed at my stupor.

"You never told me I was taking over a *freaking mega-wedding*!"

"What did you expect?" Hailey went on, inspecting a book as she spoke. "She's Victoria Atteridge."

"Atteridge?" The room spun. I planted my hands on the desk, trying to ground myself. "As in—" No. There was no way.

"Yeah. Atteridge Hotels. Her guest list is actually pretty tame for her status." Hailey's voice sounded far away as the magnitude hit me. "You have access to my Gmail and all my client info. How is this the first time you're realizing this?"

"Because," I hissed, "you have all your clients listed by first names. I didn't go diving in with background checks. I just assumed your clients were like . . . regular people." I put my hand on my chest, sure a blotchy rash consumed the pale skin. "How in the heck did you get a deal with Victoria Atteridge?"

The Atteridge was a luxury hotel franchise with locations in the Woodlands, Houston, and Galveston. But I knew they had branches all over the world. I'd seen the towering hotels as a kid and always wanted to stay in one. We never had, and as an adult, I understood why, with their cheapest room at three hundred a night, their most expensive upwards of two thousand.

"Wow," Hailey huffed. "You really have no faith in me."

I scoffed. "You started calligraphy like three days ago, so excuse me for being in shock."

"Look, I don't know why you are making such a big deal out of this. I already addressed all the wedding and shower invites. The hardest part is done. You just have a few tasks left."

"I'm making a big deal," I said between my teeth, "because this *client* is practically royalty, and I don't want to mess up any part of her big day."

"Listen, before you go on a doom spiral, just go to that meeting with her. Feel out the situation."

"Hailey—"

"Please. I know I have no right to put this on you, but this business has meant so much to me. I don't want to see it tank yet. I just need you to finish this client, and then I'll start opening my business to people in Florida."

"You're right. You don't have a right to put this on me," I said, feeling the full weight of her absence. She looked like I'd struck her. Those big blue eyes I'd always been jealous of seemed to get even bigger—puppy dog begging big. I sighed, relenting, of course, because I was always a huge softie when it came to her. "But I will at least go to the meeting."

"Thank you! Thank you!" She paused her praise as something like doubt crept across her features. "But you know you have to pretend to be me. Right?"

"What? Why?" We hadn't discussed this when I agreed to take the job.

"Because wouldn't you be pissed if your calligrapher quit and sent in her little sister instead?"

I snorted. Hailey was only fourteen months older than me, and I'd had over a decade longer of practicing calligraphy. "Yeah. You're right. She has no idea I'm the better calligrapher."

"I want you to bottle up this confidence for the next time you have a panic attack over Victoria's wedding."

My mom, who usually left Hailey and me to work things out for ourselves, shook her head. She neatly placed a stack of clothes into a box and then turned to face us. "I don't think it's a good idea to have Emily pretend to be you, Hailey."

"Me either," I said. "Besides, how would that even work? Haven't you two already met?"

"No. I met with the first wedding planner, Darcy. But Darcy was replaced by Amanda."

"Why? What happened?"

"I don't know." She shrugged. "Probably couldn't hang."

I swallowed. *Great. Victoria is possibly a bridezilla with a penchant for firing the wedding staff. What could go wrong?*

"So," Hailey continued, "it shouldn't be an issue."

"What about social media? She could already know what you look like."

"My accounts are private. I don't accept requests from clients, not that she has sent a request anyway."

"Yeah, but anyone can see your profile picture."

"Which is?"

I thought about it. She hardly ever changed her profile picture. The one she had now for Facebook and Instagram had been taken years ago when she visited Enchanted Rock. The photo was of her back, arms outstretched as she looked at the landscape. Her red hair, the same color as mine, nearly glowed in the setting sun.

"The Enchanted Rock picture," I answered.

"And faceless. I have no plans on changing it."

"This . . . could work," I mused.

"It could," she said, smiling. "Oh, before I forget." She nodded toward a box at the foot of her bed. "Take that home with you. It's for a couple of her projects. There's printouts of exactly what she wants. It's very basic—should be no problem for a *pro* like you."

"Oh good." I rolled the packing tape loudly across a box. "So, I just have to . . . do all the work."

"Oh my god!" I laughed at her exclamation. "I am done with all your complaining. You are totally killing the vibe Mom and I had before you got here."

"I think Florida life has ruined you. Everything has to be a party now."

"I was always like that," Hailey said, dropping another book into the box before sticking her tongue out at me.

"Speaking of Florida, when are we going to meet Braxton?" Mom asked.

"Yeah," I said. "I have a few words I'd like to exchange with the man who stole my sister."

Hailey snorted. "I don't know. He's busy establishing his business in Key West. I'm sure you'll be able to meet him soon."

"What's he like?" I asked.

"Hmm. Well . . . Let's see. He's sweet, loves shrimp po boys, and dreams of owning a jet ski. He's really . . . sweet."

Sweet. That didn't seem like Hailey's usual bad-boy type, but Hailey threw on a playlist of throwback boy band tunes before I could comment.

I finished packing the desk and decided to peek at the projects Hailey had waiting for me. The printouts lay on top of a pile of jean jackets, and under those was a large object wrapped with paper, which crinkled as I revealed a lantern with a weathered wood frame.

The first printout had a picture of a name scrawled across the back of a jean jacket, then it listed the names of Victoria's bridesmaids. According to the email, the personalized jean jackets were to be gifts for Victoria's gals.

It would be a flirty, fun project, which is why the somber message for the lantern took me by surprise: **This lantern is lit in loving memory of Poppy.**

What a beautiful tribute for a lost loved one. I didn't know if I'd be able to keep Victoria as a client, but I could at least do this for her. Carefully, I rewrapped the lantern and closed the box, my fingers itching to complete the project.

Chapter 8

I found myself a blundering mess on the day of the meeting with Victoria. I'd spent the previous night putting the finishing touches on the bridesmaids' jackets. They'd looked good before, but I'd decided to add some rosettes. The jackets looked amazing now; the tiny flowers rounded out the names beautifully, but I hadn't gotten to bed until after one in the morning.

I was running on coffee and adrenaline. I spilled the aforementioned coffee on my sweater, deleted an important document, and nearly forgot to attend a meeting. When I wasn't a walking, talking disaster, I stared into space, rolled a pen, or studied the notes I was supposed to take, only to find I'd been doodling with calligraphy instead. I couldn't stop fretting about the meeting.

It had been a little over two weeks since I'd found out the client I'd agreed to take over was none other than Victoria Atteridge, and the questions in my brain had only gotten louder by the day.

What if she knew I wasn't Hailey?

What if she put a whole truckload of work on me that I couldn't handle?

What if my skills didn't match her expectations?

The saving grace of the day was Beck's absence. I enjoyed a quiet, non-competitive swim and meetings without snarky remarks. I did find myself looking over to his usual spot. Frequent sights of his empty chair made me realize I looked in his direction way too often. And, if I was honest, the morning dragged without that secretive smirk of his or the one-eyebrow raise he used as a question mark.

With the afternoon blocked out on the calendar as personal PTO, I left and made the short drive to The Atteridge's corporate office. I'd seen the building before, tall and shining as if to say *we do important things here* just by the translucence of the windows, but I'd never noticed the subtle *Atteridge* over the doorway.

A secretary checked me in. Judging by the languid once-over, she seemed skeptical that Victoria would have a meeting with the likes of me—which, okay. That stung. Maybe I shouldn't have worn the maxi skirt clad in daisies.

Now worried about my situation *and* my outfit, I rode up to the eleventh floor in an elevator with mirrors as immaculately clean as the exterior of the building. Did the window washers also clean the elevators? The quality of work and attention to detail astounded me.

The view of myself, however clear, was not the prettiest. I'd lost some coloring, my already pale face paling. My freckles practically popped out like a jump scare. A rogue strand of hair fell across my face, but I held a box of the newest projects—the pane of glass, jean jackets, and lantern—so I couldn't smooth it into place. Instead, I tried blowing it back into submission.

I'd just blown the strand to the side when the elevator dinged. The eleventh floor seemed to follow the theme of the rest of the corporate office: shiny. Chrome and mirrors detailed every surface. A set of white couches sat on a fluffy rug, a cloud of comfort in all the steely, almost sterile, space. On the couch, one person waited with their back turned to me.

In front of the waiting area, a receptionist sat behind her glass desk. "How may I help you?" she purred.

If the lobby-level receptionist was the gatekeeper, this one was the hostess warm with a plate of cookies.

"Hi," I answered, shifting the weight of the box in my hands. "I'm Hailey Lane, Victoria's twelve-thirty."

A chrome vase filled with white roses reflected my image, saying *liar, liar, liar.*

"Okay, Hailey. I'll let her know you're here."

I went to nod my thanks to her, but the person on the couch behind her stood and turned. My mouth went dry.

Because standing there in one of his perfectly pressed shirts was Beckett—Beck, Senior-level Asshole, looking at me, mouth ajar, a brow cocked.

At least he looked as shocked to see me as I was to see him.

"What are you doing here?" I asked, voice low but demanding. I got closer to him, trying to keep out of earshot of the receptionist.

"Waiting to meet with my sister." He pointed to the large door beyond the sitting area.

"Your sister?"

Then it hit me.

Beckett A.

Not asshole, as it turns out.

But Atteridge.

Beckett fucking Atteridge.

I feared I'd turn black and white like a fifties sitcom if any more color drained from my face.

"Victoria is your sister?" I squeaked, unable to manage anything else utterly intelligible.

My thoughts tangled in an incoherent mess. Of all the cruel jokes played by the universe, this took the cake.

He nodded, then cocked his head to the side. "Why are *you* here? And why did you introduce yourself as Hailey?"

Shit.

The door beyond the sitting area opened. Its gargantuan height reminded me of the door before a boss fight in a video game. I'd never been any good at games.

A woman in a pencil skirt and a billowy, sophisticated blouse held open the door. Her brown curls spilled out of a clip. Same color and texture as Beck's. And then there was the sharp jaw and eyebrows. She was Beck's sister, alright. Victoria Atteridge.

"Hailey?" she asked.

I tried my best to smile. I nodded, not trusting myself to speak just yet.

"Come on in." Then she looked at Beck. "I promise, you're next. This is the last one."

I looked back at Beck, who stared like he was seeing me for the first time. He was seconds away from sounding the alarm. And why wouldn't he? His personal pain in the ass stood in his sister's office, claiming to be someone else. He could out me. He *should* out me. Ruin all my plans with one sentence: She's not who she says she is.

He held all the power.

Victoria looked between Beck and me, sensing the tension.

"Do you two . . ." Victoria started, ". . . know each other?"

"Please be cool about this," I whispered.

A moment passed, and I could see the questions on his brow, the conflict nearly molten in his irises. Those eyes didn't leave me as he answered his sister. "We're . . . old friends," he finally said. He looked at me like he could read my thoughts if he tried hard enough. "We were just catching up."

"It was nice to see you again," I said to Beck, my voice sounding like a robot because I apparently had no chill.

Victoria turned as someone in her office asked her a question. I took the halt in conversation to try and move past Beck and the incredibly awkward situation I'd placed myself in, but before I could get by, Beck's hand wrapped around my elbow.

"Tomorrow, at work," he said with calm authority, "you're explaining everything, *Hailey*."

He let go, and I walked toward Victoria's office on legs that suddenly felt like they belonged to a newborn giraffe.

The meeting with Victoria came upon me like a Texas thunderstorm. Gusts between Victoria and her wedding planner, Amanda, flew by me with such speed and force that I barely had time to respond. They batted back and forth about the timeline and the checklist. *All of which were still on schedule,* Amanda had said, beaming at me.

Then came the remaining items on the checklist, lighting up the sky with possibilities, only to be followed by the booming doubt in my head, telling me I wouldn't be able to deliver.

God, Hailey acted like she'd sealed and finished this project by completing the invites, which I'm sure was no easy feat. But she forgot to mention the work for the actual big day: a five-foot mirror for the seating arrangement, place cards, and a collection of signage.

Needless to say, Hailey had left out some items on the to-do list for Victoria's wedding. I'd been blindsided, but then I bristled at myself. This was so typical of Hailey. She'd always been the kind of child to ask Mom to buy the supplies for the project due the following day, and she'd still ace the damn thing. How could I be mad at Hailey for using the process that always worked for her?

The whole time, I just kept nodding and smiling like an idiot because what other choice did I have? Look confused and overwhelmed that Hailey, whom I'd already introduced myself as, had agreed to all these things? A better, braver person would have fessed up, but I couldn't find the courage. I realized it had to do with something Victoria lacked. Because, for all their similarities, Victoria did not have the same playful glint in her eyes that Beck had. Though she gave a pleasant enough smile, her eyes told a different story. Her eyes said she was the CEO of a Fortune 500 company, and she had to make decisions as such. Strike first and strike hard, Cobra Kai style.

And surely her power reached far. If Beck decided to tell her my real name, would she attack my career? Let The Arlow Group know just how little integrity one of their associates had. It seemed like a stretch, but was it really?

Just in case, I kept my mouth closed and tried to ignore my clammy hands and sweaty brow. I simply had to survive the meeting. Later, I could devise a legitimate excuse for why I couldn't finish the job. Maybe I'd say I had to take care of a sick relative, or I'd contracted leprosy, or I'd decided to join a convent to atone for all my sins. The last one wasn't a bad idea at the rate I was going. I'd at least tell her soon, I decided. That way, she'd have time to find someone else to do the job.

Reviewing the contract she'd made with Hailey, I knew two things: one, Victoria could afford anyone in the city for calligraphy services, and two, Hailey owed me a lot of money for taking on this job. The amount only made my anxiety skyrocket. Those numbers said a lot was at stake here.

I couldn't wait to get far away from Hailey's deal with these people, that binding contract, and that list of unfinished items. Beck looked up as I exited Victoria's office, but I fled the scene, riding down the elevator with my back against the wall, heaving in breaths.

As soon as I got to the car, I called Hailey. She needed to know I couldn't do this job and why.

She answered with a bright, "Hey!"

"So, you know Senior-level Asshole? The one who took my job?"

"Of course. He's enemy number one."

"He's Victoria Atteridge's *brother*. He knows I'm lying!"

"What?"

"He was there in another one of his perfect shirts, trying to use Superman vision to read my mind."

"Superman can't read minds."

"You are missing the point!" I screamed at her.

"How about you slow down?"

I did not heed that advice. "Even if he wasn't there, I can't do this job, Hailey." My voice accelerated as I tried to keep up with my racing thoughts. "She needs an experienced team of calligraphers for this job. Not an unseasoned me . . . I have to quit this job and do it soon so she has enough time to find a replacement."

"Why do you think you can't do this?" she asked slowly, delicately.

"Because I have a million things going on at work. Because lying makes me uncomfortable. Because I'm out of my league. Because . . . Because I'm not you!"

"You don't need to be me."

"Please, please don't ask me to do this, Hailey."

Silence stretched between us before she finally conceded. "Okay. I won't." I could tell she was trying to hide it, but her disappointment threaded through anyway.

"I'm so sorry," I choked, the stress of the day getting the best of me. "I know how much your business means to you."

"Don't be sorry. It was unfair of me to ask you to do this."

I felt marginally better after we came up with an excuse for why we had to drop out of the contract. Hailey was prepared to offer a full refund if things got ugly.

But after we hung up, I couldn't stop thinking about the look on Victoria's face when I handed over the three projects I'd brought to the meeting.

Victoria loved the jackets. She'd exclaimed excitedly at the signage and the vibrant sweeps behind her soon-to-be new last name and wedding date. Seeing her stony professionalism break for my art made my heart ascend on hummingbird wings.

When she'd unwrapped the lantern, her face fell to something more reverent. Her fingers ever-so-gently traced the name at the bottom. I knew my lettering and my style inside and out, but I'd had to practice Poppy's name on paper several times before the paint pen ever touched the lantern. I just felt a lot of love and a lot of pain behind the gesture of the lantern. I wanted to honor that.

As tears welled in Victoria's eyes, I wondered, not for the first time, who Poppy had been and what had happened to her. I didn't know anyone in our generation with that name, so I assumed Poppy to be a grandmother, perhaps. Victoria had cleared her throat, eyes still shining as she thanked me.

I dwelled on that moment so much that when I got home, I dove right into the box of hexagon tiles Victoria had sent with me. The soon-to-be place cards were marbled with one half dipped in gold—a beautiful project, just begging to be completed.

And that's how I spent the evening, ignoring important work emails to finish one last project for Victoria's wedding.

Chapter 9

Knowing full and well that I was running from my problems, I skipped my morning swim, opting to pick up kolaches for the team instead. I'd have to talk to Beck at some point, but it wouldn't be in the frigid lanes of Power Gym clad in a swimsuit. That much I knew.

Because I'm apparently shameless, I also ran a little late to our team meeting. Just enough that I interrupted Wesley's weekly reminder to update our time sheets with my kolaches. No one seemed upset by the disturbance. No one except Beck.

Ted reached for the lone jalapeno kolache, but I yanked the box back. "Come on, Ted," I said as Anna snatched the kolache. "You know preggos get first dibs."

She gave me a knowing look. She recognized my breakfast offering as stalling because I'd called her last night while in the fetal position on my couch, staring at my finished forty tiles, which meant I still had one hundred and eight place cards to go, and I hadn't even cracked open a single email for work.

I told her everything. When I got to the part about Beck being in the lobby, she said, "How did you not know he is an Atteridge? It's all anyone ever talks about in the breakroom."

To which I had practically screeched, "When do you ever see me taking a break, Anna?"

She conceded and allowed me to finish my story without further interruptions. When my word vomit finally concluded, I'd expected the scolding of a lifetime. Instead, she'd clapped—an actual applause, commenting about how surprised and impressed she was. When I told her I was going to have to give up the job, she'd told me, and I quote, "You'd better not bitch out, Emily. This is your chance."

I'd made no promises but told her I'd take her vote into consideration.

Then she'd told me not to worry about Beck—that she was ninety percent sure he had a thing for me, and if he hadn't ratted me out yet, he wouldn't.

Looking at him now, I wasn't so sure.

He glowered at me from his chair as I made my way around the table with the box, but I just smiled. Beck couldn't very well pull the Spanish Inquisition on me when we had witnesses. He'd have to play nice for a little while, at least.

I took the only empty seat. The one next to Beck. "Hungry?" I asked, opening the box toward him while Wesley continued prattling on about the importance of documenting our time.

Beck gave me a long, inscrutable look, then shook his head. "Maybe after the meeting," he whispered, an eyebrow cocked.

Damn it. He wasn't going to let this explanation thing go.

I pretended to be pensive. "Hmmm. I don't know if they will be available then," I whispered back.

"Emily, did you have something to add?" Wesley asked, calling me out like a student who'd interrupted his lesson.

I shook my head and feigned being very interested in taking notes.

Unfortunately, Beck was interested in taking notes as well. He passed me his notebook, a question at the top. And now I was getting some major high school flashbacks.

Are you even a real calligrapher?

I wondered how best to tackle this situation, which was Beckett Atteridge. I could take the high road: apologize, be upfront, let him know I planned on backing out of the job anyway. Then I thought about Hailey, the woman I'd decided to try to be more like. She wouldn't take the high road. She'd be a smartass about it. I decided her way sounded a little more fun.

What do you mean by real? I lettered back, using the prettiest faux calligraphy I could manage with the felt-tipped pens I had on hand. Then, I added some curly leaves, delicate berries, and a blooming flower. As Wesley turned around to point to the projected Excel sheet, I thrust the notebook back at Beck and capped my pen with a little smirk.

He appraised my lettering. Then, he scrawled his response below mine before placing the notebook back in front of me just as Wesley looked at Ted, answering a question about an upcoming deadline.

So why are you lying to Victoria about your name?

Are we really doing this? I thought. *Here? On notebook paper? Fine.*

Why are you sitting in this boring ass meeting when you could have a corner spot in Daddy's office?

As soon as I plopped the notebook under Beck's nose, I realized I'd made a grievous error. Partly because I'd gone too far with the wording of my question but mostly because I hadn't checked to see what Wesley was doing when I'd passed the notebook.

And he looked right at us.

No. Not us. *Me.* Because Wesley wouldn't call out the poster child of the team, now, would he?

Fuck.

"What's going on over there?" Wesley asked, trying to keep a playful tone, but the annoyance sprang through like weeds between sidewalk cracks. "Care to share with the group?"

My mouth fell open. I tried to form an explanation, but all I could think about were the incriminating words I'd written, specifically how I'd described Wesley's meeting. I waited for Beck to stand up and proudly read from his notebook, effectively dismantling my career.

Instead, he surprised me with his calm and cool reply. "I was just confirming with Emily that the deadline you had for the workflow is on the 29th." He gave an apologetic smile. "Sorry, I didn't want to interrupt the meeting to ask."

The answer he paved was so smooth. It left no reason for anyone to question further. Wesley went back to the meeting, and I should have paid attention. Instead, I kept thinking how Beck would have had no problem pulling off this double-life thing that I struggled with.

To my relief, Beck didn't try to pass any more notes during the meeting. Unfortunately, as soon as it concluded, he followed my pace packing up, matching the closing of my laptop, the capping of my pen, and the stacking of notebooks and papers. It was like the office version of synchronized swimming.

Everything was tit for tat, even our exit into the hall.

"Do you have a minute?" Beck asked, still matching each of my steps.

"Nope. I have a meeting with finance in five."

"I was being polite by asking. You forget I have access to your Outlook calendar, *Hailey*."

"Keep your voice down," I said between my teeth, then forced a smile at Susan as she shuffled past us to get to her cube.

Beck huffed out a breath, then grabbed my elbow, once again—I noted—this time steering me toward a half-empty office. Someone from management was moving up a floor. Lucky them. Unlucky me. The door shut behind us, leaving me alone in a room with Beck, a filing cabinet, and three columns of boxes. Said filing cabinet and cardboard Jenga towers blocked access to the rest of the room, serving to cage Beck and me together. He may as well have pulled me into a supply closet.

"I won't take up much of your time," he said, placing his laptop and notebook onto the filing cabinet. The movement reminded me of when the earrings come off before a catfight.

Wanting to free my own hands, I put my things onto the low-est—therefore the least risky—stack of boxes. Only once my hands were free, I didn't even know what to do with them. I tried sticking them in my pockets and then remembered. *Oh yeah, I'm a woman. And therefore, pockets on slacks are a luxury I do not have.* I ended up crossing my arms over my chest.

He slipped his hands into the pockets he actually had—point one for Beck and men everywhere. "What is going on?"

In the heavy silence, I tried to start the speech I had prepared for this occasion. I had an apology ready. And then I planned on assuring him that he didn't need to worry his pretty little head about it any longer because I would be stepping down from the job—passing the torch to the next lucky calligrapher. But there was a hardness to his eyes that made me pause.

His shoulders and eyebrows lifted as if to say *well, out with it.* "Is this some sort of elaborate scam?"

Scam?

The word sent a jolt like ice water to my veins. Because scams were serious. Scams ended up on the news with the authorities involved.

An apology and stepping aside felt like an admission to guilt. And yes, I'd lied about my first name and pretended to be my sister, but it was nothing malicious, not to the caliber Beck had imagined based on how he'd cornered me in this abandoned office.

Just as quickly as the fear arrived, anger ate it alive. "Do you seriously think I spend my free time scamming people, Beckett? Full-time business analyst. Part-time villain?"

"I don't know, Lane. I wouldn't have thought that was your M.O. But it's pretty weird that you are introducing yourself as someone else."

"It's just a first name, Beck. Ask her for the calligrapher's last name. It's still Lane."

"So, when she sends the money—it goes to your account?" I paused, and it was just enough to convince him he was onto something. "Are you the person she hired?"

I stood there, frozen. I considered lying, but these were direct questions. A misstep and I'd get caught in the web I'd spun. But more than that, his eyes lasered onto mine. He would see the lie as soon as I uttered it.

He took a step closer. "Why are you pretending to be someone else?" His deep voice hummed along my bones and seeped into my veins.

To my credit, I didn't back down from his intimidation tactic. Instead, I took my own step, shrinking the distance between us. "You are trying to protect your sister," I said, matching his almost-whisper, "and I'm trying to protect mine."

His eyebrows furrowed at that. "What do you mean?"

The truth will set you free, but it might also shoot you in the back and bury you in a shallow lot next to your ancestors. I proceeded with caution, not sure which way the wind would blow just yet.

"My sister, Hailey, owns Lettering Lane. She started this wedding but for . . ." I thought about her ditching Victoria's wedding to spend her days tanning in a string bikini with Florida Man and landed on ". . . personal reasons, I'm stepping in to help your sister with her big day and save my sister's business from tanking. This way, no one loses."

"And you feel qualified to do this? Are you as good as your sister?"

The question made me pause because I could letter in my sleep. I'd done favorite song lyrics on brass plates and simple messages on teacups. I'd personalized headbands for the entire running club during high school. I'd addressed all the graduation invites for my family. And the gifting over the years: personalizing shoe boxes, perfume bottles, supply boxes—you name it. There was no guesswork to my style.

I had more experience than Hailey—twelve years' worth.

"No," I answered. "I'm better."

He appraised me. And under his gaze, my insides turned runny. He was handsome. There was no getting around it. I wish the enemy-asshole side of him canceled out the good-looking side, but no. My damn hormones were going wild at how close we stood—so close I could feel his breath on my temple, could get high off that fresh soapy scent of his, could notice the way his Adam's apple bobbed past that lone freckle on his throat.

"So," I said a little too breathily, in desperate need of conversation to keep from floating away on balloons inflated with pheromones. "Are you going to rat me out to your sister?"

"That depends," he answered, reaching past me to get to the door. Just that one movement, where he had to lean further into my space, made the air thin out in the room.

"Depends on what?" I asked a little dreamily while he reached for his things on the filing cabinet.

"On how you do with the mirror this weekend?" he said, stepping past me to get into the hall.

The lack of his breath and his scent and his proximity cleared the haze I'd been in, allowing me to finish the conversation like a normal functioning human and not a Pepe le Pew floating toward Penelope.

"What are you talking about?"

"The mirror that you are writing the seating chart on," he replied, annoyed. Like, if I'd been Victoria's real calligrapher, I'd have known immediately what he was referring to.

"No. Yes." I shook my head and put out my hands with a frustrated sigh. "I know about the mirror."

"Good, because I told Victoria I'd drop it off at your place." My eyes widened, but he kept going. "You know, since we're old friends." He made a show of looking around to make sure no one else occupied the hall. "Sorry," he mock whispered, "Since *Hailey* and I are old friends."

"Wait—" I started because, damn it, I wasn't supposed to be taking on more of this job. I was supposed to quit. I was going to quit.

"I have to go," he said. "I actually do have a meeting in five minutes." He stopped at the end of the hall to add, "But I'm sure we'll have plenty of time to talk on Saturday, Lane."

Chapter 10

Perched on the arm of my couch, I frowned down at my phone while waiting for Hailey to reply to my string of texts listing all the reasons why I messed up colossally by not already quitting Victoria's job. When she didn't answer in a reasonable time frame—under three minutes—I called her.

"I was about to text you back if you could wait just a freaking second."

"That's it!" I declared as if she hadn't said anything. "I'm just going to call Victoria."

"Emily—"

"Tell her the truth, have her call off her brother, avoid a whole mess of embarrassment."

While I spoke, I folded my favorite fleece blanket and tossed it over the back of the couch. Then I stepped back, decided it looked too stiff, unfolded it to a rectangle, and draped it over the armrest. I'd spent way too much time scrubbing the apartment to a *this-is-just-a-model-home-no-body-lives-here* clean, only to go back and rough it up a smidge to make it look like someone actually lived here—a very tidy someone.

I should have been working on reconfigurations since I'd lost a half-day, meeting with Victoria, but I was dusting the blinds instead.

"He's already bringing the mirror," Hailey said calmly as if working with a spooked horse. "Why don't you just see how this project goes?"

"And if I mess it up?"

"What kind of marker are you using on the mirror?"

Damn it. She had me, and I knew it. I sighed. "Acrylic."

"I don't have to tell you that acrylic wipes clean with any old window cleaner."

"I know. I know! But I was going to quit. That was the plan."

"You're right," she said, in a tone that warned me this conversation was about to take a back road through the ugly parts of town. "That *was* the plan. But then you let your coworker get you all riled up. And why is that?"

"I don't know," I said, straightening a framed picture of my mom, Hailey, and me. Then I backed up, wanting to swat my own hand. I didn't care what Beck thought about my apartment. "He's just—"

"Hot?" Hailey supplied at the same time I said, "Intolerable."

"What?" I asked, thrown by her off-topic answer and how she'd even leaped to that conclusion based on our conversations about him. Also, at how—objectively—correct her guess had been.

"He's hot. Isn't he?"

"God, Hailey. This guy stole my promotion and caused extra work for me because he's careless. He's Beckett, Senior-level Asshole. My office nemesis. Enemy number one. Remember?"

"I haven't heard one denial about his hotness. So, my assumption was correct. The enemy thing only magnifies that. Trust me. All of BookTok agrees." I glared at her stupid, adorable face in the frame on my wall as she continued, "So, poor baby. You have to spend the next few hours with the office hottie while you do calligraphy—your favorite activity on the planet."

"At this point, I'd rather spend the afternoon making voodoo dolls of you and Beck."

A knock at the door made me jump. "Shit! He's here. I wasted my time to back out on calling you."

"Always a pleasure, babe."

I opened the door to a dressed-down Beck, and damn it if the T-shirt and blue jeans didn't look even better on him than his Atteridge-worthy button-downs. Being able to see the floral work on his arm certainly didn't hurt.

"I didn't know you lived on the third floor when I offered to deliver this," he declared, slightly breathless.

I stepped aside so he could carry the large rectangle wrapped in cardboard.

"You should try carrying the groceries up."

"I'll pass. Where do you want this thing?" he asked, hauling the mirror into the living room.

I motioned toward a bare wall. While Beck worked, cutting the monstrosity of a mirror free, I couldn't help but watch his T-shirt stretch over the muscles in his back. Muscles that were hard-earned from punishingly fast laps in the pool. I forced myself to turn away. He hadn't even been in my living room for three minutes, and I was already ogling him.

He straightened after cutting the last of the tape and unveiling the mirror, which looked like it had fallen straight out of the Baroque period. It was a piece of art on its own—with its swirling gold frame.

I felt panic rise like bile in my throat. This thing belonged in a museum, not in my modest apartment.

"This apartment definitely looks like your place," Beck said, distracting me from the welling dread of touching a marker to the masterpiece before me.

I frowned. "What do you mean?" I asked, immediately thinking of the water-stained ceiling, crinkled blinds, and discolored carpet. Insecurity buried itself in my chest. I should have gotten those things fixed and spent more money on making my apartment feel like a home, but I didn't because I obsessively saved for that down payment on a future house. I'd be there in a couple of years if I kept the course, but I didn't feel like explaining that to Beck.

He gestured around vaguely. "The pastel colors." Then he pointed at the blanket I'd draped over the couch. "The flowers."

"The flowers?" I asked, eyeing the print—made to look like watercolor—with its dots of lavender and bunches of baby blue hydrangeas.

"Yeah. Whether it's your skirt or just a headband. You always have some sort of flower on you."

A blush heated my cheeks. He'd stunned me, noticing anything at all about me that wasn't centered around being clumsy or pushy or something equally annoying.

I looked down at my outfit. Today I wore a plain white shirt and olive green shorts. My pointer finger rose, ready to object to his observation. But there on my wrist was the watchband I'd picked out for today—the design had cacti and wild desert flowers. My mouth opened, just to snap shut.

Then I used that finger to point at the carnations inked on his arm. "So do you."

Beck's lips flattened to a straight line. "You got me there." He leaned against my desk, and God, why did it feel so sensual to see him in my living room?

He nodded toward the mirror. "How long is this going to take? I'm just wondering how long I need to brace myself for your emotional abuse."

I eyed the pages of names I'd printed from Victoria's RSVP list. Luckily—with it being a destination wedding in Costa Rica—only 148 of the 230 invited had RSVP'd. Still a lot of names, but considerably less than I'd imagined. "A few hours. Minimum."

"Do you mind if I sit at your desk? Or do you have a corner and a Dunce cap you'd rather me use?"

"Are you sure you want to stay? I don't even have a TV."

Beck eyed where a TV would normally go, but across from the couch sat my desk, and next to that was a wall of shelving that would rival an entertainment center in size. Paper and supplies of all sorts filled each cubby to the brim, like a mini-Hobby Lobby right in my own living room.

"It's not that I don't watch shows and movies. I do. On my phone all the time," I said, feeling the need to defend myself from looking like a complete weirdo. "I just only have a limited amount of space in the apartment."

"And you chose what mattered to you," he said as though he was seeing a new side of me.

"Yeah, exactly." It felt weird to agree with him, even weirder at the way my stomach felt all fizzy with his approval.

"I don't need a TV," Beck said, pulling his backpack around so he could reach inside to get to his laptop. "Three hours should be enough time to knock out those reconfigurations."

I blinked. "I was supposed to do that."

"I know, but you seem like you have a lot on your plate."

I started to protest, but I really was drowning. "Yeah, okay. Thanks." I motioned toward my desk. "Make yourself at home."

I moved my mirror kit and RSVP list out of his way, allowing Beckett Atteridge to get comfortable in my living room.

I wasted no time cleaning the mirror and taping my guidelines. It was the actual placing of my marker against the mirror that made me pause. Oh, how out of place the mirror looked, sitting by a mystery stain on the carpet, not two feet from a roach trap.

I fought the urge to yank Beck by the collar and demand he take the mirror back to Victoria.

I can't do this.

I'm going to fuck this up.

My thoughts went south quickly, the delusion of pulling off this job dissolving with the reality of the situation. What was worse, I had an audience. While he seemed busy working, my hesitation felt palpable, thick. I didn't want him to realize my alarm because nothing said unqualified quite like fear.

I huffed out a breath and then thought of Hailey's advice: *Try on my life.*

What would *Hailey do in this situation?* She wouldn't second guess herself. She'd throw on some nineties rap, put her hair in a high pony, and get it done.

I decided to give Hailey's method a try. Just go for it. I opted for my own style of music, a playlist of punk music stripped down to acoustic guitar with vocals devastatingly soft and raw. Beck's eyes slid over as I started it up, but to my surprise, he didn't object. Then came the rest of the ritual—pulling my hair into the nest of a low bun and lighting my favorite pineapple-scented candle for good measure.

Along the edges of the tape, my reflection peered back at me. The girl in the mirror might have had more freckles and darker eyes than Hailey. Her cheekbones weren't as defined, and her nose wasn't quite as long. But she did have Hailey's confidence. And why shouldn't she? I thought back to my conversation with Beck earlier in the week. I'd done this before, not to this magnitude, but I'd completed mirror projects dozens of times. More importantly, I trusted my skills.

An hour into lettering, Beck's deep voice made my marker slip on the glass.

"Can I bother you for—" he stood, looking at the streak I'd made. "Oh, shit! Did I mess you up?"

I laughed and wiped it away easily. "It's fine."

He let out a breath. Then he seemed to get distracted, watching me work. So much so that he left his initial question behind.

I had just started the calligraphy for table five when he spoke again, "You're lifting your marker up." He said it like he'd finally caught me—the fraud he knew me to be the entire time.

". . . And?"

"And isn't that . . . cheating?"

"You are thinking of cursive." I finished the word and turned to him, my head cocked. "You know, I think you're the one who is unqualified here. How can you determine if I'm a legit calligrapher if you don't know the first thing about it? Could you have bothered to . . . I don't know. Do a quick Google over calligraphy practices?"

He narrowed his eyes at me, but the corners of his lips turned upward. "Mind if I get a drink?" he asked, not entertaining my review of his qualifications.

"Sure." I used my marker to point as I said, "Cups are in the cabinet by the fridge. You can take your pick of water, coffee, or almond milk."

"How will I ever decide?" he said with mock enthusiasm.

"Yeah, I forgot I was having royalty over. Sorry I didn't stock the fridge just to your liking, Mr. Atteridge."

But he hadn't even heard my dig. He froze, staring at my cups. For a split second of horror, I thought a roach had gotten into the cabinet.

But then he pulled out a mug and said, "This is fantastic."

He turned it toward me. With one glance, I knew which one he'd found. An Excel spreadsheet wrapped from handle to handle. Overlaid on that, the words *Freak in the Sheets* stood out in bold black letters.

I think I died a little at that moment. Or perhaps knocked a decade off my life. I turned back to the mirror to hide my face from him, only to get a look at my scarlet cheeks behind the lettering I'd completed.

"That was a gift from Hailey," I mumbled like an apology.

"I think I'd like her," Beck said, filling the mug with water instead of using a glass like a normal person.

"Everyone does," I said, going back to lettering. "I'd offer to set you two up, but she's run off to Florida with her boyfriend of two whole months."

Beck was quiet for a few beats, and that's when I realized my error.

"Is that why she can't finish Victoria's wedding?"

I risked a glance at him in the mirror. His eyes locked on mine, waiting for an answer.

"Yes." I turned to face him, afraid to ask my next question but needing to know the answer. "Does that make you mad?"

His fingers tapped on the mug as he decided. "I think it would if I weren't staring at your work right now." He stepped closer, once again seeming mesmerized by my lettering. "How long have you been doing this?"

"Since eighth grade."

"What makes a thirteen-year-old want to do something like calligraphy?" he asked, leaning against my shelf.

"It's a long story."

Beck looked at his watch. "Don't you have two more hours on this thing? Can you talk and letter?"

I thought about telling him no, and it would be three more hours if he didn't stop bothering me. But the truth was, I kind of wanted him to know this part of me. Maybe because I wanted him to understand where my passion stemmed from, so he'd understand how seriously I took my craft. Or maybe some small part of me wanted Beck to know this side of me so I could gauge his reaction.

"The year before, we were homeless for a little while." Out of the corner of my eye, I noticed Beck stiffen. He'd probably been expecting an answer like, *I needed some cutesy lettering to go with my Lisa Frank pictures, or I wanted to ask a boy out to the dance, so I wrote him a pretty letter.* Homelessness didn't seem like a pathway to calligraphy. "Everything about calligraphy is controlled," I explained. "And after months of uncertainty, I just wanted something in my life to be structured."

Most people backed up when I told them about that time of my life. It was human nature to shield your eyes from the pain, from the harshness of reality. I think most people meant well; they simply didn't know how to respond to that statement. I didn't tell many people about being homeless, but those I did would often say things like, *Look at you now. What a success story.* Or *Things happen for a reason. It looks like everything worked out in the end.* They wanted to flip the script, give it a fairytale ending, and then move on.

Not Beck. He didn't back up. He leaned in.

"What happened? Why were you homeless?"

"At the time, my mom was a teacher," I said, surprising myself by starting a story that I usually guarded so closely. "But she dreamed of living off her art. One day, she thought she got her big break when someone bought a painting for quite a bit of money. She broke her teaching contract so she could focus solely on her art. She sold a few pieces after that but none for nearly as much as that first sale.

"Eventually, she ran out of money for rent. Some guy she met from an art class offered to let us stay with him for a while. Long story short, we felt the term 'starving artist' firsthand, and Mom's art buddy . . ." I thought of how he'd screamed at me when he'd found me admiring his pens. How he'd told my mom the painting she'd spent weeks on was a far cry from art. Or how he had come home from a gallery and thrown a vase against the wall, littering the floor with amethyst-colored shards. "Well, he wasn't nice."

"Did he . . ." Beck swallowed, and his voice was gruff when he spoke again. "Did he hurt you?"

"No, not physically. It's just, my mom is a gentle soul. She never raised her voice at us. So, moving in with someone so angry was frightening." I tilted my head as if I could empty the memory of his hollering with the movement. "We didn't stay with him long. He kicked us out when it was clear my mom's paintings wouldn't fetch a steep price anytime soon. We lived out of our minivan for a while." The memory sat like a stone in my stomach. I could have spent hours telling him about that experience. But I didn't want to be dragged back to that place, even if just mentally. "My mom eventually found a job teaching at an art studio, but it was a while before things felt steady."

"What about your dad? Where was he in all this?"

"My mom was a single parent. I've only known my dad as a sperm donor and a spotty child support check."

"So that's why you haven't pursued calligraphy as a career before this?" Beck guessed.

I nodded once, then started to write the next name on my list. "Living off your art is just too risky."

Out of the corner of my eye, he seemed to mull that over, chewing on his cheek.

I ducked my head. "What about you? I want to know why you don't have an office next to Victoria's. Aren't you second in line for the throne?"

Beck scoffed. "My story isn't nearly as interesting. I can't work for my father."

There was nothing simple about not getting along with a parent. I wondered what kind of history they had—what initial force had driven them apart, what barbs had made them keep that distance.

"Why not?"

Beck shrugged, but the topic seemed heavy for him. "I think I'd be a bit of a disappointment."

I wanted to ask him to elaborate, but his short answers told me he was about to shut down. I steered the conversation in a different way. "Do you visit your sister, Victoria, often?"

"As of late, yes." He seemed to brighten marginally at the subject change. "She's having problems with the system they use. It's outdated and inefficient. She's requested a change, but some of the older crowd is resistant."

"Doesn't she own the company, though?" I asked, imagining anyone telling the fierce Victoria Atteridge *no*.

"Yes and no. She is getting ready to replace my dad as CEO and is doing most of the job's heavy lifting to get ready to take it. But she still answers to other members of the board. She can't go making a bunch of changes to the company without pissing off a lot of valuable team members. So, she asked me to help show her what the system could do if change was implemented. And honestly, there is a lot of opportunity. Things could be more accurate, quicker."

"Easier," I offered, finishing a name and removing the next row of masking tape.

"Exactly."

I looked over at him, surprised to have agreed with him again, even about something so basic. Then he smiled, so I smiled, and I realized I'd just had a pleasant conversation with Beck, one that even dove a bit deep. The realization made me pause, and I wondered if Beck was contemplating the same enigma because he pushed off the shelves, muttering something about needing to get busy on those reconfigurations.

I started on the next name with a zip of urgency.

Hours later, I stood, ankles and hips popping from the relief of stretching out after being crouched at such a weird angle to get those names at the bottom. Taking a step back, I took in the completed project and knew I was right to trust myself, to trust my skill. The calligraphy had near-perfect symmetry, with each letter consistent in size and shape.

It looked like my lettering belonged on that mirror.

It looked like it deserved to be showcased at Victoria's wedding.

Beck appeared beside me, taking a long while to size up the mirror. I watched his reflection as his eyes slowly rolled from line to line, studying my work. And for some weird reason, I felt nervous about his opinion. *Beck's.* The man who thought calligraphy and cursive were the same thing. I shouldn't have cared what he thought.

But for whatever reason, I beamed when he responded with, "This is good, Emily."

"Like professional, I'm not a fraud, good?"

"Like you should ditch The Arlow Group and start working with your sister full-time good."

My smile faded.

"What's wrong?" he asked, eyes on mine in the reflection before turning to me.

"I can't do your sister's wedding." I picked at a streak of white marker on my hand as an excuse not to meet his gaze. "She has to find someone else."

"Why?" he asked, voice quiet. "You did such a great job."

"I should have never pretended to be Hailey, and I shouldn't have put you in a position to lie to your sister. I was going to call it all off, tell your sister everything. But then you made me mad, cornering me at the office. I wanted to show you I'm not some con artist."

"Okay," he said. "Well, you showed me. I know you are a true calligrapher . . . even if you cheat by picking up your marker."

I ignored his attempt to lighten the mood. "Even so, I can't do this. I wanted to pretend that taking on Hailey's business had no risks. But there are. This is your sister's big moment. If I screw this up—" I blew out a puff of air.

Beck paused for a moment. "I promise, I'm not trying to shit on what you do." He put out his hands, a universal sign of, *I mean you no harm.* "But it's calligraphy, right? It's not like the wedding is going to be called off because the menu isn't written in elegant cursive, right?"

I decided to take the high road and not remind him of the differences between cursive and calligraphy. "I understand the service I offer is not a cornerstone for the big day, but I also know your sister has probably thought about her wedding for a long time. I don't want to be the one to disappoint her expectations."

"So don't." He gave me a daring look, and I realized how close we stood. My body tingled at the idea of him being less than an arm's reach away. I could touch that freckle on his throat, trace the tattoo on his arm, and run my fingers through his curls.

God. What is wrong with you? I internally shouted at myself, then made myself busy cleaning up the mirror. Beck increased the distance, going to my desk to get his backpack.

"So, you are encouraging me to lie to your sister?" I finally asked.

He slipped his laptop into his backpack, but not before tilting his head in contemplation. "No. You already did that yourself. I'm simply telling you to keep it up."

I scoffed.

"Look." He shouldered his bag. "You enjoy calligraphy. Enough to fake your identity at the chance to keep at it."

I gave him a look.

"I guess I'm just saying that this seems like your chance. Why don't you see what you can get away with?"

He grabbed the cardboard slats and a roll of packing tape from his bag, getting to work on wrapping up the mirror.

I thought about it. I had the live lettering left for Victoria's wedding as well as the signage: menu on a chalkboard, directions to the reception, and things like that. It would be difficult to finish them because work was the crying baby that always wanted to be held, but if I managed my time and skipped out on some sleep, I could get it done. It was possible.

The idea of the live lettering made my stomach somersault, but if I quit now, with the shower being in two weeks, Victoria might be unable to find a replacement in time. At this point, staying on as her calligrapher seemed like the right thing to do. Even if it meant I had to keep lying.

But then there was Beck. I didn't know if I could trust him to keep my identity a secret.

"So, you're not going to tell your sister about me?" I asked after he finished rolling the tape vertically.

"No."

I eyed him, suspicion swelling at the glint in his eyes. "That seems awfully generous of you, Beckett."

He winced at that. "Please. Only my father and my ex call me Beckett. And no. Not generous." He took his time lifting the mirror, a smile widening on his face. "You'll just owe me one."

Chapter 11

After Beck's dare to keep up the façade, I texted my sister and mom, letting them know my decision to stay on as Victoria's calligrapher.

Hailey turned my phone into a tiny fiesta. Celebratory emojis popped up like confetti on the screen.

Mom: In case you get nervous about where you are going, remember where you've been.

I cocked my head at my mom's proverb-like message, but then the pictures started rolling in. First, it was of a book held open to reveal a quote written in bold—something I'd lettered a few years ago. Then came the picture of the pumpkin with our last name across the folds. And on and on the pictures came of all the work I'd done in the past: a mug for my choir director, a globe with a quote about wandering, and a chalkboard sign for my mom's art classes.

By the time I reached the last picture, a set of ornaments with jolly phrases, my eyes stung. I could do this. I knew because I'd been doing it for years.

Mom's texts powered me through the next week and a half when I worked on a drink menu board for the wedding. Progress was achingly slow, but I worked on it whenever I had a little extra time after work, sometimes sacrificing sleep to finish bigger chunks. One morning, I woke before my alarm—something that never happened—and seized the opportunity to finish it.

As I sat back and examined the board with its swooping subsections and severely straight drink options, I allowed myself a moment to appreciate my work. It had come out better than I expected.

Then, I looked at the time and jumped up. I had about seven minutes to squeeze my ass into my swimsuit and fire up the Keurig.

·❤ · ❤ · ❤ · ❤ · ❤·

Beck inched his way into the water as I approached the lane. Feeling on top of the world for finishing a project and still making it to the pool mostly on time, I dove right in.

When I came up, adjusting my goggles, he stared at me. "God!"

"What?" I asked. It was an effort to force my mouth open, muscles steeled with the shock of the cold water.

"How do you do that?"

"Do what?" I barely managed to keep the shivering under control.

"Just dive in. I have to let each inch adjust to the temperature. And even then, it's a struggle."

"Sometimes you have to get in before you're ready."

Beck shook his head and looked at the opposite wall, avoiding my gaze. "I think it's a little different for guys."

My cheeks warmed at the thought of him and his. . . more sensitive parts. I kept my head down as I snatched my pair of Aftershocks, which had landed next to his headphones when I dropped them to dive in.

"Well," I said, "at the rate you are going, you'll probably be up to your shoulders by the time we start our morning meeting. Might have to join us on Zoom."

"Ha, ha," he answered dryly.

I dove back in, swimming away before he could hear my giggle. Halfway down the lane, I trod water to turn my headphones on. I hadn't even made it to the other side when I realized it wasn't my music assaulting my eardrums but Beck's. I'd accidentally grabbed his headphones. I actually had the exact song loaded on mine, but while my version was gentle and stripped-down, Beck's was a cacophony of electric guitar and growly screaming. I pushed the next button, hoping for something better, but no. Same deal, just a different song.

As soon as I made it to the other side, I ripped them off, my ear drums seeking relief. Beck popped up next to me. He held out a hand for his headphones, thrusting mine at me as if they would burn him if he held on any longer.

"It's like my music but declawed and neutered," Beck said, his perfect features pinched into a disgusted expression. It was kind of cute on him, in an annoying way.

"Well, your music is like my music shotgunned an energy drink and got a face tattoo."

"Enjoy your lullabies," he said, nose still scrunched, body posed to push off the wall.

"Enjoy your hearing. While you can."

At that, he smiled and kicked off the wall in a flawless butterfly stroke.

Still stinging from the burn to my music, I found myself trying to catch up to him. As if that would stick it to him. Not that it mattered because I never came close. His strokes were effortless. When I stopped for a drink at the same time he did, I struggled to keep my breathing under control. On the other hand, he acted as though he had gone for a walk instead of swimming eight hundred yards at the speed of a shark.

"How the hell," I started between gulps of air, "do you do that Aquaman turn in the water?"

He laughed. "The flip turn?"

"Yes! That thing."

"It's easy."

I gave him a look.

"Here, I'll show you." He floated on his back and did a slow backstroke to give us some space, and I definitely did not get a good look at the way his abs worked with the movement, or the thick line of hair that started at his lower stomach and disappeared into his swim trunks. He flipped back over, treading as he explained, "When you approach the wall, you are going to duck your head as if swimming down, but instead, tuck your knees into your chest. Then, kick off the wall while twisting back to your original position. But now facing the opposite side. Obviously."

"Obviously," I mumbled as if anything were obvious about the directions he'd given.

I watched closely as he modeled the movement, slower for my benefit but still a blur of twists in the water.

"Okay," he said after surfacing. "Your turn. Remember to curl, twist, and kick."

I thought about refusing. But the flip-turn looked pretty cool. Besides, I still felt invincible after finishing the menu board. Sure, I'd master the flip turn on the first try. I approached the wall, swam down, and twisted into some sort of mess, causing water to burn through my sinuses. I surfaced, coughing.

Yeah. Real easy. Natural, even—like folding a fitted sheet.

I expected Beck to laugh at the attempt, but instead, he came ready with suggestions for improvement. I didn't know which was worse.

"Not a bad first try. This time, make sure to blow water through your nose with the twist."

I did. And though my nose was spared the burn, upon completing the twist, I kicked out, only for my toes to touch seemingly endless water.

"Okay. This time, get closer to the wall. You have to get almost right up to it."

I did get close, so close I looked up in time to see the tiled concrete an inch from my face. And smacked right into it. The wall was not forgiving.

"Are you okay?" he asked as I came up.

I ripped off my goggles and swim cap, rubbing my forehead with a string of curse words.

"Fine." I pressed a palm to the ache in my skull and winced.

I opened my eyes and found him looking worried. "Let me see."

In other circumstances, I would have pushed his hand away, but the tenderness in his voice surprised me.

I'd never gotten a good look at the color of his eyes before. I knew they were brown, but that word seemed too dull to describe what I was looking at now. *I* had brown eyes. Beck's eyes were fresh earth or a cup of coffee on a fall morning—caramel swirled in hazelnut—lively and surprisingly warm.

"Ouch," he said, eyebrows drawn. "Unfortunately, I don't think it's bad enough to justify missing work."

I started to laugh, but it died down as his feather-light thumb grazed my forehead and lingered at my hairline. His eyes drifted back to mine, then trailed down the bridge of my nose.

"What?" I asked, rubbing the area in search of a blemish.

He smiled. "You have so many freckles." And at that, his eyes seemed to follow the trail out to my cheeks and then down to my lips. I stopped breathing as I realized how close we were, how entranced we both seemed by the proximity. Beck snapped out of it before I did, removing his hand and retreating a couple of feet. He cleared his throat. "Let's give the flip turns a break for today. Okay?"

He was back in the water before I could utter a response. The next several laps, I saw how fast he could go in the water. Beck torpedoed past me continuously, and he didn't stop again until he finished his workout.

When I approached the bench with my things, Beck was already there with a towel wrapped loosely around his hips while he checked his phone. I'd seen his stomach before, and I knew he still had swim trunks under that towel. But as beads of water rolled down that middle line separating his abs, my jaw slackened, and heat bloomed in my lower belly.

I snapped my eyes back to his face, chiding myself for drooling over Beckett Atteridge, Senior-level Asshole.

He scowled at his phone.

"What's wrong?" I asked.

"Nothing," he said, tossing his phone into his gym bag. But as his zipper got caught, trying to close it, he exhaled loudly and relented. "Victoria and my ex are best friends. So I expected her at the wedding. I didn't, however, think she'd come all the way from California for a wedding shower. But Victoria said she RSVP'd."

It shocked me to see Beck lose his composure over an ex. It turned out Poseidon was a mere human like the rest of us.

"You still have feelings for her," I guessed.

A sticky sensation spread across my chest, and I surprised myself when I put a name to it: jealousy—something I had no right to feel about Beck.

"No. It's not like that." He huffed out a frustrated breath. "It's just awkward."

"Because Victoria and your ex are close?"

"Best friends since college. Victoria introduced us a couple of years ago when Reagan moved to Houston for a job. She hadn't counted on us hitting it off." Beck looked at the swim cap in his grip. "She begged me not to pursue anything with Reagan, afraid our relationship would complicate their friendship." He smiled faintly. "But I think her making Reagan forbidden only made me want her more," he said, running a hand through his curls.

"So, you dated anyway and broke up?" I finished as I toweled off my calves.

"It's a little more complicated than that, but essentially, yes."

"Complicated how?"

It felt weird, peering into Beck's past. We weren't close enough for a conversation about exes, but I could hear the tinge of pain in his voice. I had to know more.

"Last year, Reagan and I decided to spend Thanksgiving apart." Beck sat on the bench next to me, gazing at the still water as he spoke, "My mom wanted me at their place. Reagan wanted to go back to her parents' house in California. It wasn't a big deal. We'd decided we could spend Christmas together without family.

"But while she was there, she sent me a text saying, 'Last night was amazing. Can't believe we did that with my grandma in the next room.'" I winced, but Beck kept going. "I called her right away. Obviously, she hadn't meant to send the text to me, but I thought it was innocent—like maybe her friend had come over, and they got high in her grandmother's sewing room.

"To Reagan's credit, she told me the truth—that things were getting serious between her and another guy. She told me *Tom* already had a job in Santa Monica. That she didn't feel at home in Texas, and she didn't feel like herself when she was with me."

My head snapped in his direction. "What a shitty thing for her to say."

He shrugged. "We'd been talking about buying a house in California together, but I'd just started a new job in Houston and told her I didn't feel right quitting so soon. I had no idea how homesick she was . . . That's always weighed on me. And what she said about not feeling herself when with me—what kind of person does that make me?"

"Don't do that," I said, waiting until he looked back into my eyes so he could see how serious I was. "She got caught and was justifying her actions, probably as much to herself as she was to you."

I realized, too late, that my tone held the bitter bite of someone who'd been a victim of cheating.

He looked at me, head cocked slightly to one side. "Were you cheated on too?"

"Yeah," I conceded.

"You're kidding."

"Nope. Found my boyfriend fucking his, 'I swear, there-is-nothing-going-on-between-us,' friend on his couch."

"What an idiot."

The response came so quickly, it made me blush. Like he couldn't believe anyone would cheat on me.

"Well, the same goes for your Reagan," I said. "Anyway, at least I wasn't in love with Chad. Things must have been serious between you and Reagan if you planned on moving to California with her."

Beck avoided my gaze. "In any case, please don't mention any of this to Victoria. I never told her the full story, only that it had been a mutual decision to end things."

"You don't think your sister should know?"

"No. Victoria asked us not to go out with each other. We ignored her request. So, it's up to both Reagan and me to keep things civil."

I considered that. "Why don't you bring a date?" Beck's eyes flicked to me as I continued. "She has her Tom. If you bring your own date, it will show you've both moved on. That your breakup was no big deal."

"That's not a bad idea," he said but then gave me a level look. "Except for the fact that I don't have a date on standby."

If the man walked shirtless down the waterway for only a couple of minutes, he could have a collection of phone numbers from women ready to jump at the chance to hang on his arm, but I decided to keep that little nugget to myself.

I shrugged. "Sorry, Beck. Guess it's all aboard the awkward train."

A smile spread lazily across Beck's face, and I realized my critical error—calling him his preferred name. "So, it's Beck now?"

"Don't get excited," I said, zipping my duffle. "It's going to be a case-by-case basis."

I was tempted to work through my lunch to try and keep up with the towering load. But I needed a break. And if I were trying on Hailey's life, she would work hard but play harder. Besides, of all the times I'd worked through lunch, had I ever felt caught up?

Absolutely not.

So, I closed out Excel and opened Pinterest as I enjoyed my Caesar salad. I found that even just looking at ideas for a vacation lifted my mood. I had a lot of pins on my board from a lot of different vacations. As I scrolled down, bright colors filled the screen with turquoise waters, white-sanded beaches, and fruity cocktails. I'd finally decided on Maui. Mainly because it was so green and beachy and not Florida. I had no interest in visiting the state Hailey had picked over me. Besides, if I was going to escape work by planning a dream vacation, it was go big or go home.

I clicked on a pin titled *Budgeting for Maui*. My gaze landed on the *Budget* side of the column. I frowned, already calculating how many weeks' worth of groceries and months of rent one trip would eat. I couldn't even let myself daydream about this trip without my credit card shriveling.

My mouse hovered over the X of the browser as Beck entered my cubicle.

"I'll get you the meeting notes by the end of the day," I said, waving him off.

"Did you get the text from Anna?" he asked, ignoring my attempt to get rid of him.

I flipped my phone over. I'd had it on silent so I could enjoy my lunch in peace. But, sure enough, she'd texted me.

Went in for my weekly exam and my doctor is making me go to the hospital. Apparently I'm 4 cm dilated.

"She's having the baby?" I stupidly asked Beck.

He rubbed the back of his neck. "Looks that way."

"But she's not due yet. She's still got a few weeks."

I sent Anna a quick text, wishing her luck and asking her to keep me posted. Then, the realization hit me. And it hit me hard.

Anna was gone. The last good thing about this job.

Beck leaned against the edge of my desk. "That's not too early, though, right? The baby will be okay."

"Yeah, I'm sure everything will be fine," I said, but my voice quivered ever so slightly at the end of the sentence.

"Hey, are you alright?" The tenderness in his voice surprised me. It almost made me want to cry more—like it permitted me to let my guard down.

Then I came to my senses. I refused to cry on Beckett's shoulder today. I inhaled sharply, working to rally.

"Yeah. I'm fine. Does the team know?" I deflected. "Anna was in the middle of a workflow. We'll need to divvy up her tasks."

With Beck's help, we notified the rest of the team about Anna and listed the things she hadn't been able to finish. Wesley emailed back with a, **Seems like you two have it covered.** I angled the screen so Beck could read his response.

"Looks like it's just you and me."

He drummed his long fingers on my desk as he considered Wesley's email. Between those fingers, his proximity as he leaned in close to read the screen, and his scent, my brain felt fuzzy. He wasn't even trying to be sexy, which made me all the more annoyed. His everyday actions had me all worked up.

To be fair, it had been over a year since I caught Chad cheating on me, and I'd had neither the time nor the willpower to re-enter the dating scene. So, it had been a while for me.

Still, it's not as though I had a visceral reaction to every man I encountered. Why, of all people, did it have to be for Beck?

"I know I'm still relatively new, but our team kind of sucks at acting like one," Beck said, effectively knocking me from my lustful fog.

I snorted. "You get used to it."

He looked at me. "That's the problem. I don't want to get used to it, neither should you." Beck backed away. "I'll be right back. Do *not* reply to that email."

Not even five minutes later, Beck had responded to Wesley's email.

Yep! Emily and I will knock out the workflow. We'll leave the distribution of other tasks to you, Wes! Thanks!

My jaw could have hit the desk.

"Are you crazy?" I hissed as he returned to my cubicle, laptop, and rolling chair in tow.

"I was professional." Beck nodded at the empty space next to me. "Do you mind if I work here? I think it would be easier to discuss the workflow in person rather than over messages?"

I was still stuck on his reply to Wesley. "You basically refused to do the other tasks."

Beck sank onto the chair and logged into his laptop. "Senior-level Asshole perks. Remember?"

I shook my head, but I couldn't keep from smiling. "Alright. Where should we start?"

To Beck's credit, he worked with me nonstop to finish the workflow, that is, until four-thirty rolled around. It was Thursday, after all.

Beck looked down at the time. "I'm sorry. I've gotta go."

"You know, Chili's has their happy hour on other days besides Thursday." I'd been joking, but I was also hoping he'd correct me with what he'd actually be doing.

No such luck. Instead, Beck chuckled lightly. "Thank you, Lane. You are a wealth of knowledge."

I smiled at being able to make him laugh, but as soon as he left, I sighed. We'd made a lot of progress with the workflow, but there was still so much to do.

By six, I was kicking myself for taking that lunch break. The rest of the office was empty, except for a member of the cleaning staff who was currently vacuuming the huddle room. I decided to open YouTube and start a favorite playlist, sans headphones. The music floated into my cubicle, and I took a deep breath, willing the melody to loosen me up and calm me.

It worked a little too well. Within minutes, the yawns rolled out, one after another. I needed something stimulating, louder.

I thought of what I'd said about Beck's music. *Your music is like my music shotgunned an energy drink . . .*

More energy was what I needed. I typed *Taylor Swift Rock Cover* into the search bar and got a plethora of results. I clicked on the first option—a band called Battered Keys. I rolled my eyes at the dramatic name, but the song sounded like what Beck had in his Aftershock headphones. Rock covers powered me through that workflow for about thirty minutes until a voice sounded from behind me.

"Are you listening to Battered Keys?" I jumped a good foot out of my seat, whirling to find Beck smiling like a cat. "Looks as though you are gaining some musical taste after all."

"Jesus Christ!" I fumbled to exit out of YouTube, cutting off the music. "You scared the shit out of me!"

"Sorry," he offered, "but I brought food." I registered the bags of takeout in his arms, the spiced aroma of Indian food wafting into my cube. My mouth watered as Beck plopped one of the bags on my desk. "I hope chicken biriyani is okay."

"Is this from the food truck down the street?" I opened my box and had to keep from full-on drooling at the sight of tender, seasoned chicken mixed in yellow rice.

Beck nodded. "The one that parks in front of the theater," he confirmed, smiling as he dug out the utensils.

"This is my favorite."

"I know." He passed me a fork. "Anna told me."

I tried not to read too hard into the fact that Beck had intentionally gotten me my favorite food and that I'd been a topic of conversation between him and Anna.

"What do I owe you?"

His smile lessened. "I know it's been a long day for you. Please, let me do this one thing."

"Okay . . . Thank you," I said, cautious, almost as if I expected the real Beck to show up at any moment, the one I met on his first day at the office, the one who pulled me out of the waterway, then looked down at me as if I had two heads.

But this Beck, who was making himself quite comfortable in my cubicle again, seemed anything but that guy. I took in his change of clothes: jeans and a black T-shirt. The dark shirt made the red-inked flowers pop on his arm.

His fresh shower smell was more potent than usual, and his curls lazed on his head, heavy and still a little wet. I tried to guess what he could have scheduled every Thursday that would require going home to shower before coming back up here.

"Did you . . . go for a workout?"

Beck used his fork to bat around the rice. "Something like that."

Something like that. The other action that was kind of like a workout that called for a shower after . . . Did Beck have some sort of weekly sex arrangement? My cheeks warmed at the picture: Beck sweaty, arms braced on either side of a lover.

I ducked my head, trying to appear very interested in my food. I decided I didn't want to know what Beck did on Thursdays, and Beck didn't seem inclined to elaborate. He chewed on a forkful of his biriyani.

His eyes rolled, and he moaned. "Okay," he said after swallowing. "I get the hype."

"Right?" I said, trying to enjoy my food more than the sound of Beck's moan. "Well, I guess this is good. We can knock out this workflow while we eat."

"Oh no," Beck shook his head. "I am enjoying this." He used his fork to point down at his food. "Way too much to let something like work ruin it."

I laughed, but I understood. Besides, the last three hours of nonstop configuring workflows had fried my brain, so I relented. "Okay. No work."

"So, when are you going to take that vacation?"

The question threw me off guard. "What?" I asked, mouth still full.

He gestured vaguely to the tropical elements of my cubicle. "The decorations, the canceled vacation with your sister, and then today you were on some website about Maui."

My cheeks heated. Beck had been listening to me—noticing me. I took a sip of Coke, giving my scarlet cheeks a moment to fade before answering. "I didn't realize you paid attention to what I Google."

"Well, you are on company time."

My lips pressed into a flat line. "It was during lunch."

Beck shrugged. The ease gradually melted, and the intensity returned. He wanted an answer, and we both knew I was skating around it.

"I don't know," I said finally, opting for the truth. "I can't now, obviously."

"No, not obviously. Why can't you take a vacation?"

"Because." I waved at the computer screen and the workflow as if to say, *duh*. "Work is crazy. Things are too busy right now."

"That's exactly why you need a vacation. The point of a vacation is to escape life when it's hectic."

"Wow," I deadpanned. "How profound. That should be in a fortune cookie. You got any other sage advice for me?"

"Okay," he said, letting out a small laugh and pushing his food around with his fork. Message received. He looked ready to drop the issue. Then he put the fork down and looked at me with an awfully serious expression for someone who'd said he couldn't work because he was enjoying his chicken too much. "It's just—you seem like you need a break."

I sighed. "Everyone needs a break." I decided to change the direction of the conversation before either of us could delve too far into my unhealthy work relationship and my need to excel, even if it meant hating every minute of my job. "I'll get one this weekend. I won't be working the entire time—can't."

"Why not? You got a hot date?" I'm sure he meant the questions to come out as light and playful, but the tightness in his voice was just shy of jovial.

"No." I squinted, waiting for the reason to hit him. Why *he* would also be busy. But his expression remained blank. "Your sister's shower, remember?"

"Oh! That. Yeah, that explains why *I'll* be busy this Saturday. But . . . do brides usually invite their calligraphers to their showers?"

"No. Your sister is having me do live lettering as part of the party favors."

"And that is what exactly?" he asked before taking another bite of his dinner.

"It's doing calligraphy on site. In this case, she's having me letter on Capiz shells." Before he could ask me what the hell those were, I explained, "Little round shells." I made a circle with my fingers. "Pearly, opaque. Anyway, I'm there to personalize the shells in whatever way the guests request. I'm surprised she didn't tell you." I thought of how Beck had taken a day off work to help Victoria with her company. "I got the impression you two are close."

"We are." He tilted his head to the side and gave a devastatingly handsome half-smile. "But she, mercifully, leaves me out of most wedding plans." Then the smile slid off his face and he sat up, straight and stiff. "You are going to be at the shower." I could all but see a lightbulb above his head. "And are you going to the wedding?"

"The one in Costa Rica?" I scoffed. "No."

"But you could go."

My eyebrows scrunched. "Why would I do that?" I took a long sip of Coke, waiting for him to answer.

"Because you can be my date."

I had to choke down the gulp of Coke to keep it from spraying all over my laptop. "What?" I asked around a coughing fit.

"You said it yourself. Having a date for the shower and wedding would show I've moved on."

"I meant someone else." I was still coughing up carbonation. "Not me!"

"It wouldn't be a real date." He put up his hands. "Just for pretend."

"Beck—"

"Victoria already thinks we have a history together from that incredibly weird interaction outside her office." I rolled my eyes, but he continued. "I'll tell her things rekindled when I dropped the mirror off at your apartment. And now we're seeing each other." He laughed as if amused by how naturally the narrative unrolled. "Think about it. It makes sense."

"None of it makes sense, Beck. Is Victoria going to take kindly to you dating her calligrapher?"

"I don't think she'll care as long as things aren't awkward between her best friend and her brother."

I folded my arms over my chest as I looked back at all the pieces Beck had given me, sorting them to see where they best fit. "Let me get this straight. You are asking me to fake date you until after the wedding? Because that's three weeks of acting."

"No. It would only be for the shower and the wedding. Two evenings, tops. We go back to normal when at the office. It's just a show for my sister."

"And your ex. It's a show for her too. What was her name?" I snapped my fingers as it came to me. "Reagan."

Beck shrugged. "Sure, whatever you say."

"I can't go to Costa Rica." I dropped the takeout box on my desk, too ruffled to eat another bite.

"Why? Do you not have a passport?" He frowned like I'd shattered his entire plan with a technicality.

But I did have a passport. I'd gone to Mexico with my mom and Hailey after graduation. It was the last vacation I'd taken—if you didn't count our trip to Waco a couple of years ago, which I didn't since I'd gotten food poisoning and spent the entirety of the weekend glued to the toilet in our Airbnb.

"No. I have a passport. But I can't miss work to fly across the world for a wedding."

"It's only a three-hour flight, and I'll pay for it. You could fly out that Saturday morning and be back on Sunday. You wouldn't even have to miss work since that's what you are so worried about."

"What I'm worried about is pretending to be your girlfriend, Beck." I laughed, a hysterical thing. "It is a terrible idea."

"Probably." A grin pulled wide across Beck's face. "But I think that's my decision to make since you owe me one."

My jaw dropped. I knew it. I knew that favor was going to come back to bite me. "Somehow, I feel like fake dating goes beyond that scope. That's like saying I owe you a kidney because I ate the last pop-tart in the pantry."

"Oh really, because I think fake dating is the perfect cash-in for going along with your fake identity."

I did owe him. There was no denying he'd been extra cool by not telling his sister about me. "Fine," I huffed. When his lips curved in victory, I put up my hand to halt the joy. "But we should set some ground rules."

He sat back in his chair. "Sure. What did you have in mind?"

"I'll hold your hand. Quick hugs are fine." I couldn't help it. My gaze fell to his full lips. I snapped my eyes back to his. "But kissing is off the table."

"Rule number one: no kissing." He pondered something. "What about dancing? I only ask because we are going to a wedding, after all."

The thought of my body pressed against Beck's made me dizzy. But I shook that off. It would be sweet wedding music, not ass-shaking club soundtracks. "Dancing is fine, but hands should remain at respectable cotillion-like positions."

"Fair enough," he said. "Anything else?"

"I want a separate hotel room for the night of the wedding."

"Done. We'll have to be sneaky when we part ways for the night, but it shouldn't be an issue."

I was sure we needed more ground rules, but I couldn't think of anything else. "Fine," I said, sticking out my hand for him to shake. "I'll be your fake date for the shower and the wedding."

Beck leaned in, his hand engulfing mine.

My skin tingled as I shook hands with the enemy.

Chapter 12

I crossed the shadow cast from the awning of the Galveston At-teridge—the venue for Victoria and Doug's wedding shower. My lunch roiled in my stomach.

At two hundred dollars an hour, I would be lettering for an Atteridge in front of all her friends and family. It was too much money for my worth. It was too much fame for me—Emily Lane, who worked in a cubicle and ate too much Chinese takeout and considered writing addresses on envelopes a fun night.

On top of lettering for one Atteridge, I'd be fake dating another. We'd previously agreed Beck would pick me up for the shower. I hadn't thought much of it when we'd made the plans, but sitting in Beck's Audi, engulfed in his scent, not even an arm's length away from him, had me questioning all the choices that had led me there.

How was I supposed to avoid the pull of his attraction when we'd be spending so much time together?

I took a steadying breath as the air conditioning of the lobby hit my cheeks.

I'm trying on Hailey's life, I reminded myself. And Hailey would love fake dating a hot guy. And she most certainly would not sweat doing a live lettering event for the first time. Instead, she'd hold her head high and stride in like she owned the place.

The handle of the rolling crate slipped from my grip as soon as I crossed the threshold of the ballroom. I knew this would be a nice event. I knew Victoria had the funds to throw a big party.

But this.

This was the very picture of luxury.

A velvet loveseat for the bride and groom sat in the front of the room. Perhaps throne was a better word, as the loveseat waited on a raised platform with a backdrop of fresh banana leaves and hibiscus flowers so vibrant that they looked to have been plucked in Hawaii and flown over that very morning. A neon sign added a pop of fun to the tropical stage: *All you need is love.*

Caterers had set up warmers along a long wall, and a dessert table flourished under a full balloon arch of emerald and gold. A five-tiered cake stood proudly at the top, one of those artfully naked confections.

On the tables, floating candles sat in vases of water and ferns—more greenery, more life to the room. Even the chairs were dressed well for the event, tied with neat magenta and pink bows. All of this beneath the light of grand crystal chandeliers.

For a wavering minute, I wondered if I'd been confused, that this wasn't the shower but the wedding itself. But then again, Atteridge money made Victoria a different breed from the rest of us.

A hand ran self-consciously down the side of my skirt. I'd painstakingly picked the outfit, wanting to look professional but not too stiff. I'd finally decided on a floral midi skirt and a cropped white sweater. Now I wished I'd gone with slacks and a button-down so I could blend in with the other vendors. Be a fly on the wall.

Beck noticed I wasn't right behind him and doubled back. "Hey, are you okay?" he asked.

"It's a lot." My eyes trailed along the wall of vendors.

Beck scoffed. "Victoria tends to be a little extra." His eyes roamed over my face. "You look pale, Lane." Then those eyes widened. "You aren't going to pass out, are you?"

"No!" The question surprised me, but then I remembered the meeting where Wesley had insinuated my fainting spells were a regular occurrence.

Beck didn't seem convinced by my answer. He wrenched the rolling cart from me—no easy task since I had the handle in a death grip. After he parked it off to the side, he took my hand and steered me back into the lobby. I followed him into a dimly lit side hall and then to an empty conference room.

"Sit," he commanded. Part of me wanted to be obstinate and refuse, but the rolling sea in my stomach told me to listen to him.

Water bottles lined the center of the table. Beck took one, then opened it for me. "Drink," he said before taking the seat next to me.

"Are you this bossy to all your girlfriends? Or just the fake ones?" I asked before glugging half the bottle.

"What's going on?" he asked, ignoring my attempt at humor.

I screwed the cap back on the water and then rested my forehead against the table. "I don't know if I can do this," I admitted.

"Fake dating me or the calligraphy?"

"Both. But mainly the calligraphy part." I raised my head, forcing myself to meet his gaze. "I don't think I can pull this off." I inhaled sharply. "But I have no choice. I signed up for this. People are counting on me. I can't just—"

"Hey, hey," Beck put his hand on my arm to halt the tidal wave of my voiced concerns. "You don't have to do anything you don't want to do."

My brows scrunched together. "But your sister—"

"Will live without someone signing seashells at her party." His features softened. "Again, I'm not making light of what you do. But no one is going to force you out there. If you aren't comfortable, I'll drive you home right now."

"You'd do that?"

"Of course, I would."

"But what about Reagan?"

Beck gave an amused smile. "What about her?"

I gave my own smile—a knowing one. He wanted to make her jealous, which meant he probably still had feelings for her.

"Listen," Beck continued, "it's your decision. And if you want to leave, I'll take you. But you belong here. I've seen your work. It's incredible."

I blushed, but not one to take a compliment, said, "Says the guy who thinks cursive and calligraphy are the same thing."

"You're right. I have limited knowledge of calligraphy. But how many professional calligraphers do you expect to be in attendance today?" My lips parted, ready to reply. But he was right. I felt like I could breathe deeply for the first time since I stepped into the hotel. "I suspect you are a pro at your trade, but even if you aren't, it doesn't matter. You'll be the leading authority on calligraphy at this event."

And that's how Beckett Atteridge coaxed me out of hiding and back into the ballroom. Still fighting the residual effects of imposter syndrome, I gripped the handle of my rolling cart, scanning the room for

Amanda or Victoria, and nearly jumped out of my skin when someone shrieked behind us.

"No, Jason! *Seven*. We are doing seven seats per table. Not eight!"

I whirled to find Amanda, who was not at all the composed image she'd been in Victoria's office. Now flyaways floated atop her head, escapees loose from a bun. Her blouse had come halfway untucked and not in a cute, I-did-this-on-purpose way. The blush of her cheeks looked less of a rosy and more of a *I'm* this *close to losing my shit.*

The man, who must have been Jason, seemed to read the look the same way. He put up his hands in surrender. "My mistake. I'll fix it right away."

Amanda huffed and then turned in my direction, seeming to see me for the first time. Her face fell into an attempted mask of pleasure. "Hailey, hi. We have you in that corner."

She pointed to a folded table directly to our left, not far from the entrance.

"Okay," I managed, afraid to say anything that might tip her over the edge.

"Let us know if you need anything," she said, but she was already walking toward the caterers, surely to terrorize more victims before Victoria could terrorize her.

Jason gave me a harrowing *run while you can* look. I attempted a polite smile, but at this point, it felt more like a grimace.

I unpacked supplies onto my designated table: paint pens, chalk, a sharpener, pointed pens, a case of nibs, black and gold ink, as well as painter's tape.

"You think you have enough stuff?" Beck asked.

"What were you expecting? I'd come with a box of crayons?"

"No. Maybe a few Bic pens but not crayons."

I couldn't help myself. I threw my head back and laughed. Maybe cackled is a better word. Beck's eyes crinkled at the corners with a bright, all-consuming smile. He enjoyed making me laugh, I realized. The thought sent up a flight of butterflies rebelliously and stupidly in my stomach.

"Hailey, is this spot okay?"

My head snapped in the direction of Victoria's voice. She was an absolute vision. Her curls cascaded down from a half-updo, spilling onto her back. Her coral dress fit tight, showing off her toned body.

Another woman walked in step with her on equally toned, perfectly bronzed legs. The sequins on her dress shimmered with each hip sway. She had long black hair that cascaded from a savagely tight ponytail. With piercing blue eyes and cheekbones that could cut, I didn't think anyone ever fit the word "slay" quite like Victoria's companion.

"Yes," I finally answered. "This spot is perfect."

"Good. Hailey, this is Reagan," Victoria said, indicating the model in sequins. "Reagan, this is Beck's girlfriend and my calligrapher, Hailey. They used to work together before Hailey started her business."

Beck and I had discussed the lie before he sent his sister the text letting her know he was dating one of her vendors. It sounded odd coming out of Victoria's mouth—something she believed to be true that I knew to be false—but not any weirder than her calling me Hailey, I supposed.

"They bumped into each other outside my office and have been dating since." Her head cocked to the side, but she smiled while appraising us. "I have to admit, I was surprised when Beck told me you were seeing each other, but watching you two flirt just now—I can see the chemistry."

I stiffened, and something in the back of Beck's throat made a clicking noise. He tried to cover the sound with a laugh, but it came out strained.

Reagan's icy eyes did a slow toe-to-head sweep of me. She looked unimpressed.

Yep. Nothing to see here, I thought sourly. Seeing Beck with someone as plain as me must have burned her up. I probably should have played nice, but I couldn't get over the fact that she cheated on Beck—and broke his heart.

My arm snaked behind Beck's lower back, and I grabbed his side to pull him close. In return, Beck's arm draped possessively over my shoulder. I knew he was ripped; swimming with him had told me that much, but seeing and feeling were two very different things. Every cell in my body seemed to swarm to meet the points of contact: my chest at his ribs, my hips at his thigh.

"Yeah," I said, trying my best to plaster an adoring look on my face as I looked up at Beck. "It felt like fate—running into each other again."

Beck's eyes danced. He seemed to enjoy my performance. I playfully scrunched my nose at him, and he booped it with his pointer finger. We were being nauseatingly cute.

Reagan gave a tight smile.

"Where's Tom?" Beck asked Reagan, his deep voice rumbling through my rib cage.

"We broke up last month."

"That's too bad," he said without inflection.

So much for the *they've both moved on* plan. Oh well, Victoria didn't seem fazed by Reagan being single. She was too busy smiling at us.

"Babe!" a voice called from the ballroom entrance. It belonged to a man with sandy brown hair and a sharp blue suit. Victoria's husband-to-be, I presumed. "The staff have a question about the valet."

"Be right there." Victoria smiled back at me, then gestured toward the table where I'd be doing live lettering. "And everything should be there. But if you need anything, let me know."

As her and Reagan's heels clicked toward the exit, I couldn't help but think I may have gotten Victoria wrong. She was a lot more personable than I'd previously imagined. But I guess anyone would look warm standing next to Reagan, Ice Queen.

I glanced at my watch. Only twenty minutes before the shower started. *Shit.* My mini panic attack had cost me.

Beck read the urgency in how I rushed to sharpen a piece of chalk. "How can I help?"

"Can you prime the board for me?" I said, nodding toward the chalkboard on the ground.

Amanda had let me know there would be one, so I'd already created an outline to transfer over. The message greeted guests and let them know they could get a shell inked with a name or short phrase.

"What do I do?" he asked as I handed him a piece of chalk.

"Just rub it down, lengthwise."

Beck licked his bottom lip, looking very much like he was holding in a smile. "Did you hear yourself say that?"

"Har. Har," I said, working to keep the blush off my cheeks. A valiant effort but not an effective one. "Now get to work."

"What is the priming for?" he asked, sounding genuinely curious.

"It keeps the lettering from staining the board."

"Hmm," he said as though I'd given him an interesting fact to store away. After he'd finished, he set the chalk on the table and dusted his hands.

We had the table set up and ready to go just as guests started trickling in. A guy shook Doug's hand, hugged Victoria, and then noticed Beck.

"Hey, man!" he called warmly.

Beck waved back. "How's it going, Koontz?"

"You should get out there," I said. "Mingle with your friends."

"But you're my date. And I don't want you sitting here alone." Something swelled in my chest, but I shoved it down.

"I am your date, but I'm also your sister's calligrapher. You can't be over here distracting me when I have a job to do."

"Oh, so I'm distracting?" he asked with a flirty little grin.

"Get out of here," I said, trying not to laugh and failing.

His face turned serious. "You sure you'll be okay?"

My heart stupidly skipped a beat over his concern. *He just doesn't want you to ruin the party by fainting,* I told the organ in my chest.

Not trusting myself to speak, I nodded at Beck. He backed away from the table, giving me one last smile before joining the steadily growing crowd.

With Beck—my distraction—gone, my imposter syndrome kicked back into gear. I felt like any moment, spotlights would glare down on me, and someone with a megaphone was going to call out, *She's not Hailey. And she's certainly not qualified for this!*

I swallowed back the thought and found another task, testing pens on one of the Capiz shells to find the best option for lettering. The gold popped on the shell and didn't smear like the black had. Good, I'd been hoping for that option. Something as plain as black didn't seem befitting of an event like Victoria's shower.

I looked up as Beck greeted a stylish older woman with bouncy gray curls. They embraced warmly. When Beck pulled back, he shook the hand of the man next to her. I noticed the man's eyebrows—sharp like Beck and Victoria. Judging by the stiff handshake, those were their parents. But neither Beck nor his father held a look of disdain, just reservation.

As they went their separate ways, I clocked the way his father sighed and how Beck's head bowed slightly. Things looked complicated, indeed.

Beck shook it off quickly enough. He clapped his hands over the shoulder of a man who looked to be in mid-conversation. They both smiled, but Beck's was luminous. I couldn't help it. I smiled too. *It's fine,* I thought. *He has a nice smile. So what?*

But then Beck caught me looking, and it was suddenly not fine, not at all, that I was smiling at his smile. I wanted to avert my gaze, look at other guests, check my outfit, and pretend to be busy. Something. *Anything.* But his gaze pinned me. I expected him to roll his eyes or stick out his tongue. Instead, his smile wavered slightly—as if he'd been ensnared by me as well.

"Oh wow! You do calligraphy?" My first guest snapped me out of whatever the hell that little staring contest had been.

"Yes!" I picked up a Capiz shell. "I can do a name, a favorite word, a phrase—if it's three words or less."

"Cool! Can you put my name? Lindsay—with an A."

And that's how my work began. It didn't take long for Lindsay to go back to show her friends the Capiz shell, and then I had a steady stream of guests at my table. I didn't know what I'd been worried about. Victoria may have been paying me through the nose for the service, but she was too busy to quality-check my work, and the guests were just thrilled to get something cute and personalized for free.

After the guests feasted on lunch and dessert, my line started winding around tables. It should have unnerved me: so many people, so many chances to disappoint. Not to mention, I needed to hurry to get the line down but give each shell enough care to meet Atteridge-level expecta-tions.

But once I got in my groove, I let go of all the anxiety and found I was actually enjoying myself. Usually, I saved my talents for close friends and family, but here, the guests made me feel like what I did was a big deal.

Mostly, people wanted their first or last name. One elderly lady wanted the name of a recently deceased pet on her shell. Some people wanted words like hope or faith. Sometimes, they requested tiny mantras: *be bold* or *choose happy*.

One man in line introduced himself as the groom's brother's boyfriend, Sebastian Gomez. He told me he owned a shoe store on the north side of Houston and wanted to know if I had a business card so we could be in touch for a live lettering event at his store.

I'd done it. *I* had snagged a new client. The request sent my heart fluttering until I reached for said business card and realized the only ones I had were Hailey's. Because I couldn't advertise as anyone else at this event. If I took his job, I'd have to keep lying about my identity. My heart went from fluttering to a clumsy fall, hitting every branch on the way down.

I was seriously weighing the pros and cons of legally changing my first name to my sister's when a familiar, smug face popped up next in my line. Beck had his hands in his pockets, that lazy smile on his face.

"What will it be? Beckett or Atteridge?"

I expected the names to land with bruising force. Instead, he only cocked his head to the side, letting out a contemplative, "Hmmm . . . How about *Senior* Analyst?"

I bristled. Another point awarded to Beck. I tried my best not to let it show as I dipped my nib in the gold ink and set to work on his shell.

Beck tsked. "I see you're still picking up that pen."

"You know, you talk a lot of shit for someone who waited in a long ass line to get something lettered by me." I handed over the shell for his inspection.

Senior-Level Asshole glittered under the chandelier lights.

His half-grin cracked into that full-on smile he wore so well, little crinkle lines appearing near his eyes. "I think you misspelled *senior analyst*."

"Sorry. No returns. Next!"

Beck didn't grace me with his presence again until guests began a steady trickle out the door. My table had been empty for about half an hour when he stopped by with a cupcake.

"I thought you might be hungry," he said.

"Thank you," I said, a little hesitant as I realized he'd brought me food twice now.

I bit into decadent vanilla, piled high with buttercream frosting, and licked my bottom lip with a small moan.

Beck leaned against my table, watching and waving at family and friends as they passed to leave. "So, you pulled it off, Lane."

"No one is more surprised than me," I said before taking another bite of heavenly cupcake.

"I'm not surprised at all," Beck said. My cheeks warmed at that, and it made me glad he had his back to me.

"So, are we staying until the very end?"

I noticed the vendors packing up and figured it was a sign that I could go ahead and do the same. A glance at my watch told me I needed to get my ass home so I could complete my timesheet and reply to someone from accounting about a question they had the day before. Also, Wesley wanted me to review the parameters we set for Frank one more time before we had our meeting with him the next day.

"Victoria asked the bridal party to stay until everyone else is gone." I looked at the remaining guests, who were all about our age: late twenties to early thirties. Every one of them dressed to the nines. "Probably wants to make sure everyone is on the same page about the rehearsal dinner. Or something to that effect. Shouldn't take long."

Victoria waved Beck over while Doug addressed the group. When I hung back to organize my pens, she called out, "Hailey, I want you here for this."

Hesitantly, I walked with Beck over to the table, and when my eyes snagged on Reagan's cold, blue ones, I slipped my hand in Beck's. Beck could try and shrug off her disloyalty all he wanted, but he wasn't fooling me. Reagan had hurt him. I tried not to melt as his warm hand completely enveloped mine. He squeezed once, a silent *thanks*.

When we took seats nearby, Doug addressed the group again, excitement flickering in his eyes. "As you know, the wedding is taking place in Costa Rica. But what you didn't know is that we are going up there a week early. All of us. Get ready for the best fucking time of your lives."

Victoria beamed, looking at her fiancé before turning to the rest of the group. "We are taking a week-long joint bachelor and bachelorette party."

Beck's hand gripped mine again, this time from shock.

"In Costa Rica?" someone shrieked excitedly.

"Hell yeah!" a deep voice bellowed.

Some of the guys high-fived, others clapped each other on the back.

Victoria's eyes danced with laughter. "We have it all planned out. All you have to do is pack your bags."

"And call in sick!" Doug shouted as if leading a war party. Cheering and hooting ensued.

I shot Beck a look, hoping my eyes conveyed the question shouting in my mind: *What the hell have you gotten us into?*

Chapter 13

"You know, there will be plenty of places to swim in Costa Rica," Beck said as I stopped for a drink between laps. He'd been dropping hints about the trip all week. And I got it. He needed an answer: whether I'd be joining the bachelor and bachelorette party. But I didn't have one, not yet anyway.

I downed the last dregs of coffee in my blender bottle. I planned on over-caffeinating to compensate for staying up until two forty-five after attempting to catch up on things for work. I was both still behind and tired. The idea of Victoria's wedding being over soon would excite me if it weren't for the fact that I absolutely loved completing those projects.

"Yeah, but if I stay here," I replied at last. "I'll have the lane all to myself while you're gone."

He frowned at my answer, and I took off for another lap, even though I hadn't rested nearly as long as needed. I got to the end of the lane, ready to try the kick turn one more time, but I chickened out at the last minute, stopping the movement with an outstretched hand before I could slam into the wall again.

Beck and I ended our workouts at the same time, and as soon as I'd wrapped my body in the safety of my oversized, hibiscus-covered beach towel, I approached him.

"I want to help you," I admitted.

"You do?" he asked with delighted shock.

"But I think it's a bad idea," I said. "The trip is a mere two weeks away. It will be a cold day in hell before Wesley lets us both off with such little notice."

"You are going to ask first." He'd given this some thought. "Concoct some excuse—a family emergency: Nana Beth fractured her hip, Uncle Tim has a bunion, something small but urgent. Something they can't say no to."

"You want me to lie?"

Beck gave me a look that said, *seriously?* "It wouldn't exactly be your first time, *Hailey.*"

I could have stomped on his foot for that comment. "What if they ask me to prove it?"

Beck laughed. "They aren't going to launch an FBI investigation, Lane. They are going to take your word for it. Have they ever asked you to produce so much as a doctor's note?"

"Well . . . no."

"Exactly."

"Okay. But what about you? After my debacle, they aren't going to believe you have a family emergency, too."

"No. That's why I'm going to tell Wesley the truth."

I scoffed. "You think he's going to let you off with less than a month's notice to go on a weeklong bachelor party?"

Beck didn't seem at all phased by my lack of faith. "He will. Wesley likes me." He frowned. "Or he likes the idea of me at least, an Atteridge."

Wesley did treat him like royalty. That last name probably sealed the deal for him to get the senior associate position. I glared at him as the pieces of the plan clicked into place.

"How convenient that the plan involves no lying on your part."

"I'm not as good at it as you are."

I *did* stomp on his foot for that.

"Ow!" Beck doubled over and then laughed. I stalked off toward the dressing room. "I'm kidding! Lane, wait!"

I didn't see him again until I stopped by his cube right before our four o'clock meeting. "You coming?"

"Was about to head that way."

Beck closed out of an Excel sheet and clamped his laptop shut. That's when I noticed the Capiz shell at the corner of his desk with his title in gold: Senior-level Asshole. I turned so Beck wouldn't see my smile and nearly tripped over his backpack. He kept it at the mouth of the cubicle, probably for a quick escape. It was Thursday, after all.

"Careful, Lane," Beck said in a hushed voice. "Costa Rica won't be much fun with a twisted ankle."

I shoved his backpack with my foot. "You don't need working legs to sip margaritas on the beach."

He halted. "Does that mean you're coming?"

The hopeful look on his face was cute, so I shut it down immediately. "Nope."

We walked to the huddle room in silence. I didn't mind. I'd need my voice as much as possible to get through the meeting with Frank.

"Explain one more time why this won't work?" Frank demanded, his voice already abrasive, ready to weather whoever contradicted him.

I went over the workflow again, dumbing it down as much as possible without being condescending, and, God, I should have gotten an Oscar for that performance.

"You could make an umbrella change," Frank parried.

"No. We would have to make that change in over a hundred companies."

I thought of Beck's idea to take that vacation. No way in hell that would work now. Even the royal Mr. Atteridge wouldn't be granted leave. We'd both be stuck here, trudging through these changes.

"Well, tough." Frank leaned back in his chair, fingers steepled. "Corporate office does stuff like this all the time."

"Corporate only has thirteen companies." I knew I needed to watch my tone, but we'd spent a huge chunk of time fixing parameters that Frank had originally agreed upon. He'd barely confirmed our solution would work before he wanted to make changes again.

"I don't know what to say. This isn't what we communicated, Emily."

"Actually, it is." Beck's voice surprised me as much as the authority in it. "I have our notes from a month ago, on March 24th." Beck read the meeting minutes, his voice calm and professional. I recognized them as my notes. "I sent you these the day they were taken, and I have your email stating everything looked good. Do you want me to resend the document?"

My mouth dropped. Beck was sticking up for me. Beck *had* taken my notes seriously.

"What the hell do those notes matter? We need these fixed. This is the way family office wants it done, so that's what's going to happen."

The coloring on Frank's face deepened to a dangerous—someone should probably check his blood pressure—shade.

"Now, hold on." I thought Wesley would choke on his spit the way he sputtered across the table, working to get a handle on the direction of the meeting. "Don't worry about it, Frank. I will see to these changes myself."

My head snapped in Wesley's direction. Did the king of delegating just offer to take on a project of this magnitude? Maybe I needed to take a page from Beck's book and get mouthy more often.

This seemed to appease Frank, and the meeting adjourned shortly after with tense, awkward silence. Beck got up to leave with everyone else, but I gestured for him to come over.

"Hey, I'm having a hard time with this error. Do you think you can look at it?"

By the time Beck had made it to my side of the table, we were alone in the huddle room.

"Thank you," I said. "You saved us both a mountain-load of work."

"Can you imagine?" He plopped down on the seat next to mine. "I don't know how Wesley plans to tackle it by himself. It would have taken us weeks to fix that mess."

"Especially without Anna here." My smile lessened at that. I'd squeezed in a little bit of time the day before to visit her and sweet Grace. It was amazing, holding that bundle of fresh life in my arms, but it didn't stop me from wishing Anna hadn't resigned.

"Are you okay?" Beck asked.

"Yeah, fine." I pretended to focus on closing out my Excel sheet.

"Because you look like you could use a vacation." He gave me an expectant look as though he'd dropped the perfect dad joke.

"Still on that, are we?"

"I don't get it. You've been dreaming about taking a vacation. A free one drops into your lap, and you are going to pass?"

"It's not a good time—"

"It's the perfect time."

"Work is busy—"

"It always will be. But we're almost done with this project. We can finish our end of things for the convergence. Wesley agreed to make the changes Frank is asking for. It's not a big deal."

"It is a big deal. This is my job."

"You give so much for this company. And what has it given back?"

"A salary," I said flatly. "Benefits with dental *and* vision."

"I've seen your work. You know the system better than I do. Plain and simple. They shouldn't have hired out, and they did."

That both stung and alleviated—the echo of my suspicions. He'd validated my thoughts. I worked so hard, but I didn't matter to this company.

"I need this job, Beck. I can't afford to fuck it up."

Beck's gaze skirted past me to the bottom of my screen, the time. "Shit. I have to go."

He'd made it to the door when I found my voice. "Where do you go? On Thursdays?"

Beck's hand fell from the door handle, but he didn't turn to face me. "Does it matter?"

I thought of all the possibilities I'd constructed. If he spent his Thursdays with a female companion, then *she* could go with him to Costa Rica. "It might."

Beck paused for a long time, weighing whether or not he could trust me, I realized. He caved with a sigh, facing me. "I volunteer. Teaching ISR."

Volunteer? That wasn't at all what I'd been expecting. "What's ISR?"

"Infant swimming resource."

"So . . . wait." I didn't trust my ears. Something interfered with the message before it reached my brain. "You leave early on Thursdays so you can—" I felt silly even saying out loud what I thought he'd said. "—Teach babies to swim?" I finished.

He grabbed onto the back of a chair, not meeting my gaze. "Something like that."

I gaped. "Oh my god, Beck!" I couldn't keep the awe out of my voice as if he'd produced a chunky and wrinkly Shar-Pei puppy. "You teach babies how to swim?"

"Fix whatever cute image you have in your head. Because, first of all, it's not always babies. It's six months to six years old. Also, teaching a small person how to swim involves a lot of crying."

I reined in my voice, lowering it back to its normal pitch, but I'm sure my eyes still danced with the idea of all of it. "How did you even get into that?"

"I was on the swim team in high school and college." Beck suddenly became very interested in picking at the seam of the rolling chair. This topic made him uncomfortable, though I couldn't fathom why. "I wanted to give back. It made sense."

I got the feeling he was giving me a half-truth, but I didn't press. I'd already made a monumental discovery. No further digging was required.

This bit of information complicated things because I liked this newly discovered piece of Beck. Really liked it. So much so that I had to ignore the singing from my ovaries. But this piece of intel did not fit with office enemy number one, the Beck I knew.

The one who'd taken my position.

The one who'd helped me from the waterway only to make me feel clumsy and disgusting.

The one who'd made fun of me for it later.

The one who'd misplaced my meeting notes.

The one who was competitive.

I ticked them off in my head as if presenting my case to the jury. The pretend prosecutor felt very confident in this case.

The one who was constantly messing with me. But that one wasn't entirely fair. I kind of enjoyed the banter. Besides, I dished it out too. Then the defense got a turn, casting Beck in a positive light.

He'd also been the one who could have outed me to his sister but didn't.

The one who'd come back to the office just to bring me food.

The one who'd noticed I was drowning at work.

The one who'd stuck up for me at work.

The one who'd calmed me down before my first live lettering event.

The jury was hung.

I trekked back to the stem of the conversation. Making a choice about Costa Rica had been on my mind since the shower, and it seemed like it was on Beck's mind, too.

"Pretending to date you for two days is one thing. Spending an entire week pretending to be your girlfriend in an exotic country is another. I can't go on a vacation with you," I said, with no conviction in my voice. "Think of it from an HR standpoint." I walked over to his side of the table. "We'd have an ocean of paperwork to tread since we work for the same company—on the same team."

I looked at him, daring him to disagree. It would be a mercy for him to end this fantasy. But at the same time, I hoped like hell he'd have a loophole. Because I realized for the first time I wanted this. This trip. With him.

Beck's face fell just a bit. "You're right, Emily." It was the first time he'd called me by my first name. A tingle rolled down my spine. "We couldn't go on a vacation as a couple." He took a step, leaving only a small gap between us. "It's a good thing I'll be going with Hailey." His brown eyes caught mine, searching.

I swallowed, looking for solid ground again. "And will Hailey be expected to kiss you, share a bed with you?"

I couldn't help but remember how he'd wanted to make Reagan jealous, which meant something was still there. There were greater things than my job at stake. I didn't need a heartbreak in my future.

His playful look vanished. "Our rules stay the same. You won't have to do anything that makes you uncomfortable. And we are staying in an Atteridge resort in Costa Rica. Victoria had no problem securing suites for all of us. I'll sleep on the couch."

I could be staying in a suite in Costa freaking Rica. *For free.*

With Beck.

What would Hailey do? I knew without a doubt. She'd pack her bags.

Chapter 14

Before I knew it, I was on a plane with Beckett Atteridge, bumping elbows and pulling back with little apologies. Between powering through the last-minute items for the convergence, Beck and I concocted the "family emergency" I'd used to ask for time off. We settled on me having to fly to Kentucky for my dad's knee surgery. The last time I checked, my father lived in Kentucky, but I didn't know how his knees were holding up.

As Beck predicted, Wesley approved my PTO without a single question. Then Beck put in for his vacation, adding a few more days than mine to offset suspicions, and—big surprise—Wesley approved it as well. Oh, to be the golden child.

Between our scheming, working furiously to tie up all loose ends of our project, and finishing signage for Victoria's wedding, I barely slept the past two weeks, and the time went fast. Almost too fast.

I went to switch my phone to airplane mode and found a text from Hailey.

Hailey: Tell me you got waxed!

I glanced over to make sure Beck couldn't see my screen, but he was too focused on adjusting his headrest.

Me: You are way too invested in my pretend love life.

She had, of course, been elated when I'd told her about fake dating Beck. When she learned about the trip to Costa Rica, she practically transcended to a higher plane. She thought Beck and I would have our kids' names picked out by the second day. I'd let her know, many times, that she was delusional.

Hailey: Just want to make sure you have your business taken care of before the analyst slips in.

The potent mental image set my cheeks ablaze.

"Everything okay?" Beck asked.

My phone slipped out of my hand like a wet fish, but I managed to catch it after a few fumbled attempts.

"Fine," I said. "Everything is fine."

I mashed the airplane mode and slipped it into my pocket.

"Are you sure?" Beck pressed. "Because your whole face is red."

"Yeah. It's just a little hot in here."

Beck reached up, twisting the vents in my direction. I tried not to notice the way the sleeves of his T-shirt hugged his biceps. And I tried—really hard—not to picture those arms around me. But they were mouth-wateringly masculine for such a mundane task.

"Better?" Beck asked.

"Much," I croaked.

After the plane ride, we had another three hours in the car driving from the San Jose Airport to Manuel Antonio. The view was breathtaking. Jungle plants looked ready to overtake the road at any moment. At one point in the drive, it started pouring rain. The leaves and branches bounced with the drops, dancing to the rhythm of the rainforest.

At the tail-end of the trip, the sun began its descent. Leaving the resort to shine like a beacon in the night. The property looked massive from what I could make out in the dim light. I counted five stories for the building in the forefront, and it sprawled out in either direction until it seemed to disappear into the jungle.

Attendants opened our doors, politely asking for the name on our reservation. Beck dropped his last name, and they snapped even further to attention, quickly guiding us toward our room and taking our bags.

Beck seemed uncomfortable with the five-star service, and I wondered if that was why he didn't use his last name in his email address. What must it be like living in the shadow of someone so successful, tethered by a name? I'm sure it had its perks, but it also had to be suffocating.

However, as we crossed the lobby into the lounge area of the resort, the tightness in Beck's shoulders seemed to loosen. And I felt it too. My anxiety about the trip melted away with each step. Tiki lights lit the path beside manmade waterfalls cascading into a crystal swimming pool. Palm trees towered above, and hibiscus bushes boasted pink, coral, and sunshine yellow flowers. Night sounds of the jungle gave the space a perfect white-noise effect.

If this was just the view to get to the suite, I couldn't wait to see where we'd be staying for the trip—though I had no intention of spending much time there, not when the beaches and wild jungles waited.

Victoria and her sprawling bridal party intercepted us. They toweled off and finished the last dregs of cocktails as they clambered down the walkway. Beck had informed me the rest of the group planned on coming the day before us. So, it didn't surprise me to see the group already assembled and a little toasted.

"Hey! You guys made it!" Doug called.

A guy with olive skin and dark hair stepped forward, giving Beck one of those dude handshakes that turned into a half-hug. As they did, the top of Beck's head only came to the height of this guy's jaw. I thought Beck was tall. It was a missed opportunity if Beck's friend didn't play basketball.

When Beck came back to my side, we fumbled for each other's hands until we found a comfortable arrangement. It didn't take long.

"It's Beck!"

A platinum blonde slurred before missing a step. She would have fallen if Sebastian—the shoe store owner I'd met at Victoria's shower—hadn't caught her. I almost hadn't recognized him in his banana print board shorts.

I noticed Reagan at Victoria's side right away. If she glowed at the shower, she radiated here. Her bronze skin contrasted dramatically with her white bikini—a simple design. Because, really, she didn't need anything drastic to show off the slopes of her hips, nor her perfect perky breasts. Her skin had an oily—I've been suntanning all day—kind of sheen. I suspected this was what it looked like to have all your chakras aligned.

Though I'd dressed for comfort in my stretchy shorts and a frumpy Buc-ee's shirt, she still could have drilled holes the way she stared at my hand, enveloped in Beck's.

Victoria smiled at the attendant who'd been guiding us, sending him away with a few twenties before turning back to us. "We are going in for the night. Need to be up early for our first beach day."

We stepped into line with the group. Our party of ten separated into three rows, each taking up the entire sidewalk. At the front of the pack, with Victoria, I already felt as though my every move was under a microscope.

One slip and I'd ruin Beck's illusion of being happy without Reagan, or I could expose myself as the imposter I was. Then this would all be over: Hailey's business and my chance at continuing professional calligraphy—something that had given me a new purpose, a reason to be excited.

I'd have to tread carefully.

The guy who'd dude-hugged Beck slipped between Victoria and me. "I don't think we've officially met." He stuck out a hand. "I'm Gabe, Beck's bestie."

I giggled at thinking of Beck as someone's *bestie*. "Hi, Gabe." I shook his outstretched hand. "I'm Hailey."

The use of Hailey's name as my own still felt odd on my tongue, like I had hair in my mouth, but this was the plan.

"I kept waiting for Beck to introduce us at the shower, but for a rich brat, he doesn't always have the best manners."

"My apologies. Gabe, this is my girlfriend, Hailey." Something in my stomach fizzed at Beck referring to me as his girlfriend. Even though I knew it was fake. "Hailey, this is Gabe. A pain in the ass."

I smiled. "Sounds like we'll get along great. Being a pain in Beck's ass is my favorite hobby."

Gabe's eyebrows shot up in delighted surprise. One of them had a scar running through it, which might have given him an intimidating look if not for the bright eyes and dimples. "I like her."

Beck gave me a sidelong glance, his mouth quirking into a smile. "She's pretty likable."

I blushed stupidly. *He is acting, Emily.* "How do you two know each other?" I asked, ready to get the subject off me.

"We met in high school," Beck said.

Gabe nodded. "I swept the floor with him at a swim meet, and he begged me for pointers after."

The idea of Beck being outmatched at swimming pleased me to no end.

"I don't know about *begged,*" Beck said. "I *asked* you to show me a thing or two."

"And I did. In return, he bought me a double meat at Whataburger."

"And he's been bothering me ever since," Beck said with a warm smile that completely contradicted his sentence.

In a more secluded area of the resort, a hot tub gurgled. Amongst the bubbles, a woman in a pixie cut traced the lines of her lover's goatee before leaning in for a kiss.

"Oh God," Sebastian groaned. "Are Kat and Jake still making out?"

"Hey!" another guy in the group called. "You do have a room, you know?"

The man with the goatee—Jake, I presumed—didn't stop kissing Kat to lift a middle finger. Then he pulled a giggling Kat into his lap, nipping at her lip.

My mouth went dry at the prospect of playing girlfriend with Beck here. A vision of him pulling me into his lap invaded my thoughts. I pictured my thighs wrapping around his warm torso, my stomach flush with his, and my fingers digging into his back muscles.

But Beck yanked me out of the fantasy with an alarmed, "Emily, watch out!"

Someone screamed, but before I could even get a chance to try and figure out what to watch for, Beck pulled me to his chest. Then I saw it, the slip of a snake's tail sliding into the grass.

Threat over, I turned my attention to Beck, who still held me fast. I stayed there, dazed by his sudden closeness. His breath hit my cheek, quick from the heightened adrenaline, and his heart hammered against my palm.

He'd literally swung me out of harm's way like a damn knight. Any decent human probably would have done what he did, but the damsel in distress part of my brain had all the heart eyes. I couldn't help but feel the warmth of being protected and cared for.

"Are you okay?" Victoria asked.

"I'm fine," I said.

Then, Beck seemed to remember his hands and how they still gripped my arms. He released me with a little mumble of an apology.

The platinum blonde laughed a little, turning to Reagan. "I thought you said her name is Hailey?" she said in a conspiratorial whisper.

I looked at Beck. Judging by his widened eyes, he realized it right as I did. In the heat of the moment, he'd called me Emily. The iceberg had been spotted. The Titanic was going down on her maiden voyage.

"I *am* Hailey," I said way too quickly.

I tried to laugh, but it came out forced. I reeled, grasping for an explanation, but nothing surfaced. I looked to Beck for help, but I could all but see his cogs still whirling, trying to come up with a credible excuse.

I had to say something. All eyes of the group settled on us. "Emily is my middle name. So, he calls me that sometimes."

I patted his chest like, *what a cute rascal I have on my hands.* But with the five hard pats, I hoped he received my made-up morse code. *Way. To. Go. Dumb. Ass.*

"Oh, cute," someone said.

"Hailey . . . Emily?" The platinum blonde scrunched her nose as she tested the names together.

Shit. They clashed. I immediately thought of the phrase I'd used as fashion advice in high school: black and brown makes a frown. It sounded like a name combination an eight-year-old would string together, or one parent wanted Emily and the other wanted Hailey, so to compromise, they'd picked both. In other words, it sounded like two fucking first names put together because that's what they fucking were.

"Yeah." I forced another laugh. "My parents smoked a lot of weed in the nineties."

Beck's head snapped my way. I was too chicken to look at the expression. I think I could telepathically hear him saying, *God, Lane, shut the fuck up.*

One of the guys gave a slow bro nod. "Dope."

Beck straightened, and I could see his face smooth into his normal calm, collected features.

Here came damage control. "Jesus, Vic. You may want to look into better pest control for the grounds."

Victoria rolled her eyes. "I don't know if you noticed, but the resort is backed up to a literal rainforest. There's going to be wildlife." She gestured to our surroundings. "Don't you want the full experience?"

"Does the full experience include an anaconda in my bathroom? Because, if so, I'll pass."

"If you weren't splitting a room with Hailey, I'd have that arranged." She flashed a dangerous smile that reminded me of her brother.

As the door to our suite clicked closed behind us, I gawked at our living area for the next week. Lanterns with soft lighting hung from a ceiling with exposed beams of rough wood. Sandwiched between two palm plants, a crimson loveseat beckoned. *There's room for two,* it seemed to say. The entire space looked like the wilds of the jungle had been tamed only enough for the sake of luxury and romance.

And we hadn't even seen the bedroom.

I started flipping switches on a nearby wall, hunting for brighter, we're-just-friends-lighting. Before I could fret too much about spending the evening hours of this trip alone with Beck in a space created exclusively for honeymooners, he popped the romantic vibe with, "Real smooth, Hailey Emily."

And there he was. The senior level-asshole I knew so well.

"Oh, so it's *my* fault *you* called me the wrong name?"

"I was going to fix my mistake before you went full-on kamikaze." Beck strode to a coffee table, where the attendants had dropped off our bags. "All I had to say was. 'Oops. My mistake. I meant to say Hailey.'"

I knew he was right. Knew in my bones the fix could have been so simple, but I wouldn't give him the satisfaction. "Yeah, and I'm sure your sister would think so highly of you, forgetting your date's name."

He laughed, digging in his duffle. "Who cares? Anything would have been better than you declaring your name is Hailey Emily. It sounds made up."

"Because it is!" I said, exasperated. "And was it my finest moment? No. But if they remember anything from tonight, it will be that you saved me from a snake." I strode to my suitcase so I could do something with my hands instead of using them to throttle him. "Besides, while you calculated a response to fix the error, I could almost see a loading bar behind your eyes. Just a tad suspicious, Beckett."

"Oh, great. We're back to *Beckett*," he said flatly.

"Yes, we need things to reset, treat each other like we normally would. Keep things uncomplicated."

"That's what you want? To go back to competitive coworkers?"

"Yes, because you almost never call me Emily." And because sweet, laid-back Beck muddled my brain and lowered my guard. "At work, it's Lane this and Lane that. But today, when Lane would have been an appropriate response, you decided to call me Emily."

"I'm sorry. I was a little distracted, trying to keep a jungle snake from biting your ankle."

I swallowed a lump of pride because, as infuriating as Beck was, I had to say it, "Thank you, by the way."

Beck headed toward the bathroom, an armful of clothes and toiletries. "I did the world a favor. We can't have Hailey Emily on a headstone, can we?"

The lock of the bathroom snicked shut, and I let out a growly, "Asshole!"

I rolled my suitcase into the bedroom and nearly tripped over my feet. Rose petals littered the bed, and a bucket of champagne waited on the nightstand. Forget this space being for honeymooners. The suite was an artfully crafted love shack.

"Jesus!" I plucked the petals off the bed at a feverish pace, tossing them in the trash before moving the champagne to the kitchenette.

At least Beck had been right about there being a couch. It sat on the opposite wall from the bed, right before the glass doors to the balcony.

I went outside to check out the view. My flip-flops carried me across a wood-planked deck. I wrapped my fingers around the rope of a hammock as I gazed at the rainforest beyond. I could hear it more than see it. For a minute, I closed my eyes and just listened. Crickets, cicadas, and tree frogs were plentiful in Texas, but the sounds seemed amplified here. And Houston certainly didn't have the howling noises—different from a coyote's call. I remembered an article about monkeys in Costa Rica.

I smiled. Beck could be an ass all he wanted, but I was finally doing it—enjoying a vacation.

Chapter 15

The next morning, my alarm went off, and it took me several moments to blink away the dream that immersed me before I remembered, yes, I was in Costa Rica, sharing a room with Beck. I sat up, ramrod straight, only to find the couch empty.

Last night, I'd unpacked my belongings and sorted them in the dresser drawers. I padded over there now, then pulled out my swimsuit, some khaki shorts, and something Hailey had given me to match her for our trip in Florida: A pink shirt with the words **VACAY** scrawled beside a hibiscus flower.

Getting dressed, my blood seemed to buzz through my veins with nervous, excited energy. Today would be spent under the sun without a single spreadsheet, IT ticket, or meeting that should have been an email. At the same time, I'd have to be vigilant and remember I was supposed to be Hailey while also attempting to connect with people from a wholly different social class than my own.

Topping off my outfit with a floppy sun hat, I circled the suite, wondering where Beck was. Maybe he'd gone to get breakfast. Or, more likely, he'd found the resort's gym. I rolled my eyes. I knew he dedicated himself to the lanes, but I didn't think he'd been one of those psychos who kept up their fitness regimen on vacation.

As I was about to give up and head to the lobby, I noticed the hammock's sway outside and realized someone occupied it. A tuft of curls spilled over the edge on one end. On the other, a bare leg hung out.

On the way to the balcony door, I tripped over Beck's duffle and barely caught myself. After regaining my balance, I slid the bag over with my foot.

"You really shouldn't leave your stuff on the floor," I said to Beck as I joined him on the balcony.

The jungle greeted me as loudly as it had the night before with calls of all sorts, reminding me how wild this place was. A breeze moved through the trees, sending a ripple through the emerald expanse.

"Good morning to you too, Lane," Beck said in a voice still gravelly from sleep. He turned a page in the book on his chest. "Didn't realize you were such a neat freak, but I should have guessed."

"I am not a neat freak," I huffed. "I read an article about tourists leaving their bags on the floor only to find lizards or cockroaches in the cozy compartments of their suitcases."

"We're in a luxury resort." He turned his book over, using his leg as a bookmark. "I don't think we have to worry about pests in the suite."

I leveled him a look. "Did you already forget about the snake?"

He smiled wickedly. "How could I possibly forget, Hailey Emily?"

I chose to ignore the jab. "You should probably start getting ready if we want time to eat breakfast before sailing."

Beck picked his book back up. "I'm pretty tired from traveling yesterday. I'm going to hang back and take it easy."

I snorted. "Too tired to relax on a beach?"

"I want to have enough energy for the rainforest hike tomorrow."

"You act like we are going to be rowing to the beach."

"I'm just tired, Lane." He shrugged, turning a page. "I'll meet you guys in town for dinner."

I opened my mouth to plead with him. Being alone with Victoria, his friends, and his ex without a buffer . . . In a tank of sharks, he was supposed to be the cage between them and me. The idea left me feeling vulnerable and shy.

My mouth clamped shut before I could start begging. Maybe time away from each other was a good idea. We could use some space if we hoped to maintain any sense of normalcy between us. Even if the idea of spending the day with him had excited me. Maybe, especially because it had.

"Well," I said, "enjoy your book."

He smiled. "And you enjoy your vacation. You deserve it."

Somehow, those two sentences, so simple yet earnest, made me want to ask him if he minded if I stayed on the balcony with him.

But I knew better. On this trip, too much alone time with Beck was a recipe for disaster. Clear boundaries and distance would keep me levelheaded and guarded. So, with a heavy feeling in my stomach, I headed down for breakfast and prepared for my plunge alone with the sharks.

I met the others in a van waiting outside the hotel. They greeted me with bubbly good mornings and hellos, and I realized I'd been a little dramatic, picturing the group as bloodthirsty millionaires who spent their free time diving into a pool of diamonds Scrouge McDuck style.

"Beck staying back?" Victoria asked, not seeming surprised to find I'd come alone.

"He says he's tired from traveling," I explained, buckling up beside a man with sandy blond hair and a gym shark body.

"What a killjoy," my seat partner said, outstretching his hand for a shake. "I'm Dustin Koontz. But everyone calls me—"

"*Koooontz*," a chorus of guys called throughout the van.

He shrugged, and I laughed. "Nice to meet you, Koontz, I'm Hailey." I had to work to keep the wince off my face, lying to yet another person.

Reagan and the platinum blonde ducked into the van last. The group greeted them with the same enthusiasm they'd shown me. But the blonde flashed her palm, looking a little nauseous.

"Don't," she bit out.

"Aww, is Madison hung over?" Koontz asked.

The blonde, Madison, stuck her tongue out at him, and I had to suppress a smile. This group of friends had a rich history, and even though that made me feel like an intruder, it was also kind of fun to be an outsider, figuring out the dynamic.

We boarded a boat that looked luxurious enough to be in a Dolce & Gabbana commercial. Victoria stepped up first. She looked like she belonged in that advertisement with her white button-down and navy shorts. Though secured in a ponytail, her curls whipped wildly in the sea breeze.

The captain—a squat man with a cigarette hanging out of his mouth— introduced himself as Jerry. Jerry looked as though he'd come here on a retirement trip and decided to never look back.

I found a spot near Kat, the woman who'd been making out like a teenager last night in the hot tub. Even waiting for Jerry to get everything set up relaxed me—the rock of the boat, the sunshine on my legs, the water—so blue it didn't look real.

Once Jerry got the boat into open water, Sebastian turned to the man on his left. "Babe, this is the calligrapher I hired to do luxury lettering at the store."

"Pleased to meet you, sweetheart. I'm Nick, the groom's brother. And this guy's better half," he said, bumping Sebastian's hip playfully. Nick had perfect white teeth and flawless skin. He leaned over to kiss my hand. "He's so excited to have you at his sales event."

"Wait! That's right!" Kat put a hand on my shoulder, stealing my attention. "You were the one signing shells at Victoria's shower." She tugged on Jake's shirt. "Honey, do you remember the calligrapher?" Jake nodded at Kat's words but returned to his conversation with the guy across from him.

Kat huffed at his lack of attention. "Anyway, we are getting married next spring." She waggled a ring-clad hand at me. "Just engaged!"

"Oh! Congratulations," I said, trying to calculate how many months' rent that rock on her finger would cover.

"Do you think you have availability for addressing and some signage?"

My heart caught in my throat. It was another job. Just like that. And one I'd earned in my own right. "Absolutely!" I needed to tone down the excitement. This was supposed to be something I did all the time. I cleared my throat. "Yes, of course."

Kat gave me her email, and I promised to send her some quotes when I got back home.

As the boat glided over the glittering water, I couldn't keep the smile off my face. This vacation, these opportunities—trying on Hailey's life had breathed so much life into my own. I wondered how I would bear returning to plain Emily but shoved those thoughts way down, not letting any negativity cloud this incredible day of sunshine.

Jerry dropped anchor in the middle of the bay, explaining that we'd spend an hour here before sailing to the private beach. He let us know we were free to roam the boat or take a dip in the ocean.

Soon, Doug and Koontz started doing cannonballs and backflips into the water. Gabe poised himself at the edge of the boat, and I recognized the red tattoo on his right calf as the Ironman Race symbol. I'd had a professor in college who did those races all the time. One hundred forty-something miles of swimming, biking, and running. Of course, Beck's friend would be into that.

The girls took a more docile route. Reagan, Madison, and Kat stripped down to their swimsuits and found a place on the deck to sunbathe. Knowing I'd burn to a crisp if I wasn't careful, I rubbed on another coat of sun lotion before picking my spot to lay out like a cat.

God, I had forgotten what it was like to purely exist, to soak up the sunshine and breathe ocean air. I must have fallen asleep because I jolted awake as Jerry yelled, "We are setting sail in five minutes!"

My elbow knocked my bottle of sun lotion onto the deck, and it rolled to where Victoria sat.

I got up to fetch it, but my flip-flop snagged on a board. A quick inspection told me the middle piece had slipped from the bottom.

"Damn it," I mumbled.

Acting fast, I pulled my ponytail loose and grabbed another hair tie from my wrist. I looped one of the hair ties around the straps and pulled it through the bottom where I knotted the other one, securing the strap in place—a trick my mom had taught me when we didn't have enough money to spring for new sandals. Not the prettiest fix, but one that would probably last me for the trip, at least for the lazy beach days.

Slipping my flip-flop back on, I hoped no one had noticed my Old Navy dollar flip-flop malfunction. Especially when everyone else sported

Sax Fifth Avenue or Nordstrom Rack designer sandals. But, of course, Victoria came over, my sun lotion bottle in hand. She handed it over, wordlessly.

"Thanks."

"Did you . . . MacGyver your flip-flop?" she asked, arms crossing over each other.

"I, uh, yes."

"Remind me to keep you around," she said, a smile crinkling the corners of her eyes in a way that reminded me of Beck. "I might need a life hack or two for my wedding day."

Victoria's approval radiated inside me. "I'll be there."

With that, I felt a little less like an intruder. On the beach, we enjoyed the sand between our toes and the cool lap of water around our thighs. I listened to members of the group swapping stories about work and family. To my absolute surprise, I liked these people. I wasn't sure about Madison and Reagan because they seemed to be enjoying their little bubble of two, but being with everyone else felt easy. Maybe it was the beach breeze, the rustling of palm leaves, or the crystal waves, but the air in the gathering felt sweet and light-hearted.

Even still, I kept having this feeling like I'd forgotten something important back at the resort. It kept nagging, tamping my enjoyment. With some annoyance, I realized that the missing something was Beck. I could try to ignore it all I wanted, but only he could have made the day better. Remembering Beck would meet us in town for dinner had me grinning stupidly.

Chapter 16

Beck waited for our group at a long table. He smiled as we entered the restaurant, but his jaw slackened as his eyes dipped to the slice of skin beneath my shirt. He hadn't been at the resort when we'd returned to freshen up before dinner.

I'd chosen a high-low maxi skirt and a crop top. After being in a bikini all day, showing that sliver of skin on my stomach shouldn't have been a big deal, but as I'd put on my earrings, my shirt lifted a little higher. The idea of Beck seeing that stretch of skin had made my chest flush.

I thought maybe his eyes would linger, but I hadn't anticipated capturing his attention so fully, nor the hunger in his dilating pupils.

My body had its own physical reactions, starting with the warmth pooling under my navel.

"Beck!" Koontz yelled, slapping his hands onto Beck's shoulders, knocking both of us from the trance. "You missed out on all the fun."

Beck gave a little lopsided smile. "And it looks like you missed out on all the sun lotion." He leaned over to look at Nick. "You're a dermatologist. You let this happen?"

Nick didn't look up from the menu. "This doctor is off duty."

"He did try," Sebastian said, wincing as he eyed a painfully red Koontz. "Someone didn't listen."

Victoria interrupted the group, demanding a picture. She waved at a server, but I stood up, offering before he could set his tray down. "I'll do it!"

"You will not," Victoria said. "You haven't been in a single picture all day."

She was right. I'd been offering to take the pictures because A) I was still an outsider and, more importantly, B) I could not have pictures of me on this trip with Beck. We would never hear the end of it from HR.

"I can't be in the pictures anyway," I said, hand outstretched for her phone. "My brother thinks I'm sick. I'm missing his daughter's piano recital for this trip," the lie rolled off my tongue. I hated that I was getting better at being dishonest.

Koontz banged on the table, delighted. "Damn, Hailey! Way to take one for the trip."

"Okay, you heard her," Doug called. "No picture evidence of Hailey."

Sebastian lifted his water glass in a mock toast. "What happens in Costa stays in Costa, baby!" This earned laughter and whooping from the group.

After getting dozens of shots from dozens of viewpoints of the group, I reclaimed my place next to Beck. Weirdly enough, as the volume at the table rose, it felt as though Beck and I could have a private conversation. The deafening chatter at the table acted like walls.

Which is why what Beck said next felt especially intimate. "You look beautiful tonight."

Hearing a compliment like that from someone as gorgeous as Beck made my tongue feel swollen and clumsy in my mouth. I tried to thank him, but the server came by to take our order.

"That is a sweet arm sleeve you have, brother," Koontz said to the server.

He'd been writing furiously on his notepad but stopped to roll his arm so we could get a better look. Twin snakes wrapped upward, the ink making precise scales along the way.

"Thanks. My cousin does them at his shop down the street."

"No shit?" Koontz slapped Doug's chest. "We could get those geometric wolves we've been wanting." He looked back at the server. "What's the place called?"

The server gave him the name and location, then went back to taking our orders.

When he was gone, Victoria leaned in and said loudly, "You guys have fun. Hopefully, you don't get an infection."

"Because we are in a different country, they can't have sanitary tattoo shops?" Beck mused. "Come on, Vic. You're a little too educated for that mindset."

She shot him the middle finger. "Okay, well, remember, if you get a tattoo now," she continued, looking at Doug, "you can forget about swimming, laying out in the sun, and hot tubs."

This earned a groan from Koontz and Doug. Then the table fell into voting on whether or not the wolves would look douchey on them anyway, and I took the opportunity to have another private chat with my fake boyfriend.

"So, you ever going to add to the collection?" I asked, nodding towards the ink on Beck's arm.

"Only adding something to the negative space," he said, indicating the naked band under the flower stems. "Can't give you more of a reason to call me a tattoo guy, now can I?"

"Well, give it time. They say tattoos are like chips. You can't have only one."

The server came back in record time with the table's drink orders, setting a beer down in front of Beck and a sunset-colored cocktail in front of me.

"What did you order again?" Beck asked, smiling at my ridiculous drink.

"The Pura Vida." I'd heard the term, pure life, in the full day I'd been here. Trying the cocktail seemed part of the Costa Rican experience. "The menu described it as basically a rum punch."

One sip of the fruity, refreshing drink told me to take it slow, I could barely taste the alcohol.

I nodded toward Beck's arm, steering our conversation back to his tattoo. "It still looks fresh. You haven't had it for long, have you?"

"I got it a couple of days before I started at The Arlow Group."

Right before I met him. Wow, that seemed like a lifetime ago, him pulling me out of the water. How he'd looked so disgusted at where I'd gotten his sleeve wet . . .

My eyes snapped back to his arm, his tattoo, the same spot I'd clung to that day. "Oh my God! When you pulled me out of the water, the tattoo was still healing, wasn't it?"

He took a lazy sip of his beer and leaned back in his seat. "I told you it wasn't about the shirt."

"Why did you hold out that arm for me to grab?" I asked, appalled that I could have messed up something so permanent.

"I was too worried about you drowning to think about my tattoo. At that point, I didn't know about your aggressive floating skills."

"Did I hurt you?" I asked, ignoring his attempt at humor.

"Not badly. It kind of felt like you'd grabbed onto a sunburn. But you have to understand, my tattoo artist made me swear to keep out of the pool for three weeks. I thought my arm was going to fall off after getting Woodlands swamp water on it. At the very least, I expected my tattoo to be an inky mess."

"So that's why you were a dick," my voice matched that of someone having an epiphany because that's what this moment freaking was.

"It's no excuse," Beck said, eyes serious. "I'm sorry I was rude to you."

My mouth fell ajar. I was working to conjure a response when I felt eyes on me. Across the table, Reagan focused on us. She couldn't hear our conversation, not with the roar of the table. But she was watching.

How cruel to keep her gaze fixed on Beck. What, he'd moved on after she cheated, and she couldn't let him go? Let him be happy? I might not have been in love with Chad, the one who cheated on me, but that betrayal still cut deep. He'd found someone prettier, more lovable, better. And Reagan had done the same to Beck.

Time for her to get a taste of karma.

I leaned closer to Beck and, ever so lightly, pressed the nail of my fingertip to one of the bands on Beck's arm. From there, I followed a stem all the way to a brilliant red flower. "How long did it take to get it done?" Beck froze as I traced a petal. I could relate. Just running a finger across his skin sent a hum of electricity down my spine. "Follow my lead," I purred. "Reagan is watching."

For a long moment, I didn't think Beck had heard anything I said. Goosebumps rose on his arm as I stroked the flowers with the slightest whisper of a touch. But then he swallowed and found his voice.

"Uh, six—" he cleared his throat. "—six hours or so." I didn't know what I enjoyed more, touching him or my touch's impact on him.

I gave a sympathetic wince. "That's a long time. Did it hurt?"

"I've had worse," he rasped.

"And," I said, smiling now that I had him in a trance, sure I could get more information out of him. "What does it mean, again?"

His pupils narrowed into focus. "Nice try." He grabbed my hand to stop the movement but didn't let go. My hand felt radioactive, encased in his.

"Come on," I said, "just tell me."

"I will. After you beat me at swimming."

I snatched my hand away with an eye-roll. "We both know that's never going to happen."

"Kind of the point," he said.

"Alright. Fine. But you've left me no choice but to assume I was right all along about your flower obsession—that you grow carnations in your backyard as a hobby."

Beck's mouth quirked. "And what would be wrong with that?"

"Nothing." I sniffed. "Keeping it a secret is the weird part. You get a tattoo on a part of your body that's generally on display, then refuse to share the meaning. Why not put it someplace less . . . obvious . . . if you don't want people to know what it means?"

"Maybe I like to keep you guessing," Beck mused.

I started to retort, but our server and a team of helpers set down mouthwatering dishes before us.

Thrumming music sparked the group's curiosity as soon as we stepped into the humid night air. We followed the sound to an outside bar under colorful banners and stringed lights. The DJ had the crowd mesmerized, including our group.

Beck and I shared a worried look. We were supposed to be a couple. It would be weird if we didn't dance. And this kind of music didn't call for sweet movements—hands at the shoulders and lower back. This was ass-to-pelvis bumping and grinding.

Beck leaned close to whisper, "We can come up with an excuse to go back to the resort. I don't want to make you uncomfortable."

Right away, Reagan found a stranger in the crowd to dance with. The guy looked at her like he'd won the jackpot. And I didn't blame him. Her perky breasts peeked out of her dress just enough to still be tasteful. Not to mention the way the fabric at her backside stretched to reveal a tight ass she clearly worked hard to maintain.

It didn't bother me that she'd picked a stranger to dance with. We were in Costa Rica to have fun. It was the way she'd looked right at Beck when her dance partner ran his hand across her thigh that ignited my anger.

I took Beck's hand, leading him to the dance floor. "Nope. Not uncomfortable at all," I said, partly because that Pura Vida had been strong, partly because I wanted to make Reagan turn a shade of green, but—if I was honest with myself—mostly because I *wanted* to dance with Beck.

The first song, as it turned out, was uncomfortable.

We tried to find our rhythm and placement of hands that showed we were definitely a couple who did things like this all the time while still maintaining a respectable workplace distance.

It didn't work.

"This isn't working," I voiced.

We looked like we were eighth graders at our first dance.

Beck dipped his head so we could talk without yelling. "You said cotillion hand positions when we set ground rules. I don't want to make you uncomfortable."

"Okay, but I think that's part of the problem. No one else here is worried about their date being uncomfortable. All they are thinking about is having a good time and how to keep having a good time tonight."

"What do you want me to do?" Beck moved backward, only an inch, so he could look into my eyes. I saw the conflicted line between his brows before I even made my proposal.

"I want you to forget I'm your coworker." I licked my lips, and his eyes dipped to the movement. "And dance with me like having a good time is your only concern."

"Are you sure?" he rasped.

We were intentionally edging toward breaking a rule. This was dangerous territory.

"Yes," I breathed.

Beck spun me, pulling me in until my ass was flush against him. I gasped, lightheaded at the sudden shift. Then his hot palms met my stomach, fingers exploring that stretch of bare skin. A heaviness grew between my thighs. So much for being able to look Beck in the eye after this trip. As I ground against him to the beat of the music, I tried to find it in myself to care, to want to hold onto a scrap of dignity. But pressed against Beck, both of us sweating under low lights, dancing to Costa Rican music, my mind and my judgment were clouded by need.

It didn't even take an entire song for Reagan to notice the position change. She looked over the shoulder of her date, eyes zeroing in on Beck's fingers and where they splayed at my navel, slipping just under my shirt.

"I think our mission is complete," I said, reaching up to run my fingers through his hair and tugging lightly on his curls.

"Which one?"

By this point, his length was pressing into my ass cheek. Rock hard. The idea of him wanting me made my breath ragged.

He's been drinking. He's not thinking straight. I reminded myself. *He's not into you.*

I swallowed. "The one to make Reagan jealous. She's staring daggers at me."

"I hadn't noticed," he said before dragging his hands oh-so-slowly down my stomach to my hips.

I swallowed. "I told you. I'm detail-oriented." His laugh rumbled against my back. "I think you should owe me one," I said, trying not to get too lost in his touch. "For doing an extra good job convincing her of our infatuation."

His lips were at the shell of my ear when he asked, "What did you have in mind?" His deep voice made my stomach swirly.

"I'll think of something," I said, sounding more confident than I felt.

"How about if we ever come across your ex, I'll do the grinding?"

I laughed, a breathless thing. "Tempting." I shoved my hips back, rocking my ass against him. The move elicited a groan, and he spun me to face him. "But I was thinking you should do the process documentation for the next project." That kind of documentation called for anywhere from eighty to one hundred twenty pages of walking through each and every business process. It was an absolute nightmare. "And maybe some light groveling."

"Process documentation I can do. Groveling, on the other hand . . ."

Beck's gaze dipped to my mouth for a second time that night. I leaned closer, dizzy with want. Every cell in my body hummed with anticipation. He tilted his head, his lips a breath from mine. My eyes fluttered shut right before someone roughly bumped into us. Beck had to catch me to keep us from banging mouths.

I turned to see the culprit. "Sorry!" Madison called over her shoulder, snatching Reagan from her date before heading for the bathroom.

I took a step back, and Beck slowly released his grip on my shoulders. We'd almost broken another rule. I couldn't kiss him—the man I shared a sleeping space with tonight and an office with next week.

With a mumble, I excused myself to the restroom, following the girls' lead. I needed time to think. To cool off.

I'd barely closed the door when I heard Reagan and Madison in the stalls next to mine. "Can you believe the way she was grinding on him?" Madison asked. "I thought they would start fucking right on the dance floor."

The tips of my ears heated. I'd never been slut shamed before. And even though I hadn't done anything different from anyone else out there, I suddenly felt dirty.

"I don't want to talk about Beckett and his date," Reagan growled.

"Why?" Madison asked.

Toilets flushed, and faucets turned on.

"Because I miss him. Because he's over me. Because it hurts."

"Then get him back, Reagan. Honestly, I can't believe you haven't tried already. Look at you and look at her. Where did he even find this girl? Wandering the sales rack at Target?"

I frowned. So much for fitting in.

"You and Beck should have never broken up," Madison continued. "You two were made for each other. You were in love. Everyone could see it."

"I . . . messed up, Madison."

"Haven't we all? But I'm telling you, he'll drop his date like that—" She snapped her fingers. "—If you tell him how you feel."

"You really think so?"

Madison smacked her lips. "I'd bet my trust fund on it."

Embarrassed and oddly hurt at the idea of Beck dumping me—even though I wasn't his real girlfriend—I waited in the stall until the girls left. Then I hightailed it out of there and nearly ran into Beck near the bathroom entrance.

"Hey!" He caught my gaze, then frowned. "What's wrong?"

I opened my mouth to tell him about Reagan. He deserved to know she wanted him back. But my mouth—still tingly with the prospect of his lips on mine—said, "Nothing. I just—I'm tired. I think I'm going to head back to the resort."

"I'll come with you."

"You don't have to do that," I said. "You should be with your friends, having fun."

"I want to make sure you get there safely."

Such a basic sentiment, yet it fizzled and popped in my belly, making me feel light, bubbly. "Okay, thank you."

On the way to the resort, we got distracted by colorful souvenir shops. We ducked into one that boasted a variety of kitsch items. An entire aisle was dedicated to Pura Vida shirts.

"I think that's going to be my new catchphrase," I teased.

"Pure life?" Beck seemed to mull it over. "I'll buy you a shirt if you promise to wear it to the office."

"I'll wear the shirt to work if you get Pura Vida tattooed between the bands."

Beck rubbed the skin void of ink. "I would, but I'm saving the space for something else."

I started to ask him what he planned to put there, but he picked up an oversized shirt that looked like a cartoon print of George of the Jungle's chest and leopard undies. At the top it read, *I survived the jungle.*

"This," he said, smiling wildly. "This is the one."

I couldn't help it. I threw my head back and cackled, making the shop owner's head pop up from his doze. I offered an apologetic wave.

Beck was still looking at the damn shirt. "Can't wait for the hike tomorrow so I can come back and buy this treasure."

"Oh!" He hadn't been with us at the beach when we'd changed plans. "About that. The group had so much fun with Jerry that they paid for him to take us to a different alcove tomorrow."

Beck's eyebrows scrunched. "Who the hell is Jerry?"

"He's the captain of the boat we rode on today. He's a little bristly, but that's part of his charm."

"Oh." Beck's head dipped as he put the shirt back on the shelf. "And everyone wants to go?"

"I thought you would be happy. You were too tired for the beach today. Now you get another chance tomorrow."

Beck scratched the back of his head as he headed down an aisle of shot glasses. "I'm just not really a beach kind of guy."

"But . . . you love to swim."

"Not in the ocean."

"Are you afraid of sharks?"

"No—"

"Because you are more likely to die from a vending machine falling on top of you than you are to get killed by a shark."

"It's not a fear thing, Lane."

I waited for him to go on, but he didn't, and the silence wore heavy. I could see him mentally building a wall. And I didn't want that. So even though I was, in fact, a beach girl, I found the following words tumbling out of my mouth, "Then we let them go to the alcove. You and I can go to the jungle."

"No, Emily. It's okay. I know you had fun today."

"I did. And now I'm looking forward to doing something different tomorrow. We have beaches back home. Let's go on that hike."

Beck let the shot glass he'd been examining clink onto the counter so he could read me for what felt like the millionth time tonight. "Are you sure?"

I saw the two paths the next day as a fork in the road. I could join my new friends at the alcove. Hell, I could even tell Beck what Reagan had said, and *she* could spend the day with Beck. Leaving me a guilt-free day in the sun. However, I realized I didn't want Reagan to be alone with Beck in the jungle because *I* wanted to be alone with Beck in the jungle. I only had six more days, less than a week, of freedom, and I wanted to spend each of those days with Beck. The realization was startling.

I nodded. "I really, *really* want to see a sloth." It wasn't a lie.

Beck's eyes crinkled at the corner, matching the wide smile unfurling. "Okay, Lane. Tomorrow, we'll find you that sloth."

Chapter 17

Beck and I entered under the canopy of Manuel Antonio National Park, and—amongst the trees—I didn't feel like an observer of nature but a part of it. The jungle teemed with wildlife: unabashed bird calls followed by flashes of bright feathers, rustling bushes, monkey tails, and proud, lazy iguanas. The color of the lush green forest would have been enough. It screamed life. *Pura Vida*. I got it now. In my mind, the phrase took a turn from hokey to sacred.

Animals and insects collaborated to create a symphony. I closed my eyes for a moment and took in the music of the jungle. I had to soak in what I could because this trip was going too fast. Only six days, and I'd be back in the office. I didn't know how I was going to return to my old life after *this*.

It's fine, I tried to tell myself. I'd still have calligraphy—Sebastian's live lettering event, Kat and Jake's wedding, but the comfort didn't stick. I'd gotten lucky with those two jobs. The opportunities wouldn't arise again without proper marketing, and I couldn't swing that and keep up with work.

If anything, I didn't even know if I had it in me to do those two jobs while working at The Arlow Group. I'd barely made it out alive with Victoria's wedding. I could make it work if I had a job that didn't require me to work so late and on weekends. But I didn't.

And then there was Beck. I'd had a great time with him the night before. I hardly slept, knowing he lay in the dark only steps away. The dance—his body on mine—had awoken something in me, something that ached for him. I'd considered flinging the comforter off, crossing the room, and pulling him to bed with me. I fantasized about his chest pressed against mine, being caged by his arms.

But I didn't act on it, of course. Because I knew none of the things that had been lighting up my life as of late could last for long. Not this vacation. Not my calligraphy side hustle. Not my time with Beck. It all had an expiration date. *If anything, Beck and Reagan will probably reconcile by the end of the six days*, I thought sourly.

Neither Beck nor I did much talking during the hike. It almost felt sacrilege to interrupt the wild. Occasionally, he'd hold out his hand to help me over a branch or rock. Other than that, Beck kept his hands to himself, a stark contrast to the evening before—my backside pressed into him, his hands on my stomach, my hips. The absence of his touch left me feeling hungry, starved to experience it again.

I chided myself. *This is better. Simpler. Safer.*

But I kept catching myself stealing glances at his reaction to the scenery, kept having to step away to separate us after pulling toward him like a magnet. I wanted him. I'd known that for some time. But that didn't mean he returned the sentiment. He had Reagan to pine over, and now that I knew she wanted him too . . . Things were more complicated than ever.

I have to work with him. He's my superior, even if just by a step, I reminded myself when a passing parrot made him smile so brilliantly that something in my chest pinched.

Falling for him would mean getting my heart broken by him.

This became my anthem for the trek, but with each repeat of the mantra, it seemed to lose its potency until it faded into the background.

At one point, Beck spun me around, pointing into the trees. "There! A monkey!"

"Where?"

Beck stepped closer until his chest met my back. He put his face close to mine and readjusted where he pointed until there it was. A tiny monkey with beady eyes and a black muzzle climbed down a vine with the grace of a Cirque du Soleil performer.

A surprised giggle bubbled out of me. Beck angled his face down to see my expression, and all but a few inches separated our lips. I grasped at something, anything to pull me back to my senses.

"We have to find that sloth," I said, almost in a whisper.

It took an extra beat for my words to register with Beck, but when they did, he took a step back, suddenly aware of how close we stood. "Don't worry, Lane. I'm on it."

As soon as he pulled away, I regretted shattering the moment. What was the point of guarding myself against falling for him? I stumbled off that cliff the night before—probably sooner.

I'd been losing my footing for some time now. I'd dedicated myself to trying on Hailey's life. What would she do in this situation? I could almost hear her voice answer in my mind: *I'd let myself slip.*

After a stunning, albeit humid, hike, we finally made it to Playa Escondido—the beach portion of the park. The glimmering blue ocean spread out like a prize for *surviving* the jungle.

"God, the water looks so refreshing," Beck said, and the comment would have surprised me—seeing as he wasn't a beach person—if it hadn't been scorching out.

His shirt stuck to the front of his hard chest, soaked. He was flushed, and beads of sweat dripped down his jaw.

Without my permission, my imagination ran wild—keeping the character but changing the setting: back at the resort suite, him on top of me—sweating for an entirely different reason.

I needed to get in that water ASAP. Cool me down, alright. As our feet met the sand, I chucked off my shoes, skipped out of my socks, and flung off my shorts. Luckily, I knew the hike included the beach, and I'd worn my bathing suit underneath.

Scanning the water for a marker, I found a lady with a large hat. She stood not quite as far as the twenty-five meters for half a lap, but it would do. "Race you out to where the lady in the straw hat stands and back."

I didn't wait for him to take off his hiking clothes or even respond. I needed every advantage.

My feet pounded on the sand before meeting the deliciously cool water. As soon as I was deep enough, I dove, and for a moment, I let myself suspend—spear-shaped—in the most refreshing water I'd ever experienced. Every cell in my body seemed to sigh at the drop in temperature. Then, I made myself work, pushing my arms forward, kicking my legs, propelling through the water.

I came up for air and lifted my face, searching for my marker. The straw hat was only a little further. I kept going until I saw her figure on my right, then I dove down, trying to remember how Beck described the flip turn. Curl. Twist. Kick. No wall to push off, *so* I kicked furiously instead.

I surfaced and realized I'd successfully turned the right way. I would have given a victorious war cry if I had the energy. Instead, I pretended each scoop of water was part of a rock wall, and I climbed through. Pulling myself forward.

I couldn't see Beck. Meaning he either whipped by me so fast I hadn't caught him, or I had actually held my own (not likely, but a girl could dream). Pulling my head up, I tried to spot him, and I did. Beckett Atteridge was still on the beach. Feet planted like a palm tree.

I tested putting my own feet down and found it shallow enough for standing. I thought Beck might say he hadn't agreed to a race, or I'd lost the bottom of my bikini, or Jaws picked people off in the surf. But he just looked at me, almost sad. Then he turned, heading for the tree line.

"Beck, wait!"

I exited the water into the hot jungle air, grabbing my shirt, shorts, and shoes in one swoop. I'd barely managed to get my bottoms on when I got back on the trail. My feet thudded on the wood-plank pathway. As I rounded a corner, I had to skid to a stop to keep from smacking into his back.

"Where are you going?" I asked, breathlessly pulling my shirt over my head.

He kept walking. "I told you. I'm not a big—"

I whirled on him, putting a hand on his chest to make him stop. "Beach person?" I finished. "Who cares? Beck, we did a long hike. It's hot as the devil's taint out here. You're sweating. You're flushed. You'll feel better after a quick dip." I tried to push him back towards the beach, but he didn't budge.

"I can't."

"Why not?"

"I just can't." He looked at the trees and then back at me, pained.

I took his hand in mine. No one was watching us. I didn't have to pretend to be his girlfriend. But I wanted to be in this moment with him for whatever reason. He looked at our hands for a long while. I thought he might pull away, but he didn't.

"You don't have to tell me anything. But Beck, you can trust me with this."

A muscle ticked in his jaw, and I could see the conflict warring in those brown eyes. "It's not a pretty story, Emily."

"Tell me anyway," I said quietly.

He sighed, sliding his hand from my grasp but not stepping away. "I guess I owe you since you won."

"No." I shook my head, not wanting him to feel forced to talk about something that obviously tormented him. "That was about your tattoo."

His mouth stretched into a straight line. "They're one and the same."

I cocked my head, curiosity fully piqued now, but then stopped myself. I wanted Beck to open up to me, but not like this.

My eyes lowered to his lips, and my body automatically shifted closer to his. Images of the night before flashed across my mind, of us dancing, our bodies moving together. The ghost of his touch licked across my skin. My flesh burned to have him against it once again. And then there was the almost kiss. The thought of which had kept me up for half the night.

I needed to know how those full lips would feel pressed against mine. "You don't have to tell me." I swallowed, trying to muster up as much of Hailey's bravery as possible before I chickened out. "But it's going to cost you."

"Oh yeah?" An eyebrow rose.

"I want to scrap one of our rules." I took a steadying breath. "Specifically, the no-kissing one."

His tongue ran across his bottom lip, and my insides melted, pooling to the bottom of my stomach. "It's our number one rule."

"We've already broken the other ones," I said, stepping closer.

"You said you wanted to keep things uncomplicated." His voice was smokey, as if he was having a hard time getting the right amount of oxygen.

"I changed my mind."

"I don't want you to regret this later." But his eyes snagged on my lips, his face angling towards mine.

"Then don't do anything to make me regret it," I said, trying to keep my tone light, but I think my silent plea threaded through: *Please don't break my heart.*

Beck's hands slid across my jaw and into my hair, cradling my head before lowering his mouth onto mine.

His lips were smooth and soft as a whisper as if he feared the moment might break. Or I would. Giving and taking, we found a slow, savoring rhythm. And between the touching of our lips, we shared breaths, which was almost as intoxicating, as intimate as the kissing itself—breathing each other in. Then, Beck's tongue slid across my bottom lip, and I parted for him.

He backed me into the railing, no longer seeming to worry about the fragility of the situation. My nipples pinched at the thought of being cornered by him. Our tongues glided past each other in urgent exploration. My hands explored as well. Starting at the front of him—his chest, his ribs. Then they moved to his back, getting a good feel of those swimmer muscles—tight cords under soft skin.

He nipped my bottom lip, and I gasped.

Beck retreated half an inch. "Sorry. Did I hurt you?"

I pulled him back to me, and our lips met with bruising force. "Not a pain gasp," I mumbled against his lips.

"Fuck," he groaned into my mouth, then picked me up, setting me on the railing, mouth still on mine.

My head swam. I wrapped my legs around him, and he ran a hand from my knee up my thigh. His fingertips moved so. Achingly. Slow. But when he got to the hem of my shorts, he angled his body back and away from me, resting his head on my shoulder.

"I need a minute." His voice was sandpaper.

I was pretty sure I knew what he meant by that, but completely beside myself, I gripped his shirt and yanked him back over. I gasped at the length of his outline pressed against my center. "You want me." It wasn't a question, but I was surprised.

"Are you seriously just figuring this out?"

"I guess not," I said, thinking about the night before and the way his fingers dug into my hips as we danced, how hard he was when I pressed my ass against him. But we'd been drinking. I didn't know how much of that was really him.

He rested his hands on my shoulders. "I'd love to show you how much I want you, Emily, but I don't think the rainforest is the right place for that."

"It's probably frowned upon," I agreed, trying to get a hold of my senses though the throbbing between my legs begged for release. Who cared if the howler monkeys saw us? My mouth went dry at the prospect of him. I swallowed, trying to get the words out before I lost my nerve. "I guess it's a good thing we share a room. Maybe you can show me later."

Beck's chest heaved. His dilated pupils nearly overtook the rich brown of his eyes. "Maybe I can."

Heat crept up my chest at the possibilities of tonight.

He moved to my side, leaning on the deck's railing, his ribs expanding with a long inhale. Then, the movement stopped. "No way."

"What?" I hopped off the railing.

"Right there," he whispered. "It's our sloth."

I followed the direction of his point, eyes bouncing from tree to tree until I saw her hanging by her claws. She may as well have been a damn unicorn for the awe that fell over me.

"You found her," I said, hushed. "You found our sloth."

We watched as she pulled herself upward in a movement not quite as slow as I'd imagined.

"Are you having a good time, Emily?"

I looked at Beck, and he did that thing where he tried to read my expression. I let my smile meet my eyes as I nodded. "I'm really glad I braved the jungle with you today."

A smile unraveled, slow but wide. "Me too." He was handsome.

So incredibly handsome when he smiled. I'd known it before, but now—alone in the jungle with him, after kissing— the sight made my knees weak.

The ride back to the resort was tense and quiet. Different scenes kept playing over and over as to what Beck would do to me when we got there. I pictured the door closing behind us and him carrying me to the bedroom. Maybe we wouldn't even make it that far. I could see him setting me down on the loveseat or even the countertop. I imagined running my hands under his shirt, across his chest, then down his stomach, following tight muscles until I reached his boxers.

A pothole jolted me from the fantasy.

"Sorry," Beck mumbled.

To a passerby, he might have looked casual behind the wheel of the rental. But I noticed how he gripped the wheel, white-knuckled. It was all too easy imagining that tight hold on my shorts before he pulled them down and placed himself between my legs.

God. Get a hold of yourself.

The ride to the park had seemed much shorter in the morning. Now I ached for him, and every minute seemed to stretch out, making the twenty-minute drive torturous.

As our feet met the tile of the resort's lobby, my pulse thrummed. *Beck. Beck. Beck. Beck.* I wanted to get behind that locked door. All previous reservations be damned. Beck seemed eager as well. We walked hand in hand, but my short legs had a hard time keeping his pace.

My imagination still ran wild with all the things I hoped Beck would do to me when Victoria and the group sent those fantasies to a screeching halt.

"Where have you two been?" Victoria asked. I noticed how they all had their bags as the group sprawled over the chairs and couches in the lobby.

"I texted you this morning. We went to the national park." Beck gave her suitcase a light kick. "What's all this?"

"I've been trying to call you for the past hour."

Beck looked at his phone and then held it out for Victoria's inspection. "Sorry. Spotty service in the jungle, I guess. What's going on?"

"We're leaving. Jerry told us about this amazing place only about an hour from here—glamping in Uvita." Victoria practically glowed.

Beck didn't seem impressed. "Victoria, you can't get much better than this." He gestured vaguely to the lobby around us. "Our rooms literally jut out into the rainforest. Hell, do I need to remind you that we were attacked by a viper two days ago?" I wondered if his apprehension of this idea matched mine—wanting to pick up where things left off. Now. "Where is this coming from?"

"Beck, listen." Victoria tried to straighten his shirt by grabbing where it hung off his shoulders and pulling, but the sweat from the hike didn't allow the shirt to move much. "I have to get out of this resort. All I can think about is the service here and whether the other guests are having a good time. It's going to be a great place to get married, but I can't enjoy myself while being practically immersed in work."

"Vic—"

Victoria clapped her hands together, loud and final. "You two are going to love this place. It is so romantic."

Beck pinched the bridge of his nose. "We have a pretty big group. Are you even sure they have enough rooms?"

"They have six tents left. Reagan and Madison are happy to room with each other. Gabe and Koontz . . ." We all looked over to where the two guys slumped. "Are a little unhappy to share a bed. But they are going to suck it up in the name of the trip." Victoria gave us a light shove in the direction of our suite. "Pack your bags. We're staying there for the next two nights. The van will be here in fifteen."

Before, my adrenaline had been high with the prospect of Beck and what we might do together behind closed doors. Being packed in a van with the rest of the wedding party had doused the mood. The toll of the hike hit me hard. My body sagged into the seat, and the soft rocking of the van made my lids heavy. I hadn't meant to allow myself to fall asleep, which is why I was surprised, waking to Beck's hand cradling my head against his shoulder.

"Sorry," I mumbled, sitting upright and finding my neck muscles tense from the odd angle they'd been at.

"It's okay. I'm beat too."

The ride had been quiet—everyone else looked wiped out from another day under the sun. We stopped for dinner on the way, which meant we didn't arrive at the camp until after sundown.

Stringed lights and tiki torches lit the path to a village of yurts circled around a curvy pool with a gurgling waterfall and eclectic seating. The scene was complete with a waist-high sheet metal sign and swirly letters that read *Welcome to Tranquility*. Even exhausted, I could appreciate the serene atmosphere.

The hostess of the property showed us where we could find the community showers and restrooms. She explained that tubs were available in the yurts for a more intimate experience. My cheeks warmed, and I was thankful for the low lighting to hide it. No one else seemed hot and bothered by the words "intimate experience" because either they'd already had plenty of intimate experiences with their yurt buddy, or there was no way in hell they ever would.

Dropped off at our yurt, Beck and I paused at the threshold. *How to read that look on his face?* Bracing, maybe, some curiosity, definitely tentative. And hunger. Beck held open the flap, and I took in our living space for the next two nights.

A canopy covered a circular bed in sheer, seductive sheets. Ivy spilled from shelving around the circumference of the room, giving the space a wild, fresh feel. The bones of the yurt seemed to be made of some sort of bamboo material. Hung from the beams, works of macrame hugged glass bowls with candles. The yurt was cozy, authentic, and romantic.

The cushions around a short coffee table were the only seating. No couch. Beck would have to sleep on the floor or in the bed.

Noises from the yurt next to ours—where Kat and Jake had been placed—took my attention off the self-guided tour. From the sounds of things, they were thoroughly enjoying the intimacy of their yurt. Except, they either didn't realize their yurt wasn't as secluded as expected or, more likely, they didn't care.

My face flamed.

"Jesus Christ." Beck ran a hand down the front of his face, looking a shade red himself. "These tents are paper thin."

Then he seemed to register the bed situation, eyes landing on the cushions near the coffee table. "I'll sleep on the floor," he said.

"No. We've both had a long day. You aren't sleeping on the floor."

"I don't want to make you uncomfortable."

Silence stretched between us as I tried to read the shift in our chemistry. "Did I seem uncomfortable earlier? In the jungle?"

Something sparked in Beck's eyes, but then he shook his head. "I don't think we should act on—" He looked at the canvas ceiling, seeming to search for the right words. "—those desires we expressed earlier."

That stung. "Oh."

"I want to," he rushed to say. "I really do. But now that I've had time to cool off, I don't want you to do anything you'll regret later."

He tried to soothe the jab of his rejection, but all I heard was that he didn't want me anymore. Not the way I wanted him.

"Okay," I said because what was I going to do? Beg him to sleep with me? "Yeah. You're right. Wouldn't want to complicate things."

His jaw worked. "Right." A crease formed on his forehead, like agreeing with me pained him.

"Well, I'm going to go find those showers," I said before plunging into my bag, trying like hell to hide the disappointment on my face as I searched for my toiletries.

I knew it. I knew I'd have to share a bed with Beck at some point on this trip, but I hadn't expected the scorch of his rejection.

Chapter 18

A scraping of furniture and a well-emphasized "Fuck!" woke me from an otherwise deep sleep. I jolted upright, trying to get my bearings in a bed that wasn't mine, in a room that wasn't mine, in a country that wasn't mine, with a man who wasn't mine. It took a few blurry-eyed blinks before I could make out Beck's form in the dim room, a shoe raised over his head.

"What happened?" I mumbled, failing to make sense of Beck's raised hackles and the way his eyes were trained on the floor.

Then I saw it. Something skittering in the darkness toward the bed. I lunged and smacked it with a pillow without knowing what I attacked. I raised my fluffy sword to hit it again, but Beck intervened, eliciting a fatal crunch when he smacked the thing with his shoe.

"What the hell was that?" I demanded.

"A fucking scorpion!" Beck tilted the shoe slowly to get a look at the mess. "It dropped out of my shorts."

"Are you okay? Did it sting you?"

"No, but I am going to have nightmares about that thing crawling on my leg."

"Did you leave your bag on the floor again?" I asked, my voice flat.

Beck pointed his shoe at me, and a piece of the scorpion fell off with the movement. "I don't want to hear it, Lane."

I couldn't help the smug smile unfolding on my face. And just like that, it was easy to step into our usual cadence of banter. I could almost forget our heated moment in the humid rainforest, followed so quickly by his rejection. Almost.

"Because, you know, someone did warn you about that," I said with a lilting voice.

Beck mumbled about needing to find something to clean up the mess.

I looked at the tint of the canvas that walled our yurt. The tangerine hue hinted that the sun had barely rolled its ass out of bed.

"What time is it?" I asked, rubbing my eyes.

"A little after six. I'm sorry. I didn't mean to wake you." He double-checked the inside of his shoe before slipping it on. "Go back to sleep. Barring any other wildlife attacks, I'll be quiet."

"What are you doing up?" I asked, my curiosity overriding the need for sleep.

"The others are going to the beach today," he said like that explained everything.

"I know. I heard them talking about it last night when I went to take my shower."

"I want to get out of here before the group wakes up so they won't harass me about not going."

I trod cautiously, knowing the topic hit a nerve. "Because you're not a beach kind of guy?"

"Right," he agreed, sounding tense.

I sat back on the bed. "So, what are *you* going to do?"

"There's a trail about ten minutes from town with waterfalls and pools and a nature-made waterslide."

"Cool, can I—" I started to ask if I could go with him, but then the sting of his rejection throbbed, reminding me to shut up before I could get hurt any further. "Never mind," I said, laying back down and pulling the comforter to my chin. "Have a good time."

"Did you—" Beck paused, and he seemed nervous, actually nervous, to finish the question. "Did you want to come with me?"

I lowered the blanket, if only by a little, not ready to relax my guard. "That depends. Do you want me to come with you?"

Beck looked away. "It's selfish for me to ask you to come. This is your vacation. I know you looked forward to going somewhere beachy. You should be with the group, enjoying yourself."

I did sit up at that. "I *was* looking forward to the beach, Beck. I had a great time with the group the other day." I swallowed. Time to be brave. "But it didn't compare to the hike with you yesterday. Didn't come close."

Beck turned back, reading me with those brown eyes, looking for a lie, but he would only find sincerity. "Emily Lane," he said, "would you like to see the jungle with me today?"

"Sure," I replied, throwing the blanket off. "Someone has to save your ass from the scorpions."

The park in Uvita enchanted me just as much as the one in Manuel Antonio had, with its tangle of trees, white-faced monkeys, and the gush of water that could be heard below not long after we began our descent.

Down, down, down we trekked, holding onto the wooden railing as the stairs plummeted through the greenery.

At the office, I'd take the elevator if it could save me two flights of stairs. Here, I worried the descent would be over too soon.

The whole trip would be over too soon. Three of the seven days had already passed. By the end of today, the vacation would be half over. My stomach sank at that.

I should have been thankful. I'd done so much. Seen so much: sailed over turquoise water, sunbathed on a white-sanded beach, explored a rainforest teeming with life.

Then there were the moments with Beck: him pulling me from danger with the snake, having dinner and learning more about him in that hour over gallo pinto than I had with months at the office; the dancing—God, having him take control and grip my body; and then that kiss.

I ached for what could have been last night—if Beck hadn't shut things between us down. But he was right. Pursuing this, *us,* was a mistake. This trip, my time with him, hell, even this crazy idea to pretend to be Hailey so I could play the part of the calligrapher—it was on borrowed time. All of it.

And when the trip ended, the lock would snick back into place, keeping me in the little box I'd created for myself. The prison I'd willingly crafted with the choices I'd freely and happily made.

Go to school for business—to keep myself safe.

Stay at the job I hate—to keep myself safe.

Keep things uncomplicated with a coworker, even though I'm already developing feelings for him—to keep myself safe.

Leave calligraphy as a business for those who were more daring—to keep myself safe.

In the end, my safety net had become just that: a net. And I didn't know how to cut myself free from it, not without letting my life crumble apart in the process.

We rounded a bend, and the waterfall came into view. Water slipped past moss-covered rocks to thunder into a pool below.

I watched as a man in a red speedo used the waterfall to slide off the cliff. He jackknifed into the natural pool below, only to surface and join his laughing friends on the other side.

How did this enclosed oasis exist? How was it that people were out here living their lives so fully while I shied away from any sort of risk?

This vacation wouldn't be enough to satiate my new cravings. It would only serve as a reminder of what I had missed out on. The realization was barbed.

Beck said something, an eager look across his face, but I couldn't hear him over the roaring of my mind. He did a double take before his brows furrowed. "What's wrong?"

I waved Beck off, hastily wiping my eyes with the back of my hand. I went to step around him, but his hands paused me with a gentle grip on my shoulders.

"Lane, stop. Are you hurt?"

"No. I just—" I groaned. "Can we keep moving? I really want to get closer to the waterfall."

I tried to push him off, but he held firm. "Tell me what's going on, first."

"You'll laugh at me," I said, trying to cover my eyes, but Beck grabbed my wrists.

"Emily." His soft tone threw me off guard. I stopped fighting him and looked into his searching eyes. "Please, trust me with this," he said, lobbing back at me as I'd asked him to do yesterday.

I could have confronted him about not trusting me with his secrets. But for some reason, I wanted to tell him. I wanted someone to see me and the hurt, to understand. Even if that someone was Beck. Maybe, especially if that someone was Beck.

"I forgot what this felt like," I managed.

"Taking the stairs?" he teased, but his tone and expression were all concern. The look made my heart swell.

"To feel alive," I choked on the last word but took a steadying breath. I needed him to understand. "Not only the hike. All of this. The trip. The calligraphy." And before I could stop the snowball from getting bigger, it rolled over my resolve. "You."

And on that one word, I cracked. I worried Beck would make fun of me for being dramatic and crying, or he'd shy away from my admission of feelings for him. So it surprised me when he pulled me into his chest and held me tight.

The protectiveness, the care in Beck's grip, made my chest ache in an entirely different way. I melted there, hot tears soaking his shirt. He didn't try to cheer me up, urge me to look on the bright side, or quiet me down. He just rested his head on mine and rubbed calming circles between my shoulder blades.

I don't know how long I stood there crying or how many other tourists Beck had to assure could go around us, and that, yes, I was fine. His tone never hinted at impatience or embarrassment over his emotional hiking buddy.

But as suddenly as the crying had come, it dried up. "I'm sorry," I said, peeling myself from his solid chest. "I don't know what came over me. Oh, God, I soaked your shirt."

"Don't apologize. I thought we established that I don't have some weird obsession with shirts."

"Sorry." I laughed a little, wiping my face. "I spent so long thinking you hated me over a shirtsleeve. It's going to take a while to rewrite that narrative."

"I can wait." We walked quietly for a bit before Beck asked, "Are you okay?"

I shrugged. Then, I decided to target one of the problems—specifically, one of the problems that didn't include my feelings toward him. "I've been so looking forward to a vacation, and now I'm here, it's better than I could have imagined. All I can think about is how this will be over in a few days. Then it will be back to that cubicle—behind cell walls." I stopped, realizing how dramatic I sounded. "I don't mean to whine. Everyone feels this way on vacation."

"Emily, everyone feels that way to a certain degree. But you shouldn't be dreading work so much that it keeps you from enjoying everything else. That's a problem. You look like you are heading for a root canal every time you step off the elevator at the office. Why are you at The Arlow Group if you obviously hate it?"

"Have you ever considered it's the people I work with," I said with a hip bump. I wanted to turn the conversation around, missing the lighthearted air of our morning together.

But Beck wasn't having it. "Come on, seriously."

We'd reached the bottom of the stairs and made our way over slippery rocks to a shallow part of the nature-made pool. I plunked down, taking my shoes off with a little too much attitude.

"What do you want me to say, Beck? That I'm miserable at the trade I spent thousands of dollars in college loans to learn? That I'm fucking sick of Excel? That I've only been at the job for five years, and I'm already burnt out?"

"Yes. I want you to say those things because you have an out."

"I don't." I slipped my feet into the water and watched the ripples. "I really don't."

"Why not quit? Focus on calligraphy. You could take on more jobs that way. Let it be your bread and butter."

"Because I can't, Beck."

"I need you to help me understand why. I know what my sister is paying you for this wedding. It's more than I make in a paycheck, and it's just one wedding."

"I've told you all this already. I can't give up a stable job to pursue something flimsy. My mom tried that, and look what happened to her. The grass isn't always greener on the other side."

I squeezed my eyes shut, trying to block out the memory of restless sleep in a stuffy van with no air conditioner, my stomach hollow and rumbling. How every sound outside the van's doors would send a surge of fear down my spine. I would never do anything to risk going back to that place, to feeling like a starved animal.

We sat quietly for a long while, swishing our feet in the water until Beck finally spoke again, low and careful. "I mean no disrespect to your mom, but Emily, you are too detail-oriented to let something like that happen. Tell me you don't watch your account like a hawk. That you don't have a padded savings account? That you don't have a budget to keep you in check."

He had me pegged, but I knew the fear would always act as a gatekeeper to what could be. "I'd rather play it safe."

"Okay, then play it safe. But don't stay at The Arlow Group."

"Trying to get rid of me, are you?" I asked, looking to find that easygoing, jovial place we usually frequented together. But, again, it was a bust.

"I don't want you to feel stuck. That's a dangerous place to be. You have options. Maybe you just need to get out of that place. Hell, be a greeter at Walmart to support yourself while you get into calligraphy. Or wait tables. Something. Anything. But do me a favor and go somewhere you're appreciated. We both know you should have gotten my job, but they hired out instead. It's bullshit."

"It is bullshit," I agreed. "But it would have been a shame if they hadn't."

The air between us seemed to get thicker, like someone turned up the humidity. "Because we wouldn't have met?" Beck finally asked.

I threw a pebble into the water to give me something other than his face to look at, sure my cheeks had turned strawberry red. "Yeah," I said. "And then I'd never have gotten this free vacation."

Beck threw his head back in contagious laughter. "Speaking of this vacation," he said after regaining his composure. "It's time to upgrade this experience."

He pointed to a woman sliding down the waterfall with an elated scream, then peeled his sweaty shirt off. And damn. I'd seen him shirtless plenty of times at the gym's pool. Why? Why did the sight of his chest and those abs and that line of hair trailing from his navel still make my insides feel like cotton candy being stretched too thin?

"Wait," I said, my brain groggy from lust. "You're going in?"

"Well, yeah," he said, like *duh*.

"But it's a body of water . . . that's outdoors . . . I don't know. I'm trying to understand your rule. So, it's just beaches you avoid?"

Beck nodded, jaw tight. "Just beaches."

"Have fun, I guess," I said, leaning back on the rock, content to lay out like a lizard while watching him enjoy his adrenaline rush.

"Oh no, no, no. *We* are taking the plunge, Lane."

Before I knew it, Beckett Atteridge had persuaded me off that rock, and I found myself at the bottom of a cliff, ready to climb iron rungs.

"Wow," I said, grabbing the first of the rungs, which looked like giant-sized staples hammered half-assed into the cliff. "I'm so glad I decided to come with you today instead of going with the group to the beach," I called out flatly. "Such a peaceful getaway."

Beck halted his climb to look down at me, clearly amused by my discomfort. "I never promised a serene hike."

"If I die, donate my pen collection to a local school."

"Great idea. I'm sure teachers would make good use of your Bics."

I snorted.

"If you weren't so locked in on being dramatic, you'd see that we're almost there."

We were nineteen rungs up. I looked back, and the ground seemed to waver. I couldn't even see the faces of the people in the pool. Normally, heights didn't frighten me. But if I slipped or if one of these rungs came loose, I'd shatter a leg on the rocks. Possibly worse.

Beck, who'd already made it over the top, peeked back down to see me clinging to a rung.

His expression turned serious. "You've almost got it. Just don't look down."

"Too late," I said, but I managed to make my arms and legs move and finished the climb.

With sure hands, Beck ushered me away from the edge. "See. Not so bad. Right?"

"Now we only have to jump off this fucking cliff we just climbed," I said, eyeing the rushing water warily.

"No," Beck said, "we only have to sit and let the water push us off the cliff."

"Oh great. That's so much better, letting Mother Nature push me to my death."

"Look," Beck said, hands resting on my shoulders. "You might be able to climb back down the rungs if no one is coming, but I think slipping on the way down is more of a threat than sliding into a body of water."

I paled.

"And this way will be infinitely more fun," Beck said in an almost sing-song voice.

I gave him a face, ready to tell him that I'd meet him at the bottom, that I'd take my chances on the rungs. But then I remembered I was supposed to be trying on Hailey's life. She wouldn't think twice about a jump like this. She wouldn't analyze it. She would jump. And seeing as I only had a limited time to enjoy this life Hailey had loaned me . . .

I walked over to the rushing water, heart in my throat.

"That's it," Beck encouraged. "I'll be right after you."

"Wait. You're making me go first?"

"Yes. Definitely."

"Why?"

"Because I know I'm going to make the jump. I'm afraid you are going to chicken out and get stuck up here."

"That could be an option, though, right? Staying up here for the rest of my life. Living with the monkeys."

Beck guided me by the elbow to where the water was a gentle stream. I sat down but couldn't make myself move into the rougher water, to the part that would push me over the edge. "Emily," Beck said, and I felt myself lock onto that voice, a deep calm in all the panic. "Sometimes you just have to jump and hope for the best."

Before the fear could paralyze me, I took a steadying breath and then pushed myself into the rushing water.

I screamed as it carried me forward until I was hurdled over the cliff and free-fell toward the water. And somehow, the flip in my stomach turned my scream into a burbling laugh. At the last second, I tucked my limbs in for a safer plunge into the water, the rush of which was a shock of its own. As I emerged at the surface, the thought of Beck being greeted by the cold water had me laughing again.

And sure enough, as soon as I made it a safe distance away, I heard him hollering and laughing before the splash of water and a wave that propelled me forward.

"Jesus!" Beck gasped, joining me with a few strokes. "How is the water this cold?" He shivered.

I laughed, and the action made me sink into the water a bit. Beck grabbed my arm to help me until I could tread again. His hand's touch was so warm compared to the water around us. While finding a good rhythm for treading, I accidentally sent my body into his, my bikini-clad chest colliding with his bare torso.

My skin seemed to electrify at the point of contact, the cells swarming and coming to life. Beck's slippery, wet body against mine. It was too much. And the heaviness in his expression was confusing because he'd told me, just the night before, how he didn't want to pursue this—me.

"Sorry," I mumbled, then rushed to pull away and put distance between us.

"Why are you apologizing?" Beck said, jogging lightly to catch up to me. Because once my toes met the muddy bottom, I all but bolted to the edge of the pool. He grabbed my hand, and I turned to face him. Ready to get the conversation over with, to rip it off like a Band-Aid.

"I'm apologizing because I'm not trying to disrespect your boundaries," I said, slipping my hand out of his. "Because you made yourself clear about how you feel about me."

"Have I, Emily?" he asked, the picture of calm.

"Yes. When you said you didn't want to act on certain desires. Or the way I could only convince you to come to bed last night was by building a freaking pillow fort between us. And I know you and Reagan . . ." I pushed wet hair out of my face. This was so humiliating. "It's okay. Seriously. Let's drop it."

"No. We aren't dropping this. When I told you I didn't want to make you uncomfortable, that wasn't bullshit. I didn't ask you to come to Costa Rica to seduce you. I asked you here because you seemed like you could use a break. The last thing I want is for you to leave here with regrets, to feel less like yourself around me when we go back to sharing a lane or working together."

I thought of what he'd told me about Reagan, about how she'd told him she didn't feel like herself when they were together. "I'm not her, Beck. I'm not Reagan."

"I know," he said too quickly. "But still, you were right. We shouldn't complicate things."

"But that's the problem, Beck. They are already complicated. Tell me you can sit across from me in meetings and you won't think about this trip. Our dance. That kiss. It's too late."

Once again, conflict danced in his eyes. Had misery ever looked that beautiful on anyone else? "So, what do we do?"

I swallowed. "We jump. And hope for the best."

Chapter 19

When we returned to the yurts, we found the pool glittering and empty. Both pretty worn from the hike and our fun at the nature-made watering hole, we decided a restful day poolside was time well spent.

On the deck, we had our choice of lawn chairs, padded seats by the pool, a hammock, and what Beck went straight to—a queen-sized day bed, circular—just like the one in our room. A peach cover could be pulled over the bedding to block out desired amounts of sun, giving the chair the look of a conch. He plopped down in the middle, smiling—a king on his throne.

I laughed and took a lawn chair nearby. I was being honest when I said I thought it was too late to worry about complicating things, but I wanted to give him space—to decide on his own. However, when I tried smearing sun lotion on my back in blind sweeping motions, Beck said, "Emily, come here."

I obeyed, barely feeling the heat of the deck beneath my feet as I padded over. All my nerve endings seemed to hold their breath for Beck and his touch. As his big, warm hand glided over my back, contrasting with the cool sun lotion, I had to hold in a groan. His fingers moved slowly but firmly across muscles that ached from two days of hiking. I couldn't help but wonder how those fingers would feel in other places. I'd never be able to put on suntan lotion again without getting aroused.

"Sorry. The lotion is cold," he said, probably because I had goose-bumps, but they had nothing to do with temperature. My skin sang to his touch.

"'Ts ok," I mumbled, my whole body so relaxed, any movement asked too much, even talking, apparently.

"You have so many freckles," Beck said quietly. And he seemed to draw lines with his finger across them, creating a picture by connecting the dots. It made me shiver.

"Mmmhmm."

"This grouping on your shoulder looks like the Hawaiian Islands."

I laughed.

"They're beautiful."

My laughter stopped. His comment surprised me because no one had ever called my freckles beautiful. Okay. My mom might have when I was about seven. Butterflies awoke in my stomach, fluttering at Beck's words.

"Thank you," I said, both for the compliment and the free massage via sun lotion application. As he capped the bottle, I started to get up from the bed, giving him his spot back, but then came the voices—Koontz's loud party boy voice audible over the others. Beck pulled me down, and I let him, my head fitting on his shoulder, my side boob pressing into his bare ribs.

He's making sure we look the part—like a couple, I reminded myself. *That's what we're supposed to be.* But my heart hammered at the closeness of him, at how easy it would be for him to flip on top of me. Because, apparently, that's all I could think about this whole damn trip.

"Hey, love birds!" Doug called.

"Hey, loser," Beck lazily called back.

"We're getting some lunch and heading back to the beach," Kat said. "You two should come. There's this spot where the sandbar is shaped like a whale's tail."

Beck looked at me, seeing if I wanted to join. "Thanks," I answered, my eyes trained on him, "but we're good."

"Oh, come on!" Koontz said.

I remembered Beck trying to slip out early this morning because he knew this would happen, that his friends would want him to come along, that they, in their own caring way, would bother him about it.

I planted a hand on Beck's chest and then looked dead at Koontz. "We've got some other things planned for the day," I said with a wink.

I didn't miss the way Reagan's eyes blazed at that.

On the other hand, Koontz grinned like an idiot but put his hands up in surrender. "Say no more."

After gathering supplies and refueling on refreshments, complimentary of the campgrounds, the group headed out with as loud of an exit as their entrance had been.

"Thank you." Beck's head rolled to the side to look at me.

"You're welcome," I said, suddenly aware of how close we lay and without the audience. I sat up.

"Stay," Beck said, grabbing my hand with gentle, warm fingers. "Unless you don't want to," he added, loosening his grip.

I looked at where his hand engulfed mine. "Have you always hated the beach?" I asked when I'd finally found my voice.

"I don't hate the beach." Beck sat up, running a hand down his face. "It's . . . complicated," he said, voice tight. "Something happened when I was a kid."

It may have happened a long time ago, but the pain still looked fresh. "You don't have to talk about it. I'm sorry I brought it up."

Beck's eyes found mine. "I want you to know."

And I understood. There was something about someone looking your pain in the eye and saying, *Your ugly doesn't scare me. I'm not going anywhere.* I'd experienced it firsthand with him—more than once.

I swallowed, bracing for what haunted him. "Okay."

"When I was eleven years old, my family vacationed in Panama. On our last day, my dad ended up having to work, and my mom was taking care of Victoria—she'd come down with a nasty stomach bug. My little sister was disappointed to miss out on our last beach day. So, we snuck out."

"Little sister? I thought Victoria was older."

"I'm not talking about Victoria. I'm talking about Poppy." His voice caught on her name.

In loving memory of Poppy.

The words on the lantern burst into my mind like a camera flash. My hands went to my mouth. The story was darker than I could have imagined. Dread welled in my chest.

"We got in the water," Beck continued, eyes on the pool now. "And we were having such a great time, I didn't realize how far we'd drifted out. A wave went over both of us. And I came up laughing." He swallowed. "But Poppy was gone. I screamed her name until others started helping me search. The police were called, and my parents arrived."

I could see it. A young, scrawny Beck with his wild hair and sweet eyes, screaming for his sister. The fear he must have felt. The desperation. My heart clenched.

"They didn't find her body until the next morning, a mile down the shore from where we'd been."

"Oh God." I clamped a hand on his shoulder, my eyes burning with the effort to keep from crying. "I'm so sorry."

"For Victoria, being near the beach, the place Poppy loved most, is like being close to her. For me, going to the beach and having fun without her seems like the worst betrayal." My hand found his as he continued, "You asked me why I don't work for my dad. My sister's death broke something vital in him. *Changed* him. He was never the same after, and he certainly never trusted me again. And can you blame him?"

"Beck, you were eleven. If he is still holding that over your head, that's his problem. Not yours."

Beck squinted at the pool. "He's trying to make amends. He even offered me a job. I just feel as though nothing I do would be good enough if I worked for him."

"I hate that you feel this way," I said, the tears making good on their threats.

I wrapped my arms around him, but Beck repositioned us so he was the one holding me, his head resting on mine.

"I'm not trying to make you sad, Emily," he murmured. "Most days, I do okay. But as we get closer to the wedding, I can't stop thinking about Poppy and how she should be here. And I want you to understand. I would love to spend a day on the beach with you, but I can't. That's something I'll never be able to do with you."

"Your tattoo." I choked on a sob. "They aren't carnations or peonies. They're poppies."

He nodded, rubbing my back.

I sniffled. "So there really is no secret garden in your backyard?"

The rubbing stopped. "Does that disappoint you?" he asked, and I could hear the smile in his voice.

"A little," I said with a wet laugh.

Beck pulled back to point to the negative space between the flowers. "I'm planning on getting her name tattooed here. I'm waiting until I find the perfect font. Something that fits her. At the tattoo shop, the lettering options were either gangster blocks or seductive swirls. Not what I'm going for."

We leaned back together on the mattress, but I turned so I could trace the tattoo. It was his turn to get goosebumps. I reveled in being able to return the favor.

"She's why you teach babies to swim," I said quietly.

"When I was in high school, my therapist finally got me in the pool. I'd have a panic attack halfway down the lane and have to grab onto the rope dividers to catch my breath and calm down." The admission humanized him even more, and I ached to picture a Beck with so much anxiety. So much trauma. "But after months of swimming, I found it peaceful. I was in complete control. No fear. After I got comfortable enough, I realized I needed to do something. Honor her in some way. Keep other kids from dying. I don't even know if ISR would have helped Poppy or if what I'm doing matters. But I have to try."

"It matters," I whispered, having to fight the tears again.

He gave the slightest smile and then leaned down to kiss the bridge of my nose. For a long while, we sprawled on the bed. At some point, he ended up as a big spoon, and I ran my fingers down the stems of his tattoo until his breathing slowed, and the arm he had around my waist grew heavy.

A deafening crack pulled me from a sleep I hadn't even known I'd fallen into. The sound electrocuted my senses awake. I dug my claws into something weighted around my hips.

"Ow," a deep voice murmured in my ear.

Realizing I'd used Beck's arm as my pin cushion, I released my grip on him and pulled myself into a sitting position. We'd fallen asleep in the sunshine and awoken under an ominous gray cloud. Another boom split the sky with a flash of light.

This time, rain followed the lightning. Not a gentle, *you might want to go indoors* warning sprinkle but a Hurricane Harvey downpour. For a split second, we sat there, shocked. Not even the little shell of a cover could protect us from the onslaught of water. Rain soaked us to the bone in seconds.

"Come on!" Beck said, taking my hand and guiding me off the bed.

Our hands slipped apart as we ran across the pool deck, but Beck reached back to grab my fingers tighter before pulling me after him.

We reached the yurt dripping. Our chests heaved with the adrenaline of it all. Then we dissolved into laughter, and after a day of sharing such painful memories, it felt good to laugh. It was an ointment for the soul.

Beck's eyes danced as he stared into mine, but his smile lessened as his gaze fell to my lips. The air grew heavier. He swallowed, and I watched his Adam's apple dip past that lone freckle of his. Then he tugged me to him, his mouth colliding with mine. I was ready for the impact, my hands slipped into his hair, causing drops of water to break free from his curls and roll over my fingers, down my arms.

Everything else fizzled away, and I was lost in the press of his mouth, the taste of him—how his teeth scraped my bottom lip, careful but hungry.

We didn't need the beach. We could make a tide of our own with the way we took turns pushing and giving with our lips, our bodies. He dug his fingers into my hips, and I gasped from the pressure.

I needed him. All of him. I took the hem of his shirt and tugged it upward. Beck helped, yanking it off. Heavy with water, the shirt slapped against the floor.

Beck pulled me back as if my lips were oxygen, and he couldn't go too long without coming up for air. Our chests slipped against each other, wet from the rain yet warm from each other. It was dizzying. I wanted to feel that heat everywhere.

I went to untie my bikini top, but Beck halted my fingers. "May I?"

I nodded, not trusting my voice. I could feel myself pooling in my already wet swimsuit.

He pulled the string with delicate fingers until my top slipped down, stopping only by the band at my ribs. I'm not large-chested or even medium-chested, and I definitely couldn't hold a candle to what Reagan had in the cup department, but Beck looked at my breasts like they were lost treasure.

"So beautiful," he whispered before kissing his way down my neck until his lips rested on a nipple.

I arched my body into him as he swirled his tongue ever so gently over the bud. My other nipple ached for contact, and as if he could read my mind, he reached up and lightly pinched it.

"Absolutely gorgeous," he said, his breath tickling on such a sensitive area as he unhooked the band, completely freeing my chest.

He kissed his way back up to my lips, and my fingers trailed down that delicious bit of hair under his navel. Beck's breath hitched as I snuck a finger under his waistband, but before I could find the patience to take his shorts off completely, I sank my hand in until my fingers wrapped around him. Hard. Huge.

"Fuck," Beck said to the ceiling.

I moved my hand up and down the length of him, reveling in how that size would feel in me. It almost hurt how badly I wanted him.

I halted my exploration to remove his swim shorts completely. Beck's eyes locked on my face as I took in the sight of him: the very image of manhood. In another life, I swear he was a model for a Greek god statue.

His eyes dipped to where my bikini bottoms still hid the rest of me, and he looked ravenous. I could see his pupils flare in the dim lighting. With light fingers, Beck traced the edge where it hugged my hip. My legs nearly buckled at the desire that throbbed between them. His eyes caught mine, a silent question, *Is this still okay?*

I nodded. I would let Beck do just about anything to me. His fingers curled around the strings. He tugged, then peeled them off and let the bottoms pool at my feet. I stepped out and watched him consume me with his eyes.

"You have no idea how long I've wanted you," he said.

"Since the other night?" I shivered as he moved a strand of wet hair over my shoulder. "When we went dancing."

I pressed Beck backward to the bed, and he let me, nearly stumbling over a floor cushion in the process, and then he took charge, easily hoisting me up. I wrapped my legs around his waist, relishing the warmth radiating off his torso, burning away the biting rainwater.

He set me on the bed, spreading my legs so he could stand between them. His thumb brushed against my clit, and I arched off the mattress, the slightest movement both alleviating the need between my legs while simultaneously intensifying it.

"Oh, I was definitely turned on the other night," he said, rubbing me with steady circles. "But I've been wanting you for months. In your living room when you worked on that mirror." He bent to press a light kiss on my ribs. "When I confronted you for being a fraud at the office, and we stood so close, alone in that room," he said into my skin. "Honestly, I think I was a goner when I first saw you in your swimsuit, telling me I was in your lane. I've been thinking about your thighs—dreaming about being between them ever since."

Before his admission could fully hit me, he dipped a finger inside. I gasped.

"God," he said thickly. "You are so wet." He pushed the finger in until he was knuckle-deep, and at the same time, a flash of lightning lit beyond the canvas of the tent, matching how I'd felt, lit from within. He slid his finger out, only to add a second one, and I whimpered with the pressure. "And so tight." He curled his fingers in, and I clenched against him, my body taut with pleasure and need.

I couldn't get enough air, and my heart pounded so fast I thought it would leap out of my chest. While I tried to gain control of my vitals, Beck fished his wallet out of his discarded shorts. He ripped the corner of the condom package with his teeth.

I crawled backward, and Beck joined me on the bed, placing himself between my legs. One thrust, and he'd be inside. The emptiness in me was desperate to be filled. Before he did, Beck leaned over. Either arm braced on the side of my head. And then he kissed the bridge of my nose softly, tenderly.

"Do you still want to do this?" he whispered against my lips. That deep voice could be my undoing alone.

"Yes, Beck." It came out as a beg. "Anything. Everything," I managed.

His lips melted against mine. Then, he dipped his hips, thrusting into me. Slowly, so slowly, he entered. I marveled at his size, at how well he filled me.

"Fuck! Emily, you feel—" Beck pulled out then pushed back in, filling me to capacity and then some. "—*Fuck!*"

Lightning flashed outside the tent and behind my eyelids. He pulled out again, diving even deeper this time, stretching my core. I gripped his back, biting back a moan, not wanting the others to hear us. Then thunder cracked again, and I realized the rain was pouring so hard that we wouldn't be audible over the storm.

Which was good, because when Beck picked up the pace, it was no use keeping quiet. His size, his strength, was an all-consuming pleasure. When I cried out, he immediately halted.

"Are you okay?" he rasped.

I ground against him, desperate for his friction. "Please," I begged. "Please don't stop."

I saw the comprehension snap into place, and Beck was quick to please. He pulled one of my thighs higher on his hip. The angle made me see stars. There, he pounded in me with that same stamina he showed every morning at the pool. I thought of how long he said he'd wanted me. Months of pent-up energy powered him. All the tension we'd harbored between us, all that competition, with each thrust, I paid for it in the most mouth-watering, mind-melting way.

I gripped the pillow, desperate to cling onto anything, to ground myself, but it didn't take long before that perfect pressure and rhythm began to build into aching need. "Beck!"

"I know, Emily." He brushed a kiss against the underside of my jaw. Sweat dripped off him and trailed into my hairline, mingling with mine. "Come on," he panted. "I've got you." He threaded our fingers together, then squeezed my palms. He had me pinned and filled so completely. The tension pulled—knotted—tighter like it couldn't stretch any further until the entire thing unraveled. The orgasm tore through my body, and as I clenched around him, his own pleasure followed. He buried his face in my neck, groaning my name, and I didn't think I'd ever heard a better sound.

Then, he collapsed, shifting his weight so the mattress took the brunt of it, but I savored how he relaxed into me—the way his breath tickled the baby hairs, how his arm draped limply across my breasts.

While we caught our breath, I ran my fingers through his damp curls. After a long moment, he surfaced, kissing my chin, nose, and forehead before rolling off me. "Jesus Christ, Lane."

I shook my head, still in disbelief at the nirvana we'd just been through.

"I think I get it now," Beck said, staring at the ceiling.

"What's that?" I finally managed.

"Pura Vida," he said. "Because that was pure life."

Chapter 20

My mouth slid against Beck's, and he pressed his body against mine. Nothing but skin beneath the sheets—no barrier of clothes. I'm not sure if he'd initiated the kissing or if I had done it in my sleep. It didn't matter. I just knew I had to have him again. His hand gripped my ass and then trailed to my thigh. He hitched it up over his hip. I ground against him and found him rock hard.

"Please tell me this isn't a dream," he mumbled against my lips. A laugh tumbled out of me. "Actually," he said, kissing me some more, "it doesn't matter. Just don't wake me."

I would have laughed again, but he rolled on top, and the weight of him took all my attention. My mouth salivated at the idea of him being inside me again, of feeling his rhythm, of letting him wind me so tightly until I came apart in ribbons.

He positioned himself at my entrance but then pulled back, groaning. "I only had the one condom." He dropped his head to my shoulder. "The one I keep in my wallet." His voice was gravelly from sleep. "I really expected myself to behave as a gentleman," he said with a sigh.

"You've been a perfect gentleman," I replied, angling my face to kiss him again.

Beck's lips left mine, trailing down my throat. He veered off to cup and kiss my breasts. My nipples budded at the attention, but then Beck was off again, following an invisible path down my stomach.

"What are you doing?" I gasped as he sucked a spot just below my navel.

"I'm hungry," he said into my skin, and my insides turned molten under his lips.

"Beck," I breathed, toes curling as he moved farther south. His lips stopped their descent, and he ran a hand up my leg.

"God, Emily. You have no idea what your body does to me."

Heat spread across my chest as his fingers inched closer and closer to my center. "I think I have some idea," I groaned, completely at the mercy of his fingertips.

He smiled the most heartbreakingly beautiful smile at that but then turned all business as he traced the crease of my lips. I moaned, feeling myself swell for him.

"I know I said I was above groveling." He splayed his large hands on my thighs and spread me open. "But here I am. Begging," he said, voice strained. "May I please taste you, Emily?"

The question sucked all the air out of the room. My tongue felt like a dead weight in my mouth, so I nodded.

"Emily Lane, use your words." He massaged my thigh, and the pressure of his fingers made me lightheaded. "Is this okay?"

"Yes," I croaked.

He hooked my legs over his shoulders, and I reached up, fisting the sheets above my head, bracing for him. But nothing could prepare me for the luxurious sweep of his tongue across my clit, the way he sucked languidly as if savoring his favorite piece of candy.

I cried out, and Beck placed the gentlest of kisses on the most sensitive of places.

"There's no storm this morning, Lane." His low voice rumbled across my sex.

Oh God. I knew what he was saying. We only had the thin canvas walls as a barrier for sound, and we already knew how well they insulated noise thanks to Kat and Jake's demonstration.

He nuzzled my thigh. "Do you think you can be quiet until I'm finished with breakfast?"

I whimpered in response, but he showed no mercy. His tongue entered me, stroking upward. I gasped, and my grip on the bedding tightened with my effort to keep silent.

I'd had sex before, plenty of it. And most of my boyfriends could make me come most of the time. But this. *This* was different. *This* was art.

Beck slipped his tongue out, repositioning it on my center, only to push two fingers in, curling and uncurling them, bringing another current of sensation. My back arched off the bed. He was going to make being quiet as difficult as possible.

Typical, competitive Beckett.

At least, with his tongue and fingers working in tandem, I wasn't going to have to stay quiet for long. I teetered toward the edge at an alarming rate. "Beck," I groaned, clamping my hands on his head, tangling my fingers in his curls.

He paused to moan. It vibrated through me. "You taste even better than I imagined." He scraped his teeth down my clit and started suckling.

"Beck, please," I cried, unable to keep quiet. My heels dug into his back.

What I wanted him to do, I didn't know. Slow down so I could enjoy it longer? Speed up because the tension was too much? I had no idea. All I knew was I ended up being the one to beg.

This was bliss.

This was torture.

"Fuck keeping quiet," he said across my opening. "I love the way you say my name." Then he went back to feasting on me.

I bit my hand to muffle the sound, but I couldn't stay silent when the orgasm ripped through me. As I throbbed, Beck continued licking, relishing every bit of my pleasure. "Absolutely exquisite," he mumbled, then kissed his way up my stomach, my chest, and finally to my lips. It took a long time for the hammering of my heart to calm down.

Beck had begun tracing constellations of freckles on my shoulders, but as soon as my breathing was under control, I pushed him flat on his back, wrapped my hand around him, and stroked.

He exposed his throat as he pressed the back of his head into the pillow. "Emily," he gasped, "you don't have to—oh God!" I'd put my mouth around him. The competitive nature in me took charge. It was his turn to stay quiet while I pleasured him. I licked him as slowly as I could from base to tip. *"Fuck!"*

We were getting dressed when my phone rang—loud in the quiet morning air. I scrambled to answer, hoping to reach it before it woke up the rest of the wedding party in the surrounding tents—hoping we hadn't done that already with our *intimate experience.*

"It's Wesley," I said, wondering what had come up at work that warranted the early call.

Especially when I was supposed to be helping my dad with his busted knee.

"Don't answer it. You're on PTO," Beck said, pulling on his boxers.

"Don't you think it's weird he's calling me?" I asked, quickly climbing into my romper—a perfect, comfy outfit for the trip back to Manuel Antonio.

Beck found a pair of shorts in his suitcase, which lay on the coffee table thanks to the creepy crawly visitor he'd had the day before. He examined the shorts for good measure before putting them on.

My phone quieted in my hand. "See? If it was important, he'd send an email. Or he'll call again."

Beck's phone started vibrating next.

"I think it's important," I said flatly.

Beck rolled his eyes. "Of course, his phone calls would have no problem coming through," he said, tugging on a shirt before answering. "Hey, Wes."

"Beck, we need to talk." Beck had put the call on speaker, and I could hear the tightness in Wesley's voice. Driving noises blanketed the background, so something was serious enough that it couldn't wait until he got to the office. Worse, I'd never heard him get so serious with Beck. Wesley had always spoken to him as though they'd been on the same basketball team, whipped each other with towels in the locker room—the sort of tone that was saved for *the boys*. Not now.

"Sure," Beck said, reading the situation and ditching the light tone he'd answered with.

"And by 'we,' I mean you, me." He huffed out a breath. "And Emily."

My heart dropped into my stomach.

Beck's eyes flashed to mine, but he stayed cool. "Emily? Isn't she in Kansas with her dad?"

"Look, I like you. So, before you go any further, I want you to know that I've already seen the picture on Facebook. Hold on." Wesley then proceeded to place his Starbucks order.

Beck mouthed, *What the fuck?* and tapped on a Facebook notification. There were two hundred thirty-four likes on a new picture Beck had been tagged in by Madison.

And there it was. Beck and I were in our swimsuits, asleep on the day-bed by the pool. Spooning.

I turned away from it, rejecting the picture and what it meant that my boss had seen it. Having a complete breakdown, I shoved my face into the nearest pillow and screamed.

Then I pulled back, seething. Madison hadn't posted that to be sweet. She knew I didn't want my picture taken. At dinner the other night, I'd told the whole group that I couldn't let my brother find out where I was.

Only there wasn't a brother to worry about but my fucking job.

After placing the order for his chai latte, Wesley said, "So is she with you now?"

Beck looked at me, misery plain on his face.

I felt like a kid sitting outside the principal's office. No point in delaying the inevitable.

"Yes. I'm here."

"Good. I'll only have to say this once. What you two did was reckless. Irresponsible. Our relationship policy is spelled out clearly. You must be upfront with things of this nature. There are contracts that have to be signed covering consent as well as expectations should the relationship have an unsavory end. Not to mention, the two of you lied, leaving the team scrambling right before a convergence."

I bit my cheek to hold back the reply I wanted to say—that the two of us had carried the team for the past month. The team certainly had all but spent the past two workdays twiddling their thumbs because we'd already frontloaded all the work for this project.

"I'm going to do what I can, but I have a meeting first thing with HR this morning. And later with Chester." The VP of the company. I winced. "I can't guarantee you'll both be able to keep your jobs." The sentence pierced me like an arrow. *Fired. We could be* fired *over this.*

We were idiots to think we could pull this off. No, *I* was an idiot to think I could pull this off. People like Hailey and Beck always got away with stuff like this. But not me.

My head drooped to my hands. I was minutes, maybe seconds, from curling into the fetal position.

"I'll let you know what is decided. But you'll need to be available should we have contracts to send."

Great. So, the rest of the vacation would be spent checking emails to see when the axe would fall. A ringing in my ears muffled the rest of the conversation, which was fine. I'd heard enough.

If I got fired over this, would anyone hire me again? How would I buy food? Pay for rent? I pictured my belongings in trash bags stuffed in my Prius, just like how we'd bagged our things when we lived in the van.

After hanging up, Beck knelt in front of me. "Everything is going to be alright. We are going to figure this out. Okay?"

I nodded, too numb to do anything else.

A loud voice outside our yurt made me jump. "If you want breakfast, you better get it now! We leave for Manuel Antonio in half an hour!" I recognized it as Doug's voice.

"Come on," Beck said, taking my hands. "Let's get some food in us. We'll feel better." I let him pull me to my feet even though the idea of food made my stomach turn.

Outside, others from the wedding party were mumbling and cursing over Doug's rooster call wakeup. We lingered at the back of the pack with Gabe. He looked like he belonged with the cast of *The Hangover* with his mussed hair and bloodshot eyes, which was funny considering I hadn't seen him touch an alcoholic drink the entire trip.

"Are you seriously going to let that idiot marry your sister?" he groaned, rubbing his eyes.

"Well, we still have three days to stop the wedding," Beck said. "What did you have in mind?"

Gabe hooked an arm around Beck's neck, pulling him away from me. "All we do is get him drunk enough to get that tattoo he wanted. When Victoria sees the two-foot geometric wolf across his chest, she'll kill him herself."

Beck's head fell back in laughter. The sight would have made me smile had it been under any other circumstance. I couldn't help but wonder how he could laugh at a time like this.

But then I knew. He was Beckett freaking Atteridge. What did he have to worry about? If he lost this job, he'd have another one lined up within the hour. Hell, his dad had already offered him one. He had nothing to worry about.

Me, on the other hand . . .

I pictured those trash bags in my mom's van so many years ago. The Whopper someone had given us after hours of panhandling in the sun. The three of us splitting it. And how hollow my stomach felt after.

Honed in on that picture, I didn't see the stone jutting out of the pathway. My flip-flop caught on it, and the strap sprang free from the bottom, sending me sprawling forward. I reached out, trying to catch myself on the *Welcome to Tranquility* sign, but I missed, my arm scraping down its metal edge.

My palms and knees hit the pathway with a jarring thud.

"Are you okay?" Beck asked, rushing over.

"Yes, I'm—"

I sat back, pulling at my broken flip-flop to examine my failed hair-tie hack. But a burning sensation lit from elbow to wrist. I turned my arm over to reveal not a cut but a gash. Blood welled and then dripped onto the rocky path.

Beck's eyes widened. He grabbed my wrist, gingerly turning my arm over to get a better look, then sucked air through his teeth.

"Shit!" Gabe said. "That's going to need stitches."

Beck's eyes cut to mine. "He's right. This looks bad."

"Is everything okay?" Sebastian was coming down the pathway toward us.

"She needs a doctor," Beck said. "Where's Nick?"

"Still in bed. I'll go wake him," he called with a sidestep toward their yurt.

"I'll go to the lobby. See if they have a first-aid kit and find out where the closest hospital is," Gabe said, pointing a thumb back towards the hut where the rest of the group had gone for breakfast.

I watched the blood roll down my arm and coat the rocks below. My stomach lurched.

"Can you stand?" Beck asked.

I tried to say something, but my jaw felt clumsy, my lips numb.

When I didn't answer, he wrapped one hand around my uninjured forearm and put the other on my back, guiding me to my feet. As carefully and slowly as he did, I still felt the color drain from my face.

Someone joined us on the pathway, but registering the form as Nick took me a while. My vision had narrowed, and I felt like I was looking at everything through a straw.

"Hey," Nick said, "what happened?"

Beck turned to meet him, filling Nick in about my spill, but I hardly heard a thing over the ringing in my ears. The humid morning air turned unbearably hot. Thirst blazed down my throat and across my chest, making me feel nauseous. Bloodless.

I knew this feeling. And if I'd been thinking clearly, I would have sat back down on the rocks or clued Beck in.

But I wasn't thinking clearly. Oxygen wasn't venting properly anywhere in my body, the least of which to my brain. Because I just knew I needed to get inside to A/C and water and a chair. And I needed to get there now. I took a step backward toward the hut.

Beck's explanation to Nick halted. He looked at me, his brows furrowed. I could barely see him—my vision had narrowed so much.

"Emily?"

My heel edged another step back, and I plunged into darkness.

I could hear the voices long before I could see anything. At first, it was muffled and incoherent, and there were noises of scrambling before my hearing sharpened.

"Help!" *Beck's voice*, I thought. It sounded so far away. *What's wrong with him? I should help him.* Everything felt numb, fuzzy, disconnected.

"Lay her down flat." Nick's voice.

Then some movement from a soft surface to a hard one. "She didn't hit her head, did she?"

Someone grabbed my arm. Checking my pulse, I realized, the thought floating by like a distant cloud.

"No."

"Is she diabetic? On any new medications?"

"No, and I don't think so." Beck's voice. Then a pause. "She has a history of fainting, though."

He said it like a final clue had clicked into place—as though he'd been staring at a small picture but had finally backed up enough to see the complete photo montage. And he wasn't enjoying the view.

"It's always the redheads," Nick muttered.

"Nick, her lips are gray." Beck sounded unhinged.

"Jake!" Nick ordered. "Go tell the staff to call 9-1-1. Or whatever the hell it is in this country."

That did it.

"No! I'm fine!" My voice surprised me. It was detached like everyone else's. "I'm a fainter," I slurred, wading through the confusion. "It's what I do."

Someone close let out a breath. I tried to sit up, but hands on my shoulders kept me pinned.

"Don't try to move," Beck said softly.

My vision returned. Everything was too bright at first. I blinked until my eyes adjusted, and I found Beck overhead, eyes red-rimmed and jaw clenched. He looked over his shoulder.

"Jake, why the hell are you still standing there? She needs an ambulance!" I'd never seen Beck so rattled.

"Can you tell me your name?" Nick asked.

I sighed. This was going to be a whole thing. Again. "Hailey Emily Lane."

I leveled a look at Beck because only he could appreciate how well I was actually doing if I remembered to give my full *fake* name after passing out.

Beck sat back on his haunches with a sigh of relief, but he still looked on edge—like I had right after Wesley's call—he was a whisper from tipping over into a pit of despair.

That's when I noticed his knees—scraped and bloodied.

I lolled my head to get a better look. "What happened to you?"

Beck's eyes flicked to his knees. Then he gave me an incredulous look. "You fainted, you're dripping blood all over the pathway, and you are asking me about some scrapes?"

I waited.

"I saw you falling, so I slid. To catch you."

My heart throbbed.

"I shouldn't have even stepped away from you though." He raked a hand down his face. "I knew you had issues with fainting in the past, and I had you stand right after you lost blood."

"Beck." I reached for his hand. "It's okay. I'm okay."

"What's going on?" Victoria demanded. The others hovered at the hut's entrance.

I groaned. If only the growing audience would go back to their eggs and leave me to die of embarrassment in peace.

Gabe maneuvered around the group, a first-aid kit in hand. "What did I miss?"

"She passed out," Beck said miserably.

Kat gasped. "Oh my God!"

"I'm fine," I tried to sit up again, but Beck held me firm. "Really. Fainting is like a factory reset. Or a good vomit. You feel better after." No one found that funny.

"Well, unfortunately," Nick said, cracking open the first-aid kit, "excessive bleeding is *not* like a good vomit. We need to get you to the hospital to patch up this arm."

"Do we really trust the hospitals here?" I had this strange slap-happy, almost loopy feeling. "What if they use a fishing hook to sew me up, and for the pain, they give me a leather strap to bite down on."

Beck's eyes widened at the horror my imagination had jumped to, but then he shook his head—trying hard not to laugh. "We are in Costa Rica. Not an episode of *Lost*."

"You are going to the hospital," Nick said in a no-nonsense tone. "End of discussion."

As the paramedics wheeled my stretcher to the waiting ambulance, the group huddled nearby to wave us off.

"We'll see you back at the hotel," Victoria said with a reassuring smile. "Don't worry about your luggage. We'll bring it in the van."

I was glad someone thought of all the details because I'd been so whiplashed from the morning's golf cart ride through hell that I hadn't given our things a single thought.

"Wait," Nick said. "Do you at least have your passport?"

Right, I'd probably need identification at the hospital. "Shit. No." Because all but three of my brain cells had died in the wildfire that blazed through my life after Wesley's call. The last few cells were still putting out flames.

I looked at Beck. "It's in the small zipper of my carry-on."

He nodded, but Madison stopped him. "No. You stay with her. I'll get it."

Awfully sweet of you, considering your post was the catalyst for this whole mess. But then I chided myself. That wasn't fair. *We'd started this mess.*

I couldn't even regret the choice to come to Costa Rica, not after all the memories I'd made with Beck. Memories that seemed to be hardening into pillars in my mind—holding up what I hoped to be a future with him.

Madison came jogging back as the paramedics loaded me into the ambulance. "Here is her passport," she said, handing it over to Beck. Then she trained her eyes right on me. "Rae is such a beautiful middle name. Emily Rae," she said, testing it. "It has a much better ring to it than Hailey Emily. Doesn't it?"

She backed away, and the last thing I saw before the EMT closed the door was Madison's predatory smirk.

She'd opened my passport. She'd seen my name.

She knew I wasn't Hailey.

And for the second time in the span of thirty minutes, it felt like my world had bottomed out.

Chapter 21

As it turned out, I wasn't given a leather strap to bite into for the pain but a shot of lidocaine. My hospital visit in Costa Rica seemed analogous to what I'd expect in the med center.

When the doctor came in, she'd had me recline back and propped my injured arm on a pillow. I couldn't see much with the angle of my injury being on the outside of my arm. And that was fine. I didn't want to watch my arm being threaded back together like some unfortunate, too-loved stuffed bear ripped at the seam.

Beck dragged his chair as close to the bed as it could get, lacing my fingers through his. And that's where he stayed for the entire process. When the doctor plucked a pair of forceps off the tray, I eyed them warily, praying the lidocaine worked through the length of the procedure.

Beck pulled my attention away. "I have a confession," he said, his deep voice matching the somber ER. Something in my stomach dropped at the tone. My mind immediately catapulted to, *He's getting back with Reagan.* "Do you remember that day in the pool? When we accidentally switched headphones?"

I laughed both at the memory and from relief that this conversation wasn't tilting toward his ex. "You said my music was the neutered version of yours."

With light fingers, he straightened my hospital bracelet. "That night, I went home and made an acoustic playlist."

"You're lying," I said, stunned.

Beck pulled out his phone, fished around on Amazon Music, and then pulled up a playlist titled *Lane.*

If I'd been hooked up to one of those heart-rate machines, I would have flatlined. He hit shuffle, and an acoustic cover of *Iris* by the Goo Goo Dolls started playing. My eyes closed at the intro. So much love and hurt in a few measures of guitar strumming.

"I love this song," I whispered.

"Me too," he whispered back, brushing his lips over my knuckles.

Eyes still shut, I let myself get lost in the music and the assurance of Beck's presence as he rubbed his thumb over mine. And for a second, I could almost believe it was only the two of us, not in a hospital or anywhere in particular. Just together.

I knew what he was doing. He was trying to distract me from the doctor's work—from the stitches and the needle and the blood. He didn't need to do that. I couldn't feel much from the lidocaine, and I was flat on my back—so the threat of fainting had returned to minimal. But I found myself wanting to be distracted by him.

The song ended, and I opened my eyes to peer at the wonder that was Beckett Atteridge. "I can't believe you made a playlist because of me," I said, the pressure behind my eyes warning of a possible break in the damn holding back my tears.

"I like listening to it when I'm stressed."

I pictured the average workday Beck. He knocked out support tickets with ease. He rolled with the punches and changes that corporate wanted immediately implemented. Hell, he even had enough time to engage in watercooler chats with teammates, and he did it all with charm and class and a smile. Before this trip, I never would have believed that Beckett—calm, cool, and collected—Atteridge needed music to help him unwind.

But I believed it now. Especially after how close he'd come to unraveling when I fainted. Then there was what he told me about Poppy.

"I like learning things about you," I admitted.

Beck gave a half-smile, then sat up straighter, getting a better look at my arm. I assumed he was gauging how much time until the doctor finished suturing. When I tried to look too, his hand splayed over my ribs, halting the movement. He didn't want me to see—probably afraid I'd pass out again.

"She's almost done," he said in a hushed tone, then gave a supportive squeeze. "You're doing great." He sat back in his seat, resuming the caressing of my hand with his thumb. "What else do you want to know?"

I bit my lip, unsure if I wanted to ask him in case the request landed painfully. "Tell me more about Poppy."

Beck's eyes tightened. At first, I thought he'd deny me, but then he shifted in the chair. "How to explain Poppy," he said pensively.

He looked past me, and I could see the memories flashing behind his eyes.

"She was daring. The kind of kid who would slide down the banister in nothing but her underwear during a dinner party. Or would shoot spitballs at paintings in restaurants when the adults were too busy talking." A smile broke out across his face. "But she was also the biggest tattletale when it came to the little things—one of us taking her bouncy ball or calling her stupid or not giving her a turn on the Wii. She would never rat us out on the things she should have, though—the things that could get us in serious trouble.

"For instance, one time, she and Victoria were pretending to be Ninja Turtles when Victoria pushed Poppy over a planter's box in the garden. Poppy landed wrong and broke her wrist. I watched the whole thing. When the nanny ran over and questioned Victoria about what she did, Poppy insisted she tripped. Swore she did.

"Another time, I did batting practice in the house. I got carried away, and the baseball shattered my dad's favorite art piece—a scalloped glass bowl by David Chihuly."

I winced.

"Yeah. My father saw the pieces in the hall and looked a second away from having an aneurysm. He would have skinned me alive if Poppy hadn't shuffled forward, ball in hand, tears in eyes." He gave a short laugh. "The anger rolled right off him like water off a duck. He gathered her in his lap and gave her a stern, 'Poppy, you could have been hurt. We've talked about this. You can't play ball in the house.'" Beck laughed, shaking his head, and I laughed with him. "My dad acted differently with Poppy, more tender than with Victoria or me. And I don't say that for sympathy or in a woe is me, my dad doesn't love me, kind of way." He shrugged. "Poppy coming into the world changed him. And her leaving did too."

Something twinged in my chest.

"Sorry," he muttered. "Off topic."

I squeezed his hand. I'd take what I could get. "Anyway. You would have loved Poppy."

"I think I already do," I said quietly.

But I was falling for her brother too, and that really scared me. Beck's words of encouragement, the way he held my hand and tried to keep my mind off things—it was all simple. So simple. But it meant everything.

I could see a future with him at my side on my worst days: when I'd be sick or in pain or scared or a sobbing mess. I wanted it—him being there. And I found myself wanting to be there on his worst days, too.

When it all boiled down, wasn't that what everyone needed? An anchor when life tore at you with hurricane-force winds, ripping the shingles off your sanity and security. Someone to say, *I'm not letting you go. No matter how ugly things get.*

I worried about how quickly I'd let my guard down on this trip. I'd unlocked the treasure box holding my heart and left it wide open for Beck to take.

This is risky, my brain tried to say.

But my heart was too busy to listen to trivial things like logic while in Beck's hands.

The doctor finished the twenty-eight stitches, bandaged me up, and gave me a fresh tetanus booster for good measure. Then we got to go home—home being the resort.

In a weird way, the hospital stay had served as a sort of escape from what awaited us: Wesley's call. Madison's new intel. It all piled back on during the cab ride to the resort. Beck also seemed to be wading through it, staring out the window for most of the drive, absently chewing his bottom lip.

"Beck, what are we going to do?" I finally asked.

"About Wesley?"

"About Wesley. About Madison. All of it."

He sighed. "We don't know if Madison is a problem yet."

"She's going to give Victoria my real name."

"You don't know that."

I gaped at him but then clamped my mouth shut. Because he didn't know why Madison would love to watch me die in an avalanche of my lies—that it was in the name of friendship. Her bestie wanted Beck back, and she'd do anything to tip the scales. I swallowed, not able to relinquish that bit of information to Beck. Not willing to risk losing him to Reagan.

"Call it a hunch," I said.

"And if she does, we'll explain everything to Victoria. It's a weird position, but you've proved your worth as a calligrapher. I don't know why she'd be mad."

Because people don't like being lied to, I thought. But I didn't press the issue because Beck had moved on.

"And I'm not going to let you lose your job. I'll explain to Wesley. Tell him I pressured you to come if I have to."

"No, Beck."

"It's not that far from the truth. I hassled you about it enough."

"You didn't hassle me. You were just . . . persistent."

"This is all my fault." He groaned, his head falling into a waiting hand. "I never would have, in a million years, pictured the trip going like this."

Going like this? As in him kissing me in a rainforest, sharing all our deepest secrets, and him taking me during a thunderstorm, scraping the skin off his knees to catch me, holding my hand in a hospital?

Sure, there was the *We might lose our jobs* part, the *Cutting myself open and passing out* part, and the *I might lose my chance at becoming a calligrapher before I've really had a chance to begin* part.

But knowing what I knew now, I still would have come with him. "I don't regret this trip," I said, looking right at him so he could read the truth in my face for himself.

His hand slid away from his eyes. "You don't?"

I shook my head.

He reached across the middle seat to grab my hand. Then his lips pulled into the slightest smirk. "Maybe you did hit your head when you fainted."

"Maybe so," I agreed with a quiet laugh. It would be nice to have something to pin all these emotions on.

"Emily, listen. I know you are worried about losing your job and Madison ruining things with Victoria, but you are going to be fine because I am going to take care of you." He caught my eye. "Okay?"

At that moment, without a doubt, I knew I could lean fully onto him, and he would hold me up. Just like I knew the sky was blue and Houston traffic was terrible. It was a fact: Beck wouldn't let me down.

I trusted him.

"Okay," I said, then rested my head back against the seat, not entertaining a single concern, at least not until we got back to the hotel.

We approached the elevators to our suite just behind Victoria, Reagan, Kat, and Madison. They'd donned spa robes, and each of them had their hair wrapped in towels. I made a mental note to check out all the resort amenities when I got back to our suite. I might be out of commission for more beach days or jungle hikes, but I could still enjoy a facial or a long sit in a salt room. Hell, I could make the salt room even saltier with the tears over my impending job loss.

I was close enough to ask them about their spa day when Madison said, "I mean, it's creepy. Why would she pretend to be someone else?

We should call the police and have them check her basement for the calligrapher you hired."

Kat snorted. "I can't believe I was going to hire her for my wedding."

Beck's hand landed on my shoulder. "Come on," he whispered into the shell of my ear. "We'll get the next one." He wanted to shield me from their conversation. I let him pull me back a few steps from the elevator.

Then Victoria spoke in that authoritative voice of hers. "We don't know anything," she said, sounding a lot like Beck. "Except that she's been going by a different first name. For all we know, she simply doesn't like the name Emily and wanted to try something new. Or she's in the goddamn witness protection program. There are a thousand possibilities. So, let's not jump to conclusions."

I could come back from this. I could pluck one of her suggestions and run with it. There could be a plausible explanation. Beck and I could back away now, regroup in our room, and come up with a lie free of holes.

Until whatever story we webbed together got punctured by a slip-up or a discovery, and then we'd have to patch it up with another lie and another. When I'd started lying about who I was, I had planned on it being finite. It had an end date: June 24th, Victoria's wedding. But now, I wanted a future with Beck, and I didn't want to stare his sister, someone he was very close to, in the face and be dishonest.

Even if Beck wasn't involved, I'd gotten to know Victoria better from our sailing trip—this glass-ceiling-shattering badass who also loved a good life hack and *New Girl* and Camilla Cabello and drinking whiskey straight—and I wanted her to know me better too. Me. The real me.

The elevator dinged open, and I stepped from Beck's grasp before I knew what I was doing. "Victoria!"

The group whirled around, and I couldn't help but notice the glee in Madison's eyes. She looked about ten seconds away from pulling a bag of popcorn from under her robe—like she'd been waiting for this live dumpster fire all day.

"I'm sorry," I said. "I'm sorry for being dishonest with you."

Victoria padded forward in her fuzzy spa sandals, waiting.

I licked my bottom lip. "Hailey is my sister. She got a wild hair to move to Florida, and she needed someone to finish your wedding." Victoria's mouth fell open, so I started talking faster, trying to finish my story before her mind could conjure up some twisted version of the truth or Madison's words could fill the void. "She'd already done most of the work. And I've been practicing calligraphy longer than her anyway. For years longer, actually. She should have just told you the truth. *I* should have just told you the truth," I amended. "But you are an Atteridge—a huge client for my sister. And she didn't want to lose your business or the connections a big event like yours could provide. And we were afraid you'd be angry if she told you her sister was stepping in."

Victoria just blinked at me for an agonizingly long moment, her bottom lip detaching from the top as she processed my admission. Then her gaze shifted to Beck. "You knew about this?"

Beck stepped forward. "Vic—"

She put out a hand. "How long did you know, Beck? The whole time?"

A muscle in Beck's jaw jumped. Then he straightened. "Not the whole time. But long enough."

You would have thought he'd slapped her from the look on her face. "We tell each other everything, Beck." Victoria, Queen of Atteridge Hotels and Resorts, became teary-eyed. "Don't we?"

The elevator arrived again, depositing an elderly couple who looked ready for the pool.

"Come on, Victoria." Madison wrapped her fingers around Victoria's arm. "You don't need this drama so close to your wedding day."

What a statement, especially from the woman who'd probably been adding gasoline to the drama all afternoon.

"Vic, please. Let's talk about this," Beck said as they entered the elevator.

But the doors closed, separating us from them.

I squeezed Beck's hand, trying to comfort him, but found it difficult when I was hurting so much myself.

Two parts of my life met in the middle like those elevator doors: my future in calligraphy and my relationship with Victoria. Only these doors would never open again. A welder had taken my lies and used them to seal it shut in one steady stroke.

There was no coming back from this.

That night, when my tears had dried, I laid down with Beck in our suite's bed and replayed it all. Hailey and I should have come clean at the beginning with Victoria. Told her the truth and put the ball in her court. I could have shown her my work and convinced her. Maybe my sister could have offered a steep discount. Something. Anything except lying.

While my mind raced, Beck stroked my hair with light, relaxing fingers. Through it all, he stayed with me. And I wanted to keep him there, but I realized if lying had gotten me into this mess with Wesley and Victoria, I needed to come clean with Beck before I lost him too, although I might anyway.

The low lighting of the room reflected lazily in his soft brown eyes. I wanted his eyes to be mine to look into. I wanted my hair to be his to comb his fingers through. I wanted to have his hand to hold for all life threw at me. I wanted his laugh and his voice and his smile to forever be in my life.

But it wasn't up to me.

"Reagan wants you back," I whispered.

Beck's hand stilled in my hair. "What?"

"Reagan wants you back." I swallowed. "She's been shooting heart eyes at you and staring daggers at me the entire trip. And that night when we went dancing, I overheard her in the bathroom with Madison. She knows she made a mistake." My heart slammed against my chest with a *shut up, shut up, shut up* rhythm. "She loves you," I managed, even though it broke my heart to say it because I knew it might change things between us.

Beck pulled his hand back from my hair, resting it on his chest. "Why are you telling me this?" He looked hurt.

"Because this was your plan." My sternum felt like it had shrapnel in it. "To get her back."

"Was it?" Beck asked so softly I almost couldn't hear him.

"You wanted to make her jealous to win her over." Hot tears made pathways to the pillow.

Beck touched my cheek, wiping the tears with his thumb. "And you honestly still think that?" he asked, his eyes drilling into mine.

"I don't know," I said wetly. "I just—being dishonest hasn't worked out for me. I thought I should try being truthful to someone."

Beck leaned in to kiss a spot on the bridge of my nose, wiping more tears after he did. "You should rest, Emily. You've had one hell of a day."

He pulled me into him, my knee over his hip, my bandaged arm safely on his chest. We stayed there in the dark, neither of us able to sleep, it seemed.

And the glass-half-full part of me thought anything could be keeping Beck awake. His day had been just as taxing as mine. But most of me wasn't optimistic. And I all but knew he was thinking about Reagan.

Chapter 22

"You should go with them," I said to Beck, unraveling the bandage on my arm.

The group finally planned on hiking today. This was Beck's chance to hang out with his friends without feeling like a betrayal to Poppy. And this was his only chance. With the wedding only two days from now, it would be time for the bridal party to get into gear.

Even if my relationship with Victoria hadn't come to an end—with the truth blazing down like a comet making inevitable and devastating contact—I still couldn't have gone out with my arm. I couldn't risk another fall or, worse, an infection. I needed both arms for crawling on my hands and knees to Wesley, begging him to let me keep my job.

Beck, who'd been brushing his teeth, paused, looking at my reflection in the mirror. "I told you already," he said around his toothbrush before spitting and rinsing. "I'm staying with you."

"I know, but these are your friends. I don't want you to feel obligated to hang out with me. I'll be fine here."

Beck took the bandage from me. I'd made a mess of loops around my arm. His slow, steady fingers made for a cleaner roll of the bandage.

"I'm not staying with you because I feel obligated. I'm staying with you because you're the person I want to spend the day with."

A flutter rose in my stomach. I believed him. I believed he wanted to spend the day with me. I just didn't understand why he would choose to be stuck in a resort room with me over a hike in the jungle with his friends.

He squeezed antibiotic cream onto my cut and then reapplied a fresh bandage, all with a touch that suggested if he breathed wrong, he would hurt me. "But," he continued, "I want to try catching Victoria at breakfast. Talk to her about everything."

"You really think that's a good idea?"

"Trust me. This is her. She just needed time to be mad." Beck kissed the bridge of my nose. "I'm going to fix this."

With him gone, I plopped back on the bed and stared at the ceiling, pondering the choices that had led me to this tangled predicament until my phone's bouncy ringtone assaulted the quiet. My heart tried to find an exit from my chest, as I fumbled for it, sure Wesley was calling to let me know they'd be terminating me. Effective immediately.

I sighed when Hailey's name showed on the illuminated screen. *Good. I could use someone to talk to.*

"Hailey," I answered, a second away from saying, *You aren't going to believe the shit show I've been through,* when a choking sob cut through the other line. I sat up straight.

"*Hailey?* What's wrong?"

"We—we," she choked on her own words, another sob breaking through.

"Slow down. What's going on?" I scrambled off the bed, coming to a stand, to do what, I didn't know. I was a three-hour flight away, but I couldn't just sit there.

"We broke up!" she finally got through and then crumpled into sobs again.

"You and Florida Man?" I asked dumbly, still trying to make sense of what she was saying—to make sure I'd heard her correctly.

"Yes!" she said, exasperated.

"Oh, no! I'm so sorry." I started to ask what happened, but then I heard a blinker. "Are you driving?"

"This subdivision is a *fucking* labyrinth!"

I needed her to be okay. I needed her to be safe. "Pull over! Right now!" More sobbing, but the whooshing car noise quieted.

"You were right all along. I didn't know Braxton, and moving with him to Florida was the stupidest thing I have ever done. And I know that's saying a lot." She dissolved into tears again.

"Breathe. Okay?" And she did, gulping oxygen and then hiccupping it out.

After a long time, she finally seemed to settle.

"What happened?" I asked gently.

"Nothing." She blew her nose. "That's the problem. It was nothing major. Just all the things I would have noticed if I'd dated him before deciding to live with him. Like the fact that he steers every conversation back toward him. Or how he never screws the cap back on the toothpaste. It's the way he says *irregardless* as though he's so intelligent, but it's not a fucking word, Emily." She huffed out a breath. "I really can't. He may as well sell whale organs on the black market—like you warned me about—because I can't stand another minute with him."

"Hailey, I know you are sad. But breaking up is the right move if you already feel this way about him."

"I know," she said shakily. "But I just had all my shit delivered from my apartment and canceled my lease. I don't even know where I'm going to live now. It's going to be the biggest clusterfuck to get my life back on track after this. Not to mention, as much as he annoys me, we had some good sex—great sex. Like, toe-curling sex." And then she started crying again. "And I know that sounds shallow, but I thought it said a lot about our chemistry, you know?"

I chose to ignore the sex part. "Listen to me. We are going to take this one step at a time. You have a place to live—with me—until we get things situated. Let's start there. Okay?"

Hailey let out a shaky breath. "Okay."

I stayed with her on the phone until she felt well enough to drive. She agreed to head straight to my apartment and stay there until I got back from Costa Rica. I hadn't told her I planned to come home early anyway—there was no use making her feel worse with the details. And there was no way I could unload my burdens onto her when the ground beneath her feet had turned into sinking sand. Besides, I was only making things awkward. If I left, maybe Beck could find a way to have a good time with his friends—enjoy his sister's big day. The lack of my presence would uncomplicate things.

I headed out to find Beck and to tell him what had happened and my decision to leave. I had reached the bottom of the elevator bank when the doors opened on Beck and Reagan. She had her hands in his hair, her mouth on his mouth. Kissing Beck, *my* Beck. His back was toward me. I couldn't see his expression, but I could see the way Reagan was relaxed into him. Like after the longest day, she'd finally come home.

Their kiss may as well have been an icicle to the chest—cold and piercing. It took my breath away. I covered my mouth with one hand and pressed the button for our floor with the other. Then, I repeatedly mashed the button to close the door.

As the doors obeyed, I had to grip the railing to keep from sinking to the floor. I knew this would happen. I knew it. And I still let him take me to Costa Rica. Insisted he dance with me. Told him to kiss me. Had sex with him during a rainstorm.

I still let myself fall in love with him.

And then I'd damned any chance we had by telling him how Reagan really felt.

I hadn't seen it for what it was before, but by trying to be Hailey, I'd tripped some sort of cosmic breaker. Self-sabotaged my life with a careless underthrow.

I'd fabricated this lie in my head that I wasn't engaging in risky behavior by taking the calligraphy job, pretending to be someone else, coming to Costa Rica with Beck. But that's the trouble with love and ink. They leave a stain.

I always thought the universe celebrated the bold and brave Haileys of the world, but look at her now. She'd gambled everything to move in with some guy—leaped without looking in the name of love. There was nothing more romantic than that. But only if it works out, right? Now, she could only sweep up the pieces of her broken heart—her broken life.

And I'd have to do the same.

When Beck entered the suite, I noticed the quiet, guilty shuffle of his feet. But I didn't look up. Busying my hands and my attention with packing.

"Emily, I need to tell you—" he seemed to take in my open suitcase and how I had unceremoniously tossed clothes inside as if it normally wouldn't pop a vessel in my eye to not have everything carefully folded and in its rightful place. "What are you doing?"

"I have to go," I said, praying he couldn't see the tears. "Hailey needs me. She and her boyfriend broke up."

"Oh." A long pause as he processed. "You have to go now?"

"Yup," I let the last consonant pop.

The air in the room soured. I hated being so short with him, but I hated being betrayed by him even more.

He seemed to read the shift because his next question came quieter, more cautiously. "Do you need me to come with you?"

"Your sister's wedding is two days away," I reminded him. "I'll be fine."

"I can at least ride with you to the airport."

"No, Beck." I dropped my toiletry bag into the suitcase and looked at him. "This is for the best. We knew my time being Hailey had an expiration date. And honestly, it ended when Madison found my passport yesterday." I zipped my suitcase and hauled it off the bed. "Now we can go back to normal."

I made for the door, hoping for a quick getaway. I needed to put space between us so I could dissolve into tears in peace.

"Go back to normal?" He put out a hand to stop me. "Emily, where is this coming from?"

I considered telling him that it came from Reagan's plump lips being planted on his, but I'd confronted a cheater before. With Chad, I'd literally caught him with his pants down, and he'd tried to tell me, "It's not what it looks like."

Besides, was Beck really cheating? Were we even something that could be cheated on? We hadn't staked a claim. Hadn't put a label on us. So, I approached it from a different angle.

"Look at the damage we've caused! We might lose our jobs."

"You act as though that would be the end of the world. You hate that fucking job. It's killing you." He put his hands on my shoulders. "I know you're scared. And I get it, I do. But you should give calligraphy a chance. A real chance."

"I already have!" I backed out of his reach. He wasn't hearing me, wasn't understanding our situation at all. "And what a great start I've gotten off to. I've really instilled a sense of integrity—proven I'm someone my clients can trust." I laughed bitterly. "Do you think Kat and Sebastian will hire me now?"

"Forget them. You are smart and talented, and you come alive when doing calligraphy. Don't give that up. Hell, start a new company under a fresh name."

"I think this is confusing because that seems like a move I would make, but that's only because I've been trying on Hailey's life, which has gotten me nowhere. Actually, worse than nowhere." I ran a hand through my hair, knowing I should think, breathe. The conversation was a runaway train at this point, completely getting away from me. "Starting a company in lieu of a stable career isn't me. And neither is going on vacation with my coworker—fake dating him—so he can get back with his ex."

Beck flinched. "Is that what you think I'm doing?" He looked at the ground with a pained expression as he seemed to search for the words. "I'm sorry if I haven't made it abundantly clear." His eyes met mine, sharper than before, and I watched his Adam's apple dip past that freckle. "Emily, I'm in love with you."

The words struck. Pierced. Hammered. Shredded my heart. Because I wanted to believe them. I wanted to believe them so badly, but they weren't true. We'd been pretending, and it was time to wake up and face the real world.

"You didn't fall in love with me, Beck." Tears fell before I could even finish. "I was trying to be more like Hailey." My breath shuddered. "Who you fell in love with isn't me."

"No." He shook his head.

"No?"

"No," he said stubbornly. "I don't buy that. You are acting as though you have turned into a completely different person on this trip than who you are at the office—the person I first met. And that's not true."

"We shouldn't have ever done this. We complicated everything," I said, going with a different tactic. "We fucked it all up," I choked.

He stepped forward, and I knew if my head hit his chest, it would be over. My resolve would melt. I'd crumble into his arms, and he'd tell me how much he loved me, and I'd admit my feelings for him.

I wanted it so badly. The comfort of his scent. The wholeness I felt in his embrace. He'd kiss the bridge of my nose, and all the pain would evaporate—he'd be Novocain to the throbbing wound in my chest.

The tug of my longing was nearly a physical force, but I gritted my teeth and stood my ground.

Because I knew what the future held. Not today. Maybe not for a few weeks, but eventually, he'd tell me about his decision to get back with Reagan, and he'd shatter my heart beyond repair.

I needed to keep him away from me, and the first thing that came to mind was to strike first.

"Look, this was fun while it lasted." I sniffed, working to keep my face and voice even. "But I don't feel like myself when I'm with you."

I watched it hit him like a physical blow. Watched it knock the air out of him as I parroted Reagan's words. Guilt squeezed me like a vice.

I stepped past him, and he let me go—let me walk right out of his life.

Chapter 23

I learned two things while at the airport in San Jose. One, there was a storm in Houston delaying flights back home. And two, the changes Wesley had promised Frank he'd complete himself, well, let's just say he'd reverted to his old ways of delegating. My inbox was approaching maximum density at an alarming rate.

The realization left me with some choices. I could stay at the airport to see if a flight became available while shuffling around in search of better Wi-Fi to best help Wesley. Therefore, hopefully, proving my worth to the company. Or I could post up at a nearby motel with reviews that suggested it might have a pest problem but not a Wi-Fi one. The flight I had already booked left in three days anyway, which should give the storm enough time to get the heck out of town before my original flight.

I chose the latter, mostly because I couldn't stop crying and was tired of the looks I'd been getting while sobbing over my open spreadsheet.

That's how I spent most of my Thursday and Friday: plopped in the middle of a sad motel mattress. A laptop on my thighs surrounded by tissues, some chocolate I'd picked up at the airport, and my broken sandal. I'd already pulled the *chancla* on three roaches' asses. But one had scurried under the dresser before I could get him.

I tried my best to work. I really did. I needed to get into good graces with Wesley. Working through the tail-end of my vacation showed initiative and remorse. By some cosmic mercy and punishment, the long and meticulous reconfigurations took almost zero percent of my brain power. I could complete them with my limited brain space, but it also meant I wasn't distracted. Consequently, I thought about Beck the entire time.

My mind ping-ponged between him being so tender and so sweet this entire vacation to him ripping my heart straight from my chest with that kiss from Reagan. Then, the warning signs flashed behind my eyes.

I knew he wanted to make Reagan jealous.

I knew this relationship was fake.

I all but handed my heart to him on a silver platter with a polite bow and an *Enjoy your meal, sir.*

I was glad only the cockroaches bore witness to the pitiful show. After another stint of crying—this one lasting a few hours—I collapsed on the mattress and stared at the ceiling, hiccupping. A good cry takes everything out of you, carves out your insides like a jack-o-lantern, and leaves you numb. And numb is how I felt when my phone vibrated with a text. I reached for it without sitting up, patting several scrunched tissues before making contact.

I expected Wesley or my sister or, hell, even Beck. But it was Amanda's name on my screen.

"What does the wedding planner want?" I groaned.

Maybe Victoria had told her about my dishonesty. I imagined I was about to get my ass reamed out via text message. Instead, it said:

Where are you?

That was none of her business. I'd never agreed to come to the wedding as a calligrapher. I'd agreed to go as Beck's date. Beck's fake date. I tossed my phone on a nearby pillow and covered my face with the crook of my elbow, preparing for another crying marathon.

Because in another life I would be going to Victoria's wedding as Beck's date. We'd get to dance to our first slow song together and laugh at Koontz making a fool of himself, and I'd drink too many pina coladas, and I'd get Gabe to tell me embarrassing stories about teenage Beck. Then, Beck and I would stumble into our suite, a tangle of limbs.

In another life, I kept him.

In another life, he was mine.

Another text came in while I ugly cried. I ignored it, rolling onto my side, trying to hold myself together with my arms because it felt like my heart was going to leak out through a gap between my ribs.

My phone buzzed again.

"God! What do you want?" I yelled at my phone.

Amanda had sent both texts.

We have a situation.

The other text was a picture of the five-foot mirror on which I'd made the seating chart. It had a crack from top to bottom.

"Oh, fuck," I whispered into my hand. That piece had taken me hours.

She sent me another text.

Someone ignored the fragile labels on the box.

Yeah. No shit. My thumbs hovered over the phone, ready to text something akin to, *Sorry to hear that. Best of luck!* Because I had no interest in going back to that resort. I could all but picture running into Beck and Reagan—hand in hand. Or worse, making out in that hot tub like Kat and Jake had that first night at the resort.

But then I thought about Victoria. After all the deception, I owed it to her to make this right.

Me: I'm going to need masking tape, a level, an X-Acto knife, paper towels, Windex and white acrylic markers-chisel tip!

By the time I'd changed into something other than my panties and an oversized T-shirt, I had another text.

What's your location? I'll send a driver.

Chapter 24

Victoria set me up in a conference room in the resort and led me around a maze of boxes filled with wedding items: the hexagonal name plates I'd finished, glass bottles for the guests to cork their sand for a keepsake, mystery macrame pieces, and lanterns.

The new mirror was as large but not nearly as fancy as its predecessor. A rough wood bordered this mirror instead of the former gilded frame. It was probably the best they could do with the wedding so close. I wondered who'd been in charge of finding it at the last minute and imagined poor Amanda sobbing in a rental, driving down dirt streets in Costa Rica until she found a mirror large enough to fit the names of one hundred and forty-eight guests.

The original mirror lay sideways, propped against the wall. It looked as though someone had drawn a bolt of lightning down the length of it, splitting the canvas in two. My heart could relate.

"Here are your supplies," Victoria said, indicating a plastic bag on the table. She looked back at me, but I dodged her eyes, knowing mine were puffy from all the crying I'd done. "Thank you for doing this. I want you to know I'm not mad about what happened. When I talked to Beck yesterday, I told him I wasn't mad about that, not really." She smoothed a hand down her skirt and then lifted her chin. "I wish the two of you had been upfront, but what really upset me was Beck keeping secrets. We don't normally do that."

That problem had been a main source of stress only a day ago. Knowing Victoria didn't harbor resentment against my sister or me, something internal should have lifted, but my heartbreak over Beck felt too heavy.

"It's a relief you're not mad at me," I said.

"But that's not why you're upset," Victoria guessed.

I picked through the plastic bag, starting to unbox my acrylic markers. "You're getting married tomorrow. I'm not dumping my issues on you."

"Yes." She squared her shoulders. "I am getting married tomorrow. And I'm not going to sleep tonight if I'm worried about my little brother."

My ears perked up at that. What did he have to be upset about?

"Why don't you ask him?"

I'd had Amanda print the document I'd made months ago with the sizing of the letters for the mirror. I taped it up, desperate to look anywhere besides Victoria's face. She was the last person I wanted to have this conversation with.

"I've tried. He won't answer my texts. He hasn't been with the group. Every time someone goes to check on him, he's not in his room."

I shook a marker a little too aggressively. "Have you checked Reagan's room?" As soon as the words left my mouth, I regretted them.

"What?" she asked.

"Never mind. I shouldn't have said anything."

"Why would he be with Reagan?"

I tested the marker on a nearby scrap of paper, capped it, and then made myself busy unwrapping the plastic off the paper towels. I was done with this conversation.

Victoria leaned back against the conference table. "Beck used to tell me everything, but after this week . . ." She shook her head. "It doesn't matter. Please, Emily. I'm asking *you*. What happened? After everything, I think you owe me that."

I sighed. Then faced her, arms crossed. "He is with Reagan because they are back together, Victoria."

Her eyebrows furrowed. "Why do you think that?"

Not the reaction I expected, but okay.

"Because—" *God.* Why did it feel like tattling? *Fuck it. She wants the truth. She can have it.* "Because I caught them kissing by the elevator bank." She straightened, ready to interject—to defend her brother, but I put up my hands. "It's fine, Victoria. We weren't even really dating. We were pretending so that things wouldn't be awkward between you and Reagan, mostly, but also because Beck wanted to make Reagan jealous. And it worked."

Victoria looked at me like I'd started speaking in a different language. "You were fake dating?" She shook her head. "No. I don't buy that. It didn't look fake." She scoffed. "I realize I don't know you very well, but Beck is not that good of an actor."

I shrugged. "If it makes you feel better, he fooled me too." I realized my bitter tone was unbecoming, but I couldn't help it. "I thought we might have . . . something." I sniffed, working to keep the emotions contained. "But—anyway. They are back together."

The tears overflowed. I wiped at them with my good forearm, then started cleaning the mirror, ready for her to leave already. Let me finish this project and then get the fuck out of this Atteridge resort—be done with Atteridges for the rest of my life.

"They aren't back together," she said quietly.

I stopped wiping the mirror. The certainty in her tone held my attention.

"I spent the entirety of yesterday with a sopping wet shoulder because Reagan was heartbroken over Beck's rejection." Victoria appeared at my periphery, and I met her gaze. "She kissed him in one last attempt to rekindle things. And he told her he wasn't interested. That he'd moved on and hoped she had too."

My head spun. I overlaid her words with what I'd seen, looking for a hole in the version she'd been given. But it could have been that the doors to my elevator opened right as Reagan pulled him in for a kiss. It could have been that the doors had closed before I saw him push her away. But then that would mean . . .

My shoulders slumped with the realization of what I'd done.

"I hurt him, Victoria." For no reason. "I—" I sucked in a breath, feeling moments away from crumbling to the floor. "He told me he loved me. But he doesn't," I said to myself as much as to her. "He loves who I've been pretending to be while trying to be more like Hailey."

Victoria shook her head. "What does that even mean? He was in on the whole thing. He knew you before you started using your sister's name, right?"

"Not well enough to know I'm not this person who lies about her identity or to her place of work to get time off or fake dates her coworker. I'm not the girl who demands a kiss in the rainforest or jumps off a cliff or quits her job to pursue what she's passionate about."

"But you are that girl. You did those things. Didn't you?"

Most of them, I mentally agreed.

"It doesn't sound like you were trying to be your sister," Victoria continued. "You were trying to be bold. Do you think you are incapable of being brave because you are careful by nature?"

Did I think that? That I was incapable of being courageous? Normally, I'd answer *no* without thinking twice about it. But based on my feelings and actions as of late, how could I argue otherwise? Somewhere along the way, I'd convinced myself I couldn't be brave.

"I don't know you well," Victoria said, stuffing her hands in her pockets. "But I do know my brother. He's infatuated. Just the way he watches you—like he's hanging on your every word. Like you hold all the answers."

I had to stop her because those words were salt in a wound. They were a tight grip on a sunburn. They made my breath catch. I didn't need any further damage. I hurt enough. I picked up the level and masking tape to make my guidelines.

"I'd better get busy if you want a seating chart at your wedding tomorrow."

"Fine. I'll leave you alone, but first, I need to know something."

I swallowed, dreading her question.

"Why doesn't Beck go to the beach?" Again, I wasn't expecting that.

I faced her. "You know why. Beck told me that you know."

"Please, just answer it."

I glanced at the box where the lantern I'd lettered poked out. "He feels like it's a betrayal to Poppy."

Victoria looked down. It was a long moment before she responded. "He doesn't tell people that, Emily." She pushed her hands through her thick curls. "Haven't you ever wondered why the group harasses him about coming with us? Do you honestly think they'd give him so much shit if they knew?" She took a step in my direction. "If you know, it means he trusts you. It means he does love you."

I looked at the floor. The picture swam in my tears.

He loved me.

And I broke his heart.

"I really need to get started," I said. *Please, go.* I mentally begged.

"You have my number if you need anything," she said quietly.

I waited until I heard the door click shut before sinking into the closest chair and letting the tears consume me.

Chapter 25

I hated that my canvas was a mirror. I tried not to meet the eyes of the girl in the reflection. She had a blotchy mask around her red-rimmed eyes, and the light had been snuffed from her irises.

I tried to go through my ritual as much as possible. I knotted my hair in its same low bun. I shuffled the same playlist I always used for calligraphy projects. I tried to trick my mind. *It's just me doing another project.*

But it was no use. Everything had changed.

The only good thing about this heartbreak was that I didn't have the bandwidth for nervous energy. What was the worst that could happen? Misspell a name? Omit a table? Not write perfect h's?

None of that mattered. Not when my heart had been torn like wet paper and then left in my chest to mold.

An hour into lettering, my phone rang. My fingers ached for a break, but I scowled when I saw Wesley's name on the screen. I answered, shouldering it so I could roll some relief into my wrists.

"Hello?" My swollen, waterlogged sinuses made it sound as though I'd caught a cold.

Thankfully, Wesley either couldn't hear the difference between my regular voice and my I've-been-ugly-crying-since-sunrise voice, or he simply didn't care. "Emily, I saw you were able to get some of the reconfigurations done that I asked for. Thank you for taking the initiative."

Okay, off to a good start. Maybe he'll let me keep my job. Or, at least, let me come on with the janitorial staff. I could scrub toilets if it meant I didn't have to sleep in my Prius.

"Sure," I said, "no problem."

"I also wanted to see if you could head a Zoom meeting with a team from corporate so we can start process modeling on the newest project."

"Today?" I asked. My mind felt less like a brain and more like two marbles, a paper clip, and half a stick of gum. I pulled back to look at the time. It was four thirty-three already. "When?"

"At five." He seemed unbothered by the idea of giving me twenty-seven minutes to prep for a meeting I didn't know about until now. I eyed the mirror. I'd only completed a quarter of it.

"Wait." My mind reeled. If he wanted me to lead a meeting for an upcoming project . . . "So, I'm not . . . fired?"

"God, no." He said it as though our last conversation wasn't about insubordination and how he'd practically have to sacrifice his firstborn to keep us on board.

"What about the forms? HR hasn't sent me anything over."

"Surely Beck has spoken to you."

The strained silence served as an answer.

"Uh-oh. Trouble in paradise?" He chuckled, then stopped abruptly. "Beck quit this morning. I tried to talk him out of it, but he wouldn't listen."

Wesley kept talking, but I couldn't make sense of the words he'd strung together. Beck had quit?

For me?

Or to get away from me?

Both scenarios had my heart cinching painfully again.

"Anyway," Wesley said, "this is good news for you. You'll be taking over his role as a senior analyst."

I waited for his words to conjure a spark of happiness, a mote of excitement. But nothing came. This future seemed colorless in comparison to what I'd had: practicing calligraphy and being with Beck. This was the keto version of the dessert I really wanted.

I couldn't go back. Not to Emily Lane's old life, where I worked all the joy out of my day and didn't allow time for anything else. How could I, after I'd had a sample of what my life could be?

"That role should have been mine from the beginning," I said, surprising myself with the levelness in my tone.

Wesley scoffed. "Yes, well. A good deal of politics goes into hiring," he said, a mean edge to his voice. "Be glad you don't have to deal with that side of things."

The grass isn't always greener . . . a small voice tried to warn me.

Fuck that.

"I won't be dealing with any side of The Arlow Group. I'll put in my official two weeks when I return on Monday."

"Emily, let's be reasonable." He sounded panicked. "I can't lose you too."

"Sorry. I've got the rest of my troubled paradise to enjoy."

I hung up, feeling like Genie when Aladdin finally wished for his freedom. Before the cuffs of Excel barely had time to hit the floor, I was out the door.

I needed to find Beck. Maybe I *was* bold. Maybe I could be the girl he thought I was.

Just as Victoria had said, Beck either wasn't in the suite, or he wasn't answering the door. He also didn't answer his phone, but I came prepared. I took out the stationery and pen I'd taken from the lobby. Using the wall as a desk, I wrote my note:

Beck,

I really need to talk to you. I'll be in the Sunset conference room until about seven tonight.

-Emily

I slipped the note under his door, releasing it like a dandelion wish.

I finished the last name on the mirror with a sigh of relief. Then I sat back on my haunches, feeling a full thirty seconds of triumph before looking at the time: eight minutes past seven.

Beck wasn't coming. Of course, he wasn't.

I used my phone's remaining four percent battery life to secure an Uber for the three-hour trip back to my motel in San Jose. Numb legs moved me to the door. A numb mouth made small talk with the driver. Numb fingers unlocked the room at the motel. A numb heart refused to acknowledge what I'd done, what I'd lost.

Feeling gross from hours of travel, crying, and the marker on my hands, I turned on the faucet for a steamy shower, hoping to scourge the day from my skin.

But with the heat of the drops, in the solitude of the shower, my feelings began to wake back up—prickling and then sharpening.

My own words echoed in my mind. *I don't feel like myself when I'm with you.*

I hurt him. *Beck.* The same guy who'd made a playlist because of me. The one who brought me dinner when I'd been overwhelmed with work.

And then I thought about his tight grip when we danced. That freckle on his throat. His curls. Those sleepy eyes. How he let me cry on his shoulder during a rainforest hike. The way he slipped out every Thursday to secretly teach babies how to swim.

He was a good guy. A great guy. And I'd hurt him. I couldn't get that last look he'd given me out of my head—like I'd ripped his heart out and stomped on it.

I could relate. Every thought of him wrenched my heart tighter still. Until I cried so hard I gasped for breath. I didn't know how I would ever laugh or even smile again—knowing I hurt him so deeply. That I'd hurt Beck, the guy who believed in me enough to lie to his sister, the one who'd scraped his knees to keep me from hitting the ground.

I sank to the floor, hugging my legs. There I stayed, sobbing long after the water had started running cold.

It wasn't until I pulled on clothes that I heard the voices outside. I leaned my head against the door, straining to hear what the ruckus was about. They spoke in Spanish, and it didn't seem to be any kind of emergency, only voices of irritation.

I leaned back, ready to crawl into bed, when someone responded in English.

"I know, I'm very sorry. *Lo lamento.*" I knew that deep voice. My fingers fumbled on the lock as I rushed to free the chain. "I'm sorry. I'm just looking for—" I swung the door open as Beck lifted his hand to knock on a door a couple down from mine. "Someone."

His features relaxed into relief when his eyes met mine.

"What are you doing here?" I asked, not because I wasn't happy to see him but because my mind was working to catch up with Beck standing right in front of me.

He took a step forward and paused. Beneath the yellow lamplight of that stale motel, I could read the conflict there. It was in the crease between his eyebrows, the slight pucker of his lips. Even conflict looked good on him.

"I got your note," he said, holding the scrap of paper as proof. "I'm sorry I didn't make it to you in time. I was at dinner with my dad and didn't return until after you left. I tried to call you, but—"

"My phone died," I cut in, wanting him to know I hadn't purposefully ignored his calls.

He swallowed. "Victoria told me where you were staying, but she didn't know the room number," he said, indicating the door he'd been about to knock at.

I eyed the long line of doors behind him and wondered how many he'd already knocked on.

"It's a three-hour drive. Why would you do that?" I asked, tears already blurring my vision of Beck. "And why were you at dinner with your dad? Were you asking him for a job?" Beck just looked at me, those intense eyes trying to read me through my questions and emotions. "I know you quit The Arlow Group." My voice trembled as I answered for him. "But you can't work for your dad. You told me that."

He shrugged. "We're going to make it work."

"You didn't have to quit," I insisted.

"I told you I'd take care of you," he said. Those words cracked me open.

"But—" I exhaled because vocalizing it was hard. "I hurt you."

His jaw set, and he looked down. "That doesn't change how I feel about you."

I stepped toward him, unable to stand that forlorn look on his face. "Beck," I rasped, "I am so sorry. But you have to understand. I saw you and Reagan."

He straightened at that, his eyes meeting mine again. "She kissed me, Emily," he stated matter-of-factly, not a hint of defensiveness in his tone. "I told her I wasn't interested."

"I know now. Victoria said as much."

"I came up to tell you what happened right away, but you were already packing your bags." His eyes softened. "You really thought I would do that to you? After we've both been cheated on?"

I couldn't look him in the eyes while mustering the courage to say all that had been running through my mind. "Are we even something that can be cheated on?"

The question seemed to wound him further. "We hadn't put a title on it, but I thought we were . . . something."

"Beck—"

"You don't have to explain yourself." He put out a hand. "I didn't come here to try and convince you to get back with me. I never got a chance to apologize for making you feel like someone you're not. So, I'm sorry." And he looked the very picture of remorse. "I was trying to be encouraging, but I missed the mark. I never meant to pressure you to be someone you aren't. That's the last thing I want for you. I just needed you to know that." He gave me the saddest smile as he backed away. "Night, Lane."

He turned, but my voice made him freeze. "Beck, stop!" Panic gripped me. I couldn't let him go. What if I never saw him again? The idea carved a hole in my already worn heart. "If I don't feel like myself with you, it's because I'm more competitive." I laughed wetly, thinking of our days in the pool and at the office. "I'm bolder. Happier." He turned back around, and his eyes were a physical weight on me. "You make me feel like a more vibrant version of myself." I was prattling, but I couldn't stop. My feelings were tripping over themselves on the way to my mouth, all of them desperate to be heard. "I've been terrified my life will spin out of control if I don't have a tight enough grip on it, but I've realized I'd rather lose control than lose you because . . ." I wet my lips nervously. "Because I love you, too."

"You love me?" he said, breathless—like I'd knocked the wind out of him.

"I know it's unfair for me to say that after—"

Beck stopped my words by erasing the distance between us. His hands slid to the back of my head, pulling my mouth to his. He kissed me as though his lips could chase away all the hurt.

Someone in the parking lot slammed their door, reminding us we weren't alone. Beck backed me into the door, lips still on mine. He snaked a hand around my waist to twist the handle then swung us inside. The door clinked shut, and Beck pressed me to it. He braced one of his hands against the door and slid the other across my hip. I sighed, letting myself melt into him.

He kissed along my jaw and then down my neck, only to bury his face there. He took a long inhale before speaking. "I'm glad you feel all those things with me. But one day, I hope I'll make you feel safe too," he said tenderly, then placed the softest kiss on my collarbone. "Because all I ever want to do is take care of you." He planted another kiss on the bridge of my nose before looking back into my eyes. "I hate that this trip has ruined that image for you."

I immediately thought of him pulling me out of a snake's path, letting me cry on his shoulder, skinning his knees to catch me, and holding my hand in a hospital. The memories came tumbling forward all at once. I shook my head. "Beck, no—"

"I hate that you'll be going back to The Arlow Group with Wesley knowing about us," he continued. "That I talked you into lying to him."

I smiled. "Luckily, I'll only be there for another two weeks." Beck had gone to move a strand of hair behind my ear, but his hand fell to my shoulder at that. He pulled back, eyebrows drawn as if he thought he hadn't heard me correctly. "I quit too." I laughed, delighted to have shocked him. "I'm going to give calligraphy a real chance. Maybe we can even salvage what Hailey started with Lettering Lane."

The sight of Beck's smile, reaching all the way up to his eyes, seized my heart. "Emily Lane, you amaze me."

Then his mouth was back on mine as he lifted me. I wrapped my legs around his waist, squeezing him tight. The rest of the world dissolved, like sugar on the tongue.

Chapter 26

I smoothed a hand over the front of my dress and took one last look in the mirror. I'd let my hair down; the ends flowed along the front of the black V-neck. At the waist, the fabric changed. Palm leaves covered its maxi skirt. When I shifted my weight, my leg peeked out of a thigh-high slit. The bandage on my arm didn't match the outfit, but I decided risking infection wasn't worth being completely on point.

Beck had left early to rehearse for the ceremony with the rest of the wedding party, so I was on my own for the ceremony—if one could truly be alone in a crowd of one hundred and fifty people. Luckily for Victoria and her guests, the storm in Houston had broken in the wee hours of the morning. By the talk in the lobby, most of the guests had been able to get a flight in time. The core friends and family had come days early or taken their own private jets anyway.

Following the crowd to the beach, the altar came into view with its macrame curtain framed by thick bamboo. A floral arrangement of bright, peachy tropical flowers and widespread leaves topped it off. Matching arrangements sat at the end of each aisle. They looked as though locals had picked them up an hour ago, only to be carefully tamed into classy bunches by a skilled and tireless florist.

Stacked on a tower of crates, my own signage greeted me.

Welcome to our wedding.

Shoes here.

Vows there.

It was all a very expensive boho vibe. Ditch the Jimmy Choo heels, but wear the Saks Fifth Avenue dress. Not me, of course. Mine cost thirty dollars on Amazon.

I scanned the crowd, stupidly looking for a friend to sit by before remembering I'd alienated myself by lying to the ten people I knew in attendance here—Beck not included. But then there sat Sebastian, waving from his place on the third row. I turned around, sure he meant the wave for someone else. But no. He smiled at *me*.

"Sit by me," he pleaded. "Nick's the best man, and if this seat is not occupied, his pyramid scheme cousin will try to sell me whatever she's wrapped in now, and I'll end up guilt-purchasing essential oils."

I took the seat. "Can't have that. Victoria would not approve of soliciting at her wedding."

Sebastian laughed. "No, she would not." Then he leaned back in his seat, arms crossed. "I'm actually surprised you're here. I heard you caused quite the drama, *Emily*."

I flushed and watched my coral-painted toes sink into the sand. "About that. I'm sorry for lying to you."

"Victoria said you were trying to save your sister's business." He gave me an assessing look.

"That." I tilted my head. "And I wanted to see if I could hold my own in the calligraphy world." I met his eyes. "I understand if you want to go with another calligrapher for your event."

"Hell no!" His outburst caused a little white-haired old lady to turn, face pinched. "Sorry," he said to her, maybe a little too sweetly, before turning back to me. "Listen, lying about your first name was weird, for sure. But I would have sold my soul if it meant my business' success when I first started. So, I get it."

"You do?"

"Yeah. Besides, I've watched you work. I know your calligraphy is legit. Just make sure I have the right name for Venmo."

"Okay," I said, relief bubbling out of me in a giggle. Maybe Lettering Lane had a fighting chance.

We quieted down as the string quartet started playing something slow and sweet. Doug led his men to the altar. He wore a full khaki suit, but the rest of the guys had a laid-back wedding look: no jacket, and the long-sleeved shirts were rolled halfway up their forearms. I could see the edge of Beck's tattoo peeping out from his sleeve first. Nick blocked the rest of his frame until they turned a corner. I followed the trail up a bicep that had held me close last night across the span of the chest I had used as a pillow. Up the throat with my favorite freckle in the world. My eyes grazed the lips I could spend an entire life kissing but never have enough of. Then I snagged on waiting eyes.

He seemed trapped by my stare as he took his place on the altar.

You look beautiful, he mouthed.

A blush spread, flaming across my cheekbones. I looked down for a moment, then smiled. *You too,* I mouthed back.

And he did. He looked like a model for the damn button-down he wore. His picture belonged plastered on a David's Bridal billboard. I thought he had a penchant for wearing nice shirts all this time, but maybe he just made shirts look that good.

Then he smiled that charming smile of his. It made me breathless. He was effortlessly, recklessly handsome.

The music shifted again for the bridesmaids and then for Victoria, who absolutely stunned the crowd with her beauty. The dress hugged her curves intimately until fanning into a mermaid shape at the end—all in intricate lace. And the sunset definitely put on a show—streaking hot-pink and tangerine clouds across the sky, only to be reflected in the waves below. I couldn't tell you a single thing uttered by the officiant, though. I was completely distracted by the bride's perfect brother.

After the ceremony, I meandered around the reception, waiting for Beck to finish having his pictures taken with the rest of the bridal party. Right over the sand, a canopy of string lights illuminated long tables lined with candles. The area seemed to say, *Gather here. Break bread and celebrate.*

The glass sign I'd painted a lifetime ago actually looked like it belonged right along with all the other décor—something I'd created, braless while my downstairs neighbors hurled insults at each other. The sight made pride swell in me, as did the five-foot mirror guests stopped at to check their table numbers. It had turned out good—great—despite being last minute and lettered with a broken heart.

Last, there was the tribute to Poppy on a small table by itself. "I wish you could have been here," I said to the candle flickering in the glass.

What could have been sat like a stone on my chest. I could only imagine how Beck and Victoria felt.

Arms snaked around my waist, warm hands met at my navel, lips at my ear. "Jesus, Emily. This dress—" He stopped, his breath snagging, his fingers tightened around me for a moment before releasing it all in a low exhale. "Did you do this?" he said, moving to my side to get a better look at the lantern. "Or was it your sister?"

"It was me," I said quietly, watching the turmoil overtake his features.

"It's—" His fingers stretched toward the lettering, *In Loving Memory of Poppy*, but stopped not even an inch away. He wore so much in his expression: pain, regret, love, admiration. "It's beautiful." He looked at me, eyes shining in the low lighting. "Thank you."

I smiled and let him lead me to the dance floor. Beck talked the DJ into letting him pick a song, and we danced our first slow dance to *Iris*.

After a few dances, dinner, and cake, I gathered with the other ladies for the ritualistic bouquet toss.

Reagan surprised me by choosing the empty space at my side. "I'm sorry if I made things hard on you this trip."

I looked at her, expecting a patronizing look plastered on her perfect face, but she seemed nothing but sincere. "Well, not just me, but Madison too." She looked at where her friend was booty-bumping another laughing guest. "She was trying to be a good friend, but she took things too far." Reagan suddenly became very interested in straightening the sash at her waist. "Like I took things too far by kissing Beckett. I just—" For a second, she appeared close to crying but then rallied. "I really messed up with him. Fucked things up royally. And I thought I could win him back, but it wasn't my place to do that. I've missed my chance. Anyway." She tried to smile, but this time, tears welled in her eyes. "Do you think you could forgive me?"

I thought of how my fear of love almost made me lose Beck. Fear could make you do crazy things, but love was worse. Before I could answer her, something lobbed through the air at us. I caught it, blinking in surprise at the gorgeous arrangement of tropical flowers in my grasp. I handed the bouquet to Reagan.

"I forgive you," I said, then padded my way through the crowd to find Beck.

Except Beck wasn't where I'd left him with Gabe and Koontz. In fact, all the other guys had lined up for the garter toss, but Beck wasn't anywhere on the floor. I weaved in and out of guests who talked and laughed excitedly as Doug reached under Victoria's dress to pull out the garter.

I finally saw him when I reached a break in the crowd. He stood on the beach, gaze trapped in the waves not far from the tree line.

I slipped my hand in his, and we stood for several minutes, listening to the crash of the waves. Watching the reflection of the tiki torches glimmering in the tide.

"I was going to try." Beck's voice sounded croaky. He cleared his throat. "Just dip my feet in." He gestured toward the water, looking awfully nervous for Beckett Atteridge. "But I don't think I can. Not tonight. Not when Poppy should be here, and we have a lantern lit in her stead because I—" He choked to a stop on the last word.

I pulled him to me and squeezed him tightly, trying to calm the hammering of his heart. I looked up at him, and he rested his forehead on mine. "You don't have to do anything you aren't ready to do. But Poppy wouldn't want you to feel this way about the beach. Based on what you told me, she was the coolest kid ever." Beck gave me a small smile and rubbed lazy circles on my back. "She didn't want you to get in trouble over the vase because she adored you. Just like she didn't hold it against Victoria for breaking her wrist." He lifted his head off mine, and I watched my words sink in. They were words to heal, but healing was often painful. "There's no way she'd blame you for what happened. She'd want you enjoying the waves and sunshine." I gripped his hands. "You, volunteering—teaching ISR—that's honoring her. You, avoiding a place where you two used to love playing together? That's a shame."

Beck exhaled a trembling breath, watching the surf for a long while. Then his eyes met mine. "Will you uh—will you come with me?"

I squeezed his hands tighter and nodded, not trusting my voice to speak. I felt like I didn't deserve to be with Beck at a moment so crucial while simultaneously being so thankful he picked me to hold his hand.

His pants rolled up, my dress hiked in one hand, we took step after step until the tide reached out, washing over the tops of our feet. Beck stood tensely next to me for a few minutes—he was still as a statue save for his curls blowing in the wind.

But little by little, breath by breath, he relaxed. "You were right," he said, wiping away a few tears before wrapping an arm over my shoulders. "Sometimes you just have to get in before you're ready."

That statement rang true with our relationship and my pursuit of a career in calligraphy as well. I wasn't ready for any of this, but being here for Beck, facing something so great, I'd take the uncertainty. I would, every time, if it meant I'd be the one he trusted with this. To be his anchor.

I squeezed myself tighter against him. *I'm not letting go,* I willed my body language to tell him. Beck seemed to hear my silent proclamation because he laid his head against mine.

"Thank you," he whispered before planting a kiss on the bridge of my nose. I tilted my face, catching his lips with my own.

I used to love to tell myself the grass wasn't always greener. It was easier that way. Safer.

But sometimes, just sometimes, the other side *was* greener. Sometimes, it was as green as a Costa Rican rainforest. Sometimes, it was *pura vida.*

Epilogue

"Let me try yours." I leaned toward Beck's drink, but he pulled it away, taking a bite into the pineapple garnish on top.

"Why?" he asked around the fruit in his mouth. "Yours isn't good?"

"No. Mine is great." And it was. Nothing better than a pina colada right off the beach. I eyed his drink—a blue Hawaii, the same color as the waves crashing in front of us. "But yours looks better."

He smiled, handing his glass over for my tasting. "I do know how to pick them," he said, giving a sultry look as he spread out on his lounge chair.

"I see what you did there." I took a sip of pineapple heaven. "You are smooth, Mr. Atteridge."

He winked clumsily. Then his phone vibrated—Victoria's name on the screen. "Damn it. Do you mind if I take this?"

He had hardly touched his phone the whole ten days we'd been in Maui, but I knew his sister itched to have him back at work to help with a system update. He'd made himself quite valuable to the Atteridge team. He'd even managed to impress his father. They'd met for dinner last week and had been civil with each other.

"Tell Victoria hi for me," I said.

Beck answered the phone with a gruff, "What?" Then flashed me a wicked smile. The two of them loved giving each other hell about work. His eyes skated over the waves as he listened to whatever Victoria was spouting about. "I can promise you it's not an emergency," he said, rolling his eyes.

I picked up my own phone to scroll through Instagram. Hailey had tagged me in a new post. In the picture, she held up a bottle of perfume with perfect white lettering.

Her caption read: **Thank you Maurine's Fragrance for another amazing opportunity!! Only thing that could have made today better was my partner in crime. #CalligraphySisters #LiveLettering #LoveAndInk**

The last hashtag made me smile—the name of the company we'd started together. We'd had to rebrand Hailey's business after Madison spammed social media with negative reviews. It turned out Madison was an influencer, and her following reached far. Reagan eventually called her off, but the damage had already been done by then.

It wasn't good timing for Hailey, with a big breakup, and it was pretty much my worst nightmare: quitting a stable job only for calligraphy to slip out from under my feet. I had questioned my decision to quit over and over, ruminating it into the ground.

We both wallowed in despair for a couple of weeks. Then, one night, after sharing a roll of cookie dough, she said, "So what do we call our new business?"

Starting a business from the ground up proved to be one of the most difficult things I'd done. Each client came hard-earned. Then, after months of pumping the well for drops, a steady trickle took over, and before we knew it, we had a gush on our hands.

And now, a year later, Hailey had moved on from Braxton. We made enough from Love and Ink for Hailey to get her own place, which she'd filled to the brim with the most beautiful artificial plants.

I clicked to comment. **Can't wait for the next job. Watch out, San Antonio. Lane sisters are coming at you.**

Out of all the calligraphy jobs, live lettering had easily become my favorite. However, addressing Grace's first birthday invitations was a close second. Anna had been over the moon.

"Okay, okay." Beck was wrapping up the conversation with Victoria. "All that can wait until I get back on Monday . . . Uh-huh . . . I know. You will live. Bye!" Beck hung up and let out an exasperated breath.

"Is it hard?" I asked, giving him a *poor baby* pouty lip. "Being so needed?"

He melted into his chair. "Exhausting."

"Does that mean you are too tired for a last dip in Maui waters?"

Beck took another sip of his drink, then sat up to take his shirt off. "Absolutely not."

I laughed, loving how eager he'd become to swim in the ocean. Since he'd first dipped his toes in the water in Costa Rica, he'd created a long bucket list of beaches he wanted to visit. He said he had to make up for all that lost time. I said I was always down for a tropical vacation.

I stripped to my bikini and let him take my hand as we headed for the glittering water. "Just go easy on me," Beck begged.

"Come on," I said, tugging him into deeper water. A wave rolled up and over our stomachs, causing Beck to cuss and step up onto his tiptoes.

I laughed and pressed into him. "I'll warm you up."

His hands went to the back of my thighs, and he lifted me so I could wrap my legs around his waist. He angled his face towards mine. Our lips only inches apart, I breathed him in for a moment. I could have gotten drunk off his breath—all pineapple and rum.

I slid my hands to his neck and pulled him down the rest of the way, savoring the fullness of his lips and the way his tongue slid so gently across mine. My thumb rubbed over the spot where I knew his freckle to be. Beck's hands were busy too. One pressed into my shoulder blade, keeping me steady. The other moved south—into dangerous territory.

I could easily see the kiss turning more frantic, the two of us sloshing back to the shore, jogging through the sand to grab our belongings, barely giving ourselves enough time to towel off before heading up to our room to finish what we'd started.

I could see the scene so easily because we'd done exactly that just yesterday.

Reluctantly, I pulled away, extracting a low groan from Beck. "This is our last beach day," I breathed. "I want you to enjoy it."

"I want to enjoy you," he husked, playfully nipping at my bottom lip before kissing across my jaw. My eyelids fluttered.

I swallowed. My resolve was a straw house at this point. It could be blown over with the slightest suggestion. I think he realized this because after he grazed my earlobe with his teeth, he whispered, "I'm not above groveling, Emily," into the shell of my ear. I shivered under his grip. He had me right where he wanted me.

Or would have if a wave hadn't knocked us both under.

We came up laughing and sputtering. Beck pushed strands of my hair from my line of sight before kissing the bridge of my nose. My attention snagged on the newest addition to his tattoo. I curled my fingers around his forearm, holding him still to get a better look.

The new ink had been there for almost a year now, but it still took me aback. The space between the bands had been filled. Poppy's name was in my lettering, written in ink on Beck's arm. The calligraphy I'd done on the lantern for Victoria's wedding had stuck with him. He said he had to have it.

Having my handwriting on him felt so personal. More intimate than if my own name had been there. I wondered if Hailey would ever discover that Beck's tattoo had inspired our new business name: Love and Ink.

"Are you sad?" Beck asked. "That today is our last day?"

I considered that. I should have been, right? Leaving Hawaii and its perfect water and fruity drinks and hikes through luscious forests. But the best part of the trip was Beck, and we'd leave together to return home.

We'd picked a cozy house in the Woodlands, and I'd said goodbye to my water-stained ceiling, jammed door, and arguing neighbors. The sense of security I'd felt when the realtor handed over the keys to our home had been an all-encompassing warmth. For the first time in a long time, I stopped obsessing over the possibility of becoming homeless. Having our own house anchored me.

My favorite part of our home was the small flower garden in the backyard. My desk faced the window that overlooked it, which not only made for an aesthetic background for calligraphy projects but was also convenient for giving Beck shit.

"I always knew you were into flowers," I'd called out the window on a mild April morning.

Beck hadn't even looked up from his weed-pulling. "I want to remind you that the garden was your idea."

Even with our different work schedules, Beck and I still shared a lane for swimming each morning. He was, regrettably, still faster than me, but he wasn't the only one to teach babies how to swim anymore. I'd secretly taken ISR training and surprised Beck with my certification on his birthday. Now, we both volunteer on Thursdays.

My life with Beck proved to be much more than I could have dreamed. My heart swelled at the thought of it.

"I'm not sad to leave," I answered honestly, threading his fingers in mine. It wasn't hard to leave a vacation when your life back home was its own shade of paradise.

Did you enjoy this book?

S ign up for her newsletter and get a mirrored first chapter from Beck's perspective. It's on the house!

Harrietashfordwriter.com

One more thing, before you go!

I've already taken up a good chunk of your time, but would you consider submitting a review for this book? I wouldn't ask if it wasn't important. Reviews drive an author's career, and I very much like this job. Goodreads is great if you need a place to start.

Thanks again for reading "The Trouble with Love and Ink." This was my first published novel, and it is a dream come true to have it in readers' hands.

Acknowledgements

This book would not be here without my village. Thanks first to my husband. If you wouldn't have encouraged me, this book would have been dead in the water. Actually, I don't think I would know a thing about falling in love if it weren't for you. I often think about that morning in our high school cafeteria, how you asked me to be your girlfriend. Such a simple question, but I felt in my bones that the moment was much greater. It was the beginning of an incredible journey.

On the off chance that one of my boys actually reads this, thank you for being incredible. You make me want to be the best I can be.

Thank you to my parents, both by blood and marriage. You guys have supported and loved me through my wildest ideas. You've taught me the beauty of hard work and following through with plans. I'm sorry I kept this book a secret from you. I just love surprises and hope you love this one.

Kyle-Ann and Angie, thank you for keeping my secret and being some of my biggest supporters. I adore you guys. Y'all have made me feel like I could smash any barrier.

Thank you to my cover artist, My Lan Khuc. You are the sweetest, most talented cover artist in all the land. Also, to Hayley for being an incredible PR/hype queen. You have often talked me down from the ledge and openly shared your knowledge and expertise with me. I so appreciate having you in my corner. Thank you to my editor, Sherri Shackelford. You coaxed out the more beautiful language in my story. Ramona Mihai, thank you for catching all the little errors in my manuscript. Your proofreading skills reign supreme. Margaret, thank you for playing the bestie, pre-proofreader, and unofficial literary agent roles. Oh! And for being the brains and talent behind that incredible burn cake/ cover reveal. Your support has meant so much. I can't wait until your book is finished!

A huge shoutout to the Bookstagram/Booktok community. I was completely taken aback by how welcoming y'all are. I'd probably still be stuck in some agent's slush pile if it weren't for you. Thanks for bringing me out of my shell and convincing me to go indie.

Team Trouble, I couldn't have asked for a better street team. You've completely blown me away. Thank you for passionately championing my debut novel.

Lastly, thank you, dear reader. Having this book in your hands is a dream come true. There are a lot of incredible novels out there; the fact that you took the time to read mine means the world. I've got all the heart eyes for you.

About the Author

Harriet Ashford has been addicted to writing since the fourth grade and has become increasingly serious about it. She lives in Houston with her husband, two boys, and a rambunctious blue heeler. When she's not reading, writing, or herding the boys, you can find her embroidering semi-inappropriate messages onto her latest cross-stitch project.